Blood Storm

A Mitch King Mystery

Sam Waas

Blood Storm

by Sam Waas
© 2015 Blood Storm
Swartz Creek, MI 48473
Cover design by Clarissa Yeo

Tell-Tale Publishing Group, LLC
5714 Peri St
Swartz Creek, MI 48737

Praise for Blood Storm...

I just finished Blood Storm, the 2nd novel in the Mitch King series. Waas has a great way of showing the struggles that King, a divorced Private Investigator in the modern day goes through. His physical and dangerous struggles that come with the job description. His personal struggles with decisions he has made in his life that take a toll on him. And his struggles in his (somewhat lacking) love life. There are familiar characters from the first King novel, and some new faces that guide you through the story. Without giving anything away ahead of time, Waas takes you through the cases King is working on and how they invariably interact with each other. But it is not the usual hokey private eye story, and Waas even pokes fun at that genre while inside Mitch King's head. And just the right amount of comedy is sprinkled in that helps balance out some of the gore and filthy life that goes along with dealing with sick criminals and lowlifes. I am looking forward to Mitch King's next adventures.—rda, Amazon

Many thanks to my friends and family who encouraged and supported me when I was struggling with indecision on my novels.

Greatest appreciation to Bill Pronzini and Robert Crais for providing me such illustrious targets and goals toward which I could endeavor to aim.

A little more than kin, and less than kind
— Hamlet's take on family values

Chapter 1

It was nearly midnight when I stepped off the splintery wooden porch of the tavern and headed toward my car. I'd finished my tedious business with the bar owner and only wanted to get my weary self home before Houston dumped yet another rain squall on my head.

The earlier shower had let up, but water still pooled throughout the poorly lit and uneven gravel of the parking lot. I was negotiating a large puddle near a Dodge Ram when I smelled cigarette smoke and heard a muffled cough. This small distraction put me on edge because muggers often target drunks leaving taverns as easy prey. I was sober, but the robbers wouldn't care. I didn't see anyone, but reached beneath my jacket anyway, hand on the .45's grip, ensuring that the pistol was easily accessible in its holster.

A sudden movement in the shadows, a metallic click.

Something bad was going down. I stepped back, but put my foot into a chuckhole and slipped, falling square on my butt. Before I had time to cuss, fire erupted where my head had been a second before!

I was momentarily dazed from the muzzle flash and noise, then quickly scooted behind the truck's big rear tire, pulled out my pistol, clicked off the safety and stayed quiet.

My ears rang from the blast but the cycling of the pump shotgun was still unmistakable. I even heard the little tink from the empty shell casing hitting the gravel. Who it was I didn't know, but he wasn't as much a mugger as murderer. I had about two seconds before the attacker got around the tailgate for another shot.

I peered under the truck frame and saw cowboy boots creeping along on the other side, silhouetted by a distant streetlight. I aimed, fired and got lucky.

There was a grunt of pain and a man's body landed with a whump. He was wriggling around on his back, trying to point the shotgun toward me beneath the truck. I fired at his bearded face three times and rolled away to seek better shelter, putting more vehicles between the shooter and me.

No further movement from the man and nothing else immediately threatened. I hit the release and the nearly empty magazine dropped free. I grabbed a full mag from my shoulder rig and slammed it into the pistol.

I cautiously rose to my feet, peeking around the far side of a rusty Buick. As people began yelling from the doorway of the bar, I eased from behind the car, aiming my gun at the man lying on the ground, ready to fire again.

It wasn't necessary. One of my bullets got him straight through the head and tore a gaping hole in his temple where the bullet emerged. There was plenty of blood and he wasn't getting up again, ever. I took a closer look and recognized my old biker nemesis Dutch. He and I had a scuffle in Mid City last summer and he'd sworn to get even. But typical for Dutch, things just hadn't worked out his way.

A half-smoked gore-splattered cigarette lay beside his head. Dutch should have known that smoking was bad for his health.

After making certain that nobody else was trying to kill me, I clicked my .45 on safe and walked toward the bar. Everyone was calling and gesturing but I paid no attention. Things were fine until the excitement and emotional surge caught up with me, and all the steam and piss and vinegar inside went swirling away. I sagged to grab at the porch railing and plunked down on the top step, pistol dangling idly from my fingers. I gasped and choked back tears.

Chapter 2

An hour earlier, I'd been stuck square in the middle of a rainy September night, fighting traffic along Telephone Road. Right then, I hated the traffic, hated every damn car, SUV and pickup near me, hated the rain and hated Houston.

Not that it was the city's fault. Houston hasn't done anything bad to me that I haven't brought down upon myself. However, blaming others seems to be one of my better talents these days—at least that's what my friends tell me.

Vehicles roared along the wet pavement, kicking muddy spray onto my windshield. I had already gone through a bunch of washer fluid and hoped the dash wouldn't start flashing its irritating fluid low light. As though I needed another nanny in my life.

I drove at a reasonable pace, or tried to, slow enough to avoid hydroplaning and fast enough to escape being forced off the road into a drainage ditch by aggressive drivers tailgating me, drivers who evidently needed to get where they were going a helluva lot quicker than I did. Maybe they were VIPs?

The road was four lanes wide but it was jam-packed, people cutting back and forth abruptly and turning without signaling into stores, strip malls, bars and ubiquitous Whataburgers, while others of their breed pulled out right in front of me with impunity to rejoin the fray.

On any given Friday or Saturday night, about half the drivers are legally impaired, but right now I'd have voted Telephone Road an eighty percent drunk rating. Nevertheless, I tried to keep my sanity and avoid honking and flipping the bird at anybody who cut me off. After all, I was near my destination and a road rage incident would severely limit my free time. So I rambled along without visible complaint, jaw clenched and teeth grinding. Luckily, I was driving the 4Runner, which gave me at least a fighting chance with the monster trucks and behemoth SUVs. If I'd taken the MGB, I'd have long ago been squashed like a beetle at a church picnic. As it was, my Toyota was on the puny side, manufactured in a model year before the 4Runners started on steroids and overgrew their original design intent.

Rodney Crowell memorialized Telephone Road in his great Houston Kid album. And although this Houston urban highway has gentrified to some degree since the rock'n'blues fifties era of the song, Telephone Road still retains a generous component of country-western bars, biker hangouts and chancy strip joints.

I was pulling into the gravelly lot of one of those strip joints right now, but hoped that my visit wouldn't prove too chancy. Turkey John Turner, the bar's owner, was into me for some surveillance work I'd done on his divorce and phoned earlier, saying he had four hundred to pay on account. If I waited too long, the money would quickly transmute into white powder and migrate up Turkey's nose, so I decided to grab the cash while it was still green and spendable. Hence my ten pm expedition on a stormy night when I would otherwise be sanely home, watching my Lost Season Five DVDs and yelling at the screen in vain about all the corners into which J.J. Abrams had painted himself and his loyal fans.

* * *

The glaring neon sign out front of the bar proclaimed Kuntry Klub Kittens and illustrated this by a predictable flickering image of a scantily clad cowgirl twirling her lariat, but despite the shameless pun and promise of women in abundance, the lot was nearly empty, only a thin row of cars and pickups to show that the place was even open. Business at topless bars has fallen off during the recent economic downturn, inflated drink prices not being worth the treat of goggling pneumatic breasts or getting the occasional feel job. But high class entertainment always suffers in a recession.

At least the weather cooperated briefly, rain subsiding into a few furtive spritzes. I parked, got out, squished through the puddles toward the door. There was a porch of sorts and I stood there, brushed the water off my jacket and checked the lay of the Springfield .45 auto beneath. The new shoulder holster was behaving as advertised, holding the compact 1911 frame cleanly and comfortably against my ribs, no gangsta bulge. Tonight I was wearing an unlined black leather jacket, yellow mock turtleneck, black jeans and charcoal Nikes. Glancing down, I realized that maybe I was dressed like an oversize bumblebee, then decided I was just too imaginative for my own good. Or so I hoped.

I was testing my new holster tonight, a composite and nylon rig that had a gazillion Velcro straps you could fine tune ninety-six ways to Tuesday, so as to better accommodate the vagaries of your body shape, pistol size and carry preference. Previously I'd used a waistband rig for my S&W 9mm but I wanted to test this new gear in combo with the equally new and more powerful 1911 pistol before we reached authentic shoulder holster weather. That's how my pal

Tony Vee jokingly defines Houston winters, during which the thermometer plummets to a bone-chilling fifty. I also felt somehow obligated to play the tough guy role. All private eyes wear shoulder holsters, at least those in movies or TV, and who was I to buck the trend? Could get me tossed from the Shady Shamus guild. I figured I was pushing the envelope anyway, carrying a 1911 instead of a vintage Smith and Wesson .38 snubbie, but the times they are a'changin'.

Regardless of how I carried the weapon, shoulder or waist, I've come to prefer synthetic composite holsters to leather. You run around in Houston with a hunk of cowhide glued to your skin for a few weeks and Old Spice won't begin to address the problem. Homicide Lieutenant Joe Duggan, asked why he used a Shooting Systems nylon rig for his Les Baer, simply said, "Leather gets stinky." Case closed, Sonny Crockett's retro Miami Vice shoulder rig notwithstanding.

* * *

I looked across the lot. Above the endless melee of Telephone Road I could make out the glow from high-rises in the Galleria and Med Center, barely visible through the skimpy and devolving tree line and rapidly dissipating shower. People who haven't been to Houston maintain this nebulous image of the city, always hot and steamy, the only buildings in town being a corral and the now-vacant Astrodome. Everyone drives pickups or Caddies when they're not riding their favorite horse down the street, every guy has two six-guns and a big white Stetson like the crazy Texan on The Simpsons, every gal has huge blonde hair and is named Lula Belle.

This is understandable because any TV show purporting to be in Houston has obligatory stock intro footage of longhorn cattle, a rodeo or horse infested parade, even though the story may detail a new cancer cure or some oil exploration discovery. This Cowtown image is just as accurate as the Neil Simon stereotype in which everyone in New York City is divorced, works for a prestigious advertising firm and lives in a luxury loft overlooking Central Park.

Decades ago, Houston may have fit the cowboy pattern, but now it's the fourth largest city in the country and a world center for oil exploration, with engineers and other technical types in abundance. NASA adds to the techie overload. Yes, we do have our Western wannabes, most believing that ownership of a Ford F-150 confers cowboy status but for whom the term All Hat and No Cattle applies perfectly. Myself, I haven't ridden my horse to work for a couple weeks now.

As I stood on the porch, two young men came out and immediately lit cigarettes. They wore standard Southwest casual—blue jeans, sports logo T-shirts with a denim vest over and rough out boots. We smiled obliquely at one another, a brief male acknowledgement of the universally accepted search for naked tits.

One guy glanced at his buddy. "Wanna head over to Showgirls?"

"Yeah, shit, might as well," the other said, frowning back toward the bar they'd just left. "Fuck 'em if they can't take a joke." He looked at me. "Good luck in there, pal. It couldn't be deader if it was a fuckin' zombie convention."

I smiled, nodded a quiet assent and thus encouraged, they walked together, each unsteady, fell into a red Camaro and drove off weaving down the road, easy targets for a DUI arrest. But that wasn't my problem.

I got the impression that the Kitten Klub hadn't exactly delivered on its advertised sexual smorgasbord and when I stepped inside, it was obvious.

Other than a dozen scattered customers and a slightly lesser number of girls, I had the place to myself. Turkey John apparently had dancers park their vehicles in front to pad the imagined audience count, but to little effect. Not that this sparse client base would give me guilty feelings about taking money from John. The payment was long owed anyway and he was offering only a fraction of the total. I'd take the cash and be glad of it.

Chapter 3

The Kuntry Klub Kitten is decorated as an Old West saloon or more likely, somebody's secondhand and drunken concept of what an Old West bar looked like. There are faux oil lamps, many of which aren't casting their faux flames because the faux bulbs are burned out. Dusty hanks of braided rope depicting various cowboy working knots are stapled to the wall, alongside drawings of cattle brands and cheap prints of Western shootouts. The Kitten has always been ratty, even when busy, but now the seams are really showing. Nobody was onstage dancing, just the CD jukebox blaring generic country-western. In times past, the place would be overflowing with cigarette smoke, but nowadays the only bars where you can smoke are, I think, a few taverns in Ecuador. The Kitten is torpid and rundown, but at least I can breathe inside.

Some tired looking guys were sitting up front at the railing around the stage, hoping against any reasonable measure of expectation to catch a flash of shaved pussy or cop a feel from the equally tired girls sitting alongside them. The girls were flirting and drinking per their assignment but showing little enthusiasm in the task, yet that didn't deter the men, who seemed to welcome the ritual displays of affection as a challenge rather than accept inevitable rejection.

When you think about it, topless bars are among the least sexy places around, all show and no go, or at least not enough genuine sex to make it worthwhile, since vice cops keep these hangouts well patrolled, shutting them down if prostitution becomes prevalent. Any horny guy, married or not, can find himself in bed with a woman more quickly by trolling the everyday sleazy pickup bars that abound in Houston and get laid for a lot less money, too. If you're not terribly particular, you can easily find a partner to share a couple hours in a nearby hot sheet motel. It's not good for your health or personal esteem, but it's there for the taking. Yet topless bars have an established reputation for sex and the patrons tonight were damned well determined to prove their case.

The girls who didn't have customers sat arrayed along one side of a long table at the rear of the tavern in a dismal parody of the Last Supper. Actually, they keep their backs toward the wall so they can quickly spot a new customer coming in, all the better to sink their hooks into. The table is also closest to the bathroom, where the girls can duck in from time to time and snort a quick line.

I recognized two of the dancers from when I'd been here previously, mainly from their disparate tattoos. Their names were more tenuous in my memory, but I did know Darlene from a job I'd done for her and I seemed to conjure up Connie for another girl. Maybe that was her name.

Turkey John sat at the end of the table, wearing a drugstore cowboy yoke shirt straight out of a Roy Rogers movie. He had his chair tilted back, overrun cowboy boots propped up. Turner was sipping a drink and trying his level best not to do anything productive but simultaneously project an image of assertive management.

"Hey, Mitch, glad you could come." Turkey John stood up, came to greet me. I smiled inwardly, realizing why his nickname's so fitting. John Turner is tall and angular, long skinny neck and prominent Adam's apple that seems to bob up and down as he walks. His head also pigeons back and forth with each step, accentuating the turkey caricature. John hates the nickname but he'd become acclimated, knowing it was a lost cause to pretend otherwise.

We shook, and John glanced to one of the girls. "Darlene, grab Mitch a beer, would ya?" He turned back to me. "Goddamn, you look like a fuckin' bumblebee."

"Hadn't noticed."

So much for my choice of fashion. At least I was ready for Halloween.

We sat at a small table. Turkey John watched the bar intently as though something exciting would soon occur. After a while, it did, sort of. One of the girls got up wearily from her chair, stepped onto the little stage and began to sway casually to whatever music was playing. After a few stanzas, she took off her top and danced wearing only a G-string and crappy high heels. She was decent looking, trim figure and nice breasts, but she was also a bit tipsy and the heels made her wobbly and awkward. Why stilettos are supposed to be sexy on naked women I've never figured out, but it comes with the territory and is pretty much de rigueur for titty dancers and pinup girls. I'm no Casanova but I've been to bed with my share of women and the first thing they do is kick off their shoes like any normal human being.

As each girl danced, customers would reach over the stage rail and stick a dollar or two into her G-string and she'd give the guy a slobbery kiss on the cheek. To me it was about as sexy as a 1940s burlesque number but everyone else seemed to think it was the best thing going, the act rewarded with enthusiastic applause from the other girls and whichever men weren't too drunk yet to notice the action on stage.

"Seems a little slow tonight," I told John.

He waggled his hand sideways. "Kind of. Rain kept 'em home." Yeah, right.

Darlene came over with my beer. It was in a smallish glass that was none too clean, but at least the beer was too flat and tasteless for me to bother to try to drink. For that I was pleased and tipped Darlene a five.

"Thanks, Mitch." She smiled, gave me a friendly little smooch, sort of on my forehead, squeezed my arm. She looked tired, but it was a tired of the good sort, working hard to support her nuclear family, not the exhausted pallor of a druggie. Darlene never touched drugs, one reason she retained custody of her child through the turmoil of an abusive relationship and despite her somewhat raunchy occupation.

"How are things with your little boy now? What's his name, Eric?" I'd helped her out on a custody problem last year, pulled some strings with the court to get her ex-boyfriend's bail revoked and stick him back in jail where he belonged.

"Derek. Fine. Better. He's at my mom's tonight. He started kindergarten last month." Darlene's smile was less showy and more genuine now. "Thanks for what you did."

Turkey John had been listening. "Mitch is our own special Kuntry Klub deevorce consultant." He looked up at Darlene. "Hon, you better do a set now." She nodded and strolled toward the stage, glancing back over her shoulder at me, smiling.

"Darlene's got the hots for you, dude," John said. "She'll screw you blue and cook you breakfast too."

I just shook my head. She wasn't my type and not because she was a dancer. With my last disastrous relationship, dating's furthest from my mind and no woman is my type these days. "No, she's just a client."

"Reminds me," John said, reaching in his pocket, pulling out some bills and handing them to me. "Thanks."

"No problem." I stuck the money in my pocket without counting. Seeing Darlene half-naked on stage made me a little uncomfortable. Connie, the only other dancer I knew by name, was busy on her cell, nobody else gave a damn, so I thought it best to head out.

But Turkey John was, as usual, prepared to launch into a vigorous rant about his ex, may she rot in hell and hurry up getting there. Each time he tells the story, it expands into more and more fanciful accusations and it's only a matter of time before she has a seat on the Trilateral Commission and is covertly scheming to overthrow our entire American Way. Tonight I couldn't have cared less and begged off listening after about ten minutes of nonstop harangue. With the rain blowing over, business had picked up a bit anyway, and more customers meant less time for Turkey John to bore me.

I had the money, none of the girls were really cute enough to spend time with and I'd already turned down one lukewarm glass of Turkey John's house draft beer. Better to cut my losses and get the hell home. My DVD player awaited. As I stood up to go, I smiled congenially at the girls on the back table and thought I recognized the very young one at the end.

"Christ, John," I said. "Is that your daughter Allie?"

He nodded. "Yeah. My ex asked me to look after Allie tonight, has some big-shot dinner plans with Mister Perfect."

"What is she, thirteen, fourteen?" I shook my head at him. "You got any brains? Know what the fuck happens if Texas Alcohol strolls in? Shit, they'll slam your place shut and jerk your license in a heartbeat. And send Allie off to juvie. You can forget visitation till she's out of college, too."

"They ain't gonna come around tonight. Too much rain."

I shrugged. None of my affair. At least Allie wasn't dressed in stripper gear, only jeans and a pullover. I figured the dancing would start next year, Turkey John being such a peach of a guy.

I waved goodbye to the girls and headed to the parking lot for my unexpected rendezvous with Dutch.

Chapter 4

It was a carnival atmosphere after the shooting, cop cars and ambulances and CSI vans all around. A few energetic customers scooted off before the police arrived, those remaining sequestered inside, hung over and thirsty and cranky, waiting until they were cleared of suspicion and let go.

One of the beat cops remarked to me, grinning, "Hell, give 'em some more beer to keep 'em happy, then run the whole bunch downtown for drunk and disorderly." An elegant Swiftian solution. Turkey John somehow managed to spirit away his underage daughter, for which I was thankful, if only for her sake.

The Homicide lead was Sergeant Elvin Freeman, a short, slender black guy in his forties, handsome face, skimpy moustache and prematurely gray hair. He wore a stylish suede jacket over a white shirt, skinny black tie and pressed jeans. Freeman also sported a small fedora, tilted jauntily. Hats are now making a comeback, especially with sexy TV detectives. Freeman worked Homicide under Lieutenant Sorriento and I'd only met him a few times. We really didn't know each other but I'd heard good things about him. Except of course the fedora.

First thing Freeman did was to dig out a pack of Pall Malls, offer me one, which I declined. He lit up while he glanced over my credentials—investigator's license, special carry permit, driver's license. "These up to date, clean and clear?"

"All okay."

Freeman nodded, and had one of the CSI people relieve me of my pistol. The tech cleared the action and bagged the weapon, made me out a receipt. I told the tech where I'd dropped my spent magazine so he found it and bagged it, too. Everything was performed efficiently, I noticed, despite the fact that the CSI guy didn't wear dark sunglasses, wasn't rude, nor was he armed. His sole job seemed to be collecting crime scene evidence as his profession specified. Maybe he sped around town and chased down bad guys in his off hours, pretending to be a real cop?

"Assuming everything checks out," Freeman told me, "you should get your gun back after the county attorney reviews the evidence. And from what I see thus far, looks like a good shoot."

"Thanks."

Freeman proffered a disdainful snort. "Don't start getting cocky," he warned. "We still gotta check things out and you're not home free." He took a deep drag on his cigarette. "You can't shoot somebody and expect a free pass. Just hang cool and we'll see."

I quickly agreed. I had enough people out for my hide these days and didn't need another homicide investigator on my bad side, too.

Freeman stuck me in the back of his unmarked car, doors open so I could hang my legs out. One of the other cops gave me some paper towels and I could wipe off at least the top layer of grime that I'd accumulated while rolling around in the parking lot. The rain had ceased and the breeze felt good, helping me relax. Freeman left me sitting there and walked the shooting scene as they were moving the body, chatted with his team and the medical folks, came back. He had another Pall Mall going.

I reminded Freeman that I knew Homicide Lieutenant Joe Duggan and he would vouch for me, so Freeman phoned Duggan at home despite the late hour. They chatted a bit, Freeman laughed then clicked his cellphone. He grinned. "Duggan's pissed, rousted from a perfectly fucking good sleep, thanks for fucking nothing. He also said to not let that asshole King shoot anybody else for a while and to tell him to get fucked."

"You caught Joe in a good mood."

Freeman frowned at me. "You got a habit of shooting people so's I need to keep an eye on you? You're not gonna go all Hood on me, are you?" Short not for ghetto neighborhood, but for Going Fort Hood, that terrorist killing having recently replaced the phrase Going Postal in the lexicon of cop speak for crazed massacres, crude and angular though it was.

I shook my head. "Duggan's referring to this past summer. I was the guy, the shooting in the trailer park down on South Main."

"Jesus, that was a mess. I heard the prosecutor no billed. So you walked, no charges?"

"Yeah," I said. "Still, a can of worms."

Freeman took a final puff and flicked the butt onto the gravel, where it caught a puddle and hissed briefly. "Duggan said you were a total prick, though you've been less of a prick lately, but the jury's still out—the cop jury, the one that fuckin' counts." He squinted. "Still, tell me a shooting that isn't fulla shit." He swept his arm to indicate the parking lot where the technicians were working then plunked into his front seat, leaned back to rest his head. He seemed more at ease and I guessed I wasn't in too much hot water, at least not yet.

Another CSI came over, bringing the wallet they'd taken off Dutch. It was in a plastic zip lock bag, the contents that they'd tweezered out also in separate bags, all dutifully labeled. Freeman flipped the bags back and forth until he could read the driver's license. Dutch's real name was Clarence LeBrock. I'd never known it and now it mattered only to the medical examiner and family. I knew he had a younger brother somewhere, so I'd have to be watchful for the next few weeks. Freeman nodded to the tech, who gathered everything and went back to the shooting scene to collect more evidence.

The CSI tech surprisingly didn't speak in a gruff monotone, didn't order the Homicide officers around and didn't even shoot anyone. No dark glasses either. And from glancing over the crime scene, the female CSI didn't wear short shorts and a bikini halter. I guess they had a long ways to go in mimicking the TV CSI pantheon.

"So you didn't recognize this LeBrock guy till after it was over?" Freeman asked, jotting notes.

"Nope. It was dark and it was just somebody after me with a shotgun. I never knew his real name anyway. All I knew was the nickname Dutch."

"Last time you saw him?"

"June, down in Mid City. We had an altercation at a biker bar called the Shack. I was trying to get a line on somebody, Dutch didn't appreciate my snooping around, we went at it. Both of us got banged up a bit, no foul, no loss. I don't remember the exact date but I can look it up and give you a call." I omitted the other part, where my buddy Tony Vee had trussed up Dutch in the trunk of his Eldorado, brought him by my house to help wring out the name of the guy I'd been looking for.

The guy I then shot dead.

"So far as you know," Freeman said, "LeBrock, aka Dutch, had no further conversation with you, no reason to shoot you, no way to know you'd be here tonight."

"Nope. Seeing him was a complete surprise. I've had zero contact with him since then. And I was here tonight to conduct some business with the owner, John Turner. Totally unrelated."

"What kind of business?"

"Turner's no saint but he had a particularly rough divorce last year, custody battle. I did the usual, videos of his wife cheating on him, running down info on her dope dealer boyfriend. Turner's into me for about twelve hundred. He phoned, had some cash on account tonight."

"So you think Turner set you up?"

"I doubt it. I've never pressed him on the money." I glanced over at the shabby bar. "Turner's been running on a thin margin, we both knew it. So I'd mail him an invoice every month, he paid me a couple hundred now and then, no biggie. Turner might drag his feet at paying but he's not the type of guy to turn violent. It's just not in him."

Freeman scanned the traffic streaming along Telephone Road. "I don't suppose this Dutch guy was just driving by, spotted your car, got out and waited?"

"No way. He'd never even seen me drive the 4Runner and it's unlikely he'd be able to spot it from the street at random anyway, rainy and dark."

Freeman nodded. "So we gotta assume somebody dropped a dime on you, told Dutch where you were."

I shrugged. "Looks that way."

"Anybody but Turner know you were coming here tonight?"

"Not that I know of. Turner could have mentioned it to someone."

"Okay. Guess I got to chat with him. Don't go wandering off anywhere till I get back." Freeman hauled himself out of the car, scribbled in his notebook.

A uniformed cop came up, a tall stocky blond guy named Erikson. "Sergeant? I've got one of the dancers, Darlene, says she's got to talk to you, says it's important."

"Duty calls," Freeman said. He tossed his half-smoked cigarette onto the gravel and walked with Erikson toward the bar.

Chapter 5

A few minutes later and Freeman was back, grinning like a junkyard dog eating ice cream . He plunked down in the back seat next to me. "Sometimes shit happens, King."

"Yeah?"

"Yeah. This gal Darlene said one of the other dancers, name of Connie, phoned her boyfriend earlier, acted real suspicious about it, so Darlene sort of listened over her shoulder. Wanna guess what the boyfriend's name is? Or was?"

"Dutch LeBrock?"

"Bingo."

Freeman took out another Pall Mall, offered me one. I shook my head. "Never took up the habit."

"I should quit, too," he said, lighting up. "Anyway, I talked to Connie, reminded her that cellphone numbers were on record, she should save everybody time and tell me the truth about phoning her boyfriend."

"And?"

"And he knew you came by the bar occasionally, told her to let him know the next time you showed or he'd kick her ass."

"Think she knew he'd be shooting for me?"

Freeman puffed a bit, thought, shook his head. "Naw. I don't see her for that. She's all weepy now, of course, but I don't think there's a mean streak in her. I'm guessing she saw a whupping on the way for you, nothing else. She's going downtown with us, but we probably won't be filing charges."

"This lets John Turner off the hook?"

Freeman flicked away his spent smoke, shrugged. He was accumulating a nice pile of Pall Mall discards in the lot but they blended nicely with the odd thirty thousand already there. "Probably. Shit happens, like I said."

"Need anything else from me?"

"Not tonight. You'll need to come by, make a formal statement. Might want to chat with your lawyer in the meantime."

"I wish to hell this hadn't happened at all," I said.

"Tell me about it." Freeman lit another smoke. "You didn't hear me say this, but LeBrock might have some friends. You okay for self protection?"

"Glock 30 in the 4Runner, more stuff at home. I'm okay."

Freeman nodded. "You look like you can handle yourself. You got LeBrock through the ankle, one in the head." I was quiet on that, comment being unwise. Freeman got out of his car again. I got out, too. "Go ahead, take off. I'll contact you if I think of something else. And call us early tomorrow."

"Sure. And look, Sergeant, I appreciate your being straight with me. Honest."

Freeman put his hand out, we shook. "You seem all right, Mitch. Maybe you've gotten some bad rep."

"Hope so."

"I do need to tell you that some of the CSI people said you were dressed like a big fuckin' bee." He grinned. "Myself, I don't see it. You have a good night."

There went my graceful exit. I went inside to talk with Turkey John.

"What the fuck do you want?" he said. "I'll have cops crawling through here for a week. So much for turning a fucking profit."

"I'm sorry about this, John," I told him. I pulled the cash he'd given me out of my pocket, stuck it into his hand. "Consider our account square, paid in full." Before he could say anything, I turned and walked out to my car.

Everything was fine until I got home. That's when the headaches and nausea began.

Chapter 6

Shimmers of heat rose from the sticky asphalt lot and formed distorted counterfeit images of the cars and trucks squatting there. The furious sun glared at bits of chrome trim and bumper, forcing lancets of brightness from these points straight through the deep tint of my windshield.

The air conditioner of the 4Runner cycled as it compensated for the hundred degree September day and the entire vehicle registered a labored complaint, shuddering as the engine took up the slack. I wondered how much strain I was putting on the faithful Toyota machinery, how many months I was shaving off its lifespan. Cost of doing business, I figured—if you call sitting on your tail all Sunday afternoon business.

I was in eastside Houston, parked in a midsize office complex over by the Ship Channel and right in the afternoon sun because the existence of a single shade tree was anathema to an imperious enterprise philosophy that squeezed out each available square foot of rental space.

Dozens of places like this exist in Houston, everywhere in fact. Developers obliterate a respectable neighborhood, bulldozing homes and apartments that sat happily for decades. Trees ripped from their ancient roots as well, chaff blown from the millstone of egregious capitalism. Then come the concrete slabs and cheap cinderblocks and cheesy aluminum trim, long rows of generic shops and offices extruded like sausages from an infernal steampunk packing house. In these stores you can get a beer, a tune-up, life insurance, a cheap suit and a massage. And that's only the first block. Eventually the focus of commerce turns elsewhere, the strip centers fail and are flattened, making room for more homes and apartments, cycle continuing unabated. Progress they call it, but I had my doubts.

So here I sat in this abominable modernity because it gave me a good view of the back door of All Houston Pawn, where I was expecting Rudolph Barnetski and his accomplices to show up and make their delivery. Thus far, they hadn't.

I was waiting for Barnetski and his pals because he was the prime suspect in the burglary of a pawnshop where he clerked across town. Someone had broken in two weeks ago, disconnected the surveillance video and taken the guns, stereos, cameras, everything of value. Police figured it for an inside job and the insurance company agreed, but there was no clear proof. Suspicion fell to Rudy Barnetski since he was the only new employee, the others being family or having worked there years. Rudy had also been in trouble before, minor scrapes. The cops questioned Barnetski but nothing came of it, so they filed the case alongside the hundreds of other unsolved burglaries. They simply don't have time or resources to stake out every petty suspect. So the insurance people asked me to work the case.

Such jobs are the foundation of a private investigator's food pyramid. We function mostly on retainer from law firms and insurance companies, picking up the rest of our business by referrals and, once in a millennium, the walk-in client who is the mainstay of the fictional private eye.

In mystery novels, desperate and stunningly gorgeous women are endlessly trudging up the four squeaky flights to the PI's shabby office. There's so many of them they have to take a number, just like the long line of imaginary girls in the old Brit movie The Knack. In real life, clients never pick you out of a phone book at random. Who uses phone books these days anyway? Sure, my website solicits clients but I also make it clear that my bread and butter jobs come from professional sources. And anyone searching for me in a walkup will be out of luck. My office is in the front of my house.

Chapter 7

When I took the pawnshop contract, I poked around, spread some talking money and was put in touch with a snitch named Bobby Carter. From him I learned that the suspected Rudy Barnetski hung out with Randy Shindler, owner of East Houston Pawn. HPD robbery division had Shindler pegged as a fence, even though the county attorney hadn't yet put together enough evidence for an indictment, the mills of justice always grinding slowly.

Nevertheless, Bobby Carter assured me that the stolen goods would be filtered into East Houston's inventory today and Carter was probably right because he'd been asked to help lug all the stuff. Therefore, I sat, listened to a Mozart symphony and waited.

Things had been calm since the Dutch LeBrock attack. The police found everything in order, the county attorney referred the case to the grand jury without charges and the shooting was ruled justified. And because Dutch's younger brother was serving eight-to-ten in Huntsville for armed robbery, I didn't have to look over my shoulder for him. Good.

So they gave me my pistol back and I was turned loose on the streets again. My insides still churned occasionally from memories of the shooting but I was sleeping better each night.

* * *

Our rainy spell had long since disappeared and now we were into the heat cycle, typical for a Houston fall, where the weather ping-pongs back and forth between storm and toaster oven. A parallel to my personal life.

I'd already gone through the Sunday Chronicle and was kicking myself for not having brought a book or loaded one onto my new Samsung handheld. I'd virtually memorized the sports section, such as it pretends to be in Houston, and in frustration I then reread each scrap of other news, things I usually skipped, like Lawrence Zane's awful column in which he rambles endlessly about yesteryear except that he can't remember any of it. I even pored through the society page, where vapid sycophants heaped inane praise on each other's desolate socialite careers. I was told who had been seen with whom, who was summering in Tuscany and who was celebrating an anniversary at Tony's Wine Cellar. As if I gave a spotted damn.

Next, I played around with my new Samsung gadget. It's a bit smaller than an iPad, maybe less powerful, but I'd chosen it for being compact in the first place. I wasn't planning on watching 3D movies or rebuilding ancient Tyre anyway. I just wanted a handy electronic notebook, something to replace the ancient paper standby. I'd already set up my calendar and appointment schedule, which was a snap. Now I was testing how accurately the thing analyzed my cribbed handwriting and converted it to nice clean text. Pretty well, it turned out—it hadn't hiccupped once. As long as I was reasonably neat, it digested anything I wrote. This was a plus, I decided. Otherwise, I'd have blown a few hundred bucks on a fancy Etch-a-Sketch. But I soon tired of this, too. The computer games didn't interest me, surfing the Net didn't float my boat today, so I shut off the little smartphone and dumped it back into my shoulder bag.

I was bored, plain and simple. Funny thing, that. Boredom was what made me opt out of the legal profession to become a private investigator in the first place. I could still hear my father's disappointed stentorian lecture: "Mitchell, you must stay the course, apply yourself. I have served the law in my time, as did your grandfather in his, as you should now. I anticipated the day when you might place your name beside mine, King and King, Attorneys at Law. Don't turn your back on your heritage, Mitchell. Reconsider."

And reconsider I did, for five agonizing months. But I'd had enough. Despite genuine respect for my father, I was simply not cut from attorney cloth. I left law school my second year, milled around a while, taught American history at community college, briefly considered joining the FBI, then decided that becoming a private investigator might be the ticket. I could stay in touch with my friends in the legal profession yet enjoy a more exciting vocation. Little did I expect that the thrill of being a private eye would boil down to sitting alone in my car all afternoon, trying to stay awake.

Mozart's Symphony Forty-One was over. I clicked off my iPod and tried the radio, scanning idly, searching for a modicum of brightness. Nada. I couldn't listen to the Astros because they were playing the Angels tonight. And the classical station was running a fund drive, Alan Alda droning on in his nasal way about the value of supporting Public Radio. Nothing makes me change the station faster than hearing, "We'll get back to our regular programming soon, but there are plenty of phone lines open and we need to hear from you." Click.

I retrieved the iPod again, dangling where it was jacked into my dash so I could use the car stereo. I scrolled through the albums I'd ripped and came up with Michel Camilo's On The Other Hand. Sounds of his extraordinary jazz piano soon filled my ears and took an edge off the waiting. I did a few isometrics to work the kinks out and squeezed a hand exerciser to further liven up my day.

It's said that cops lead lives of stupefying tedium punctuated by rare moments of sheer panic. Being a PI is the same, minus the panic. You spend most of your time searching the Internet or digging through musty city and county records. Some assignments do require fieldwork, slightly less boring but nonetheless mundane. You sit in a MickeyD's with a microphone up your sleeve to tape an embezzler bragging to his girlfriend. You sit in a motel parking lot to grab a photo of a wayward wife screwing her boss. You sit outside a golf course and video a guy on total disability playing the back nine. Mostly you just sit. You sit and wait, drink a thermos of rancid coffee, then piss it away into an empty Gatorade bottle because you can't quit your vigil long enough to use the john at the Chevron down the street.

I was reaching for that bottle when a battered Econoline came around the corner and pulled up behind the pawnshop. Barnetski, Shindler and my snitch Bobby Carter got out.

Chapter 8

Rudolf Barnetski was a small man, barely five-six. He was wearing faded jeans and an old AC/DC shirt, ready for some grunt work. Randy Shindler, pawnshop owner and partner in this rip-off, was a tall thickset guy, fat but muscular beneath, expansive beer-gut overlapping his beltline and hanging cantilever above his well-concealed zipper. He was decked out in his finest pawnbroker regalia, slime green slacks and an ugly print shirt topped with wide paisley suspenders. Bobby Carter was average size and wore modest slacks with a neat button-down shirt. The three men had all the size and sartorial bases covered.

They looked around but didn't spot me because I was wedged between a couple of semi-trailers partway down the street. Shindler unlocked the back of his shop while Barnetski and Carter climbed into the rear of the van. Through my binoculars, I could see a stack of surround sound receivers and other gear in the truck, so I punched up Freddy Gonzales on my smartphone.

"HPD robbery division, Sergeant Gonzales speaking. How can I help you?"

"Gonzie? Mitch King here. They just showed up. You ready to rumble?" I delivered the last word with a bad Michael Buffer impression, stretching out the syllables to rumbool like I was introducing pro wrestling.

Gonzie ignored my lame attempt at humor. "How long we got?"

"Twenty, twenty-five."

"Sit tight and don't do nothin'," he cautioned. "On the way." Gonzie verified the address and hung up.

I did as Gonzie suggested and watched the three men unload their booty. Carter crouched in the truck and passed out the goods, while Barnetski and Shindler stacked the stuff just inside the pawnshop door. Shindler might have thought he'd avoid manual labor but it hadn't worked out that way and with his help they were hurrying the job and making better time than I first guessed. If the cops didn't get here soon I might need to stick my nose in.

Twenty minutes. I opened the center console and took my .45 from the padded spring clips I'd installed. It was so damn hot lately that I'd temporarily abandoned the shoulder rig and gone back to my waistband paddle holster or keeping the pistol in the console.

More action at the pawnshop. Bobby Carter hopped out of the now-empty van and slammed its door. He held a six-pack of Lone Star cans by the plastic rings, peeled off three beers and shared them with his pals. I figured they'd chug the beer and head out. The cops were nowhere, so I clicked off the radio, put the Toyota in drive and edged from my hiding place.

I ran the window down as I neared the trio and the heat blew in like a monster hair dryer set on high. Houston summers are a treat if you're into nonstop saunas and they last from May until well into October. The men's shirts were soaked through and mine would soon be the same.

Shindler quickly shut his shop door when he saw me approach and all three men stood side by side near the van. They frowned uneasily at my arrival so I put on a happy face, Mister Nice Guy on a pleasant drive. Bobby Carter recognized me right away and backed off from the other two, but he didn't say anything to blow my cover.

I put the car in park. "Excuse me. I'm turned around. Guess I'm lost. How do I get to Navigation Boulevard?"

Shindler gestured. "It's back that way about six blocks."

He pointed south and Navigation was actually east but I didn't care. Instead I opened my door and leaned out, keeping my right hand behind the door panel. "I've got a map. Can you show me?"

Shindler walked over. He was impatient but willing to cooperate in order to get rid of the pesky stranger.

I slid to the pavement and brought the pistol into view. "Okay," I told him. "Stop right there." He stopped. I kept the gun pointed down but waved it toward Carter and Barnetski. "You two stay where you are."

"Shit, I only got, like, twenty bucks on me," Shindler said. "You're welcome to it. Just don't shoot nobody."

I smiled. If Randy Shindler thought he was getting robbed, he was in for a surprise. I backed up so all three men would be covered, and as I did, stumbled on a low curb and lost my balance!

That was the opening Barnetski needed. He threw his beer at me and it splashed into my eyes as the can dinged off my forehead. It was a risky move but he did it anyway and it worked perfectly.

Shindler rushed me, slapping at my pistol with a huge fist. The gun spun out of my hand and clattered to the pavement, bouncing away. He slammed me against my car, his substantial weight knocking me breathless.

Barnetski pounced over and kicked at my ankles and knees like an enraged child.

My right leg went numb and I slipped sideways. Shindler used his thick forearm to drill me repeatedly under the chin, banging the back of my head against the Toyota while Barnetski continued his kicks. I turned to protect my groin but my eyes unfocused and it was only a matter of time until they had me down. One of them would pick up my pistol and that would be it.

No way! I summoned any energy I had, jammed my thumb hard into Shindler's throat. He jerked away momentarily, giving me room. I steadied myself and grabbed his shirt lapels, snapping his head down, my knee up. I heard his nose crack like a number two pencil. Shindler reeled drunkenly and I kicked him square in the balls. He folded over like a garage sale lawn chair.

I quickly reached over and snatched Barnetski by the hair, swung him headfirst into the Toyota's high-rise bumper. His skull made a satisfying hollow clang and he dropped.

Shindler was on his hands and knees, coughing, a stream of blood dribbling from his nose. I spotted my Springfield lying beside my front tire. The safety was still on and the pistol looked fine. I picked it up and covered Shindler, who at the time was not paying much attention anyway. Barnetski lay unmoving and Bobby Carter was standing where he'd been all along. He could have helped me but hadn't. Thanks for nothing.

I looked around. Sergeant Frederico Gonzales was leaning in the door of his cop car, grinning broadly at me.

"Sorry we were late," he said. "About ready to lend a hand but you being such a tough guy, we figured you wanted to take care of business yourself."

Chapter 9

Two cop cars had pulled up during the altercation but I hadn't seen them, distracted with fighting Shindler and Barnetski. There was Gonzales' plainclothes unit, Gonzie's partner Taurean Williams driving and a regular blue-and-white cruiser behind, two uniformed cops inside. All of them were laughing their asses off at my nearly having the crap beat out of me.

Hey, what are friends for?

Randy Shindler was slowly rising to his feet and Barnetski was moving around, moaning. I holstered my pistol and looked back to Gonzie. "You guys mind helping a little? Or should I take them downtown myself and book them for you, too?"

Still chuckling, Gonzie gestured to the uniforms, who got out and began to round up the wounded. They checked Barnetski, rendered an expert medical opinion and pronounced him in perfect condition for handcuffs. Shindler and Bobby Carter got the same. All three were patted down for weapons and stuffed into the back of the cruiser. To protect his identity, my snitch would be treated like the others at first, then released. It was a small price to pay and Bobby Carter, being the inept criminal I knew him to be, would eventually land back in jail on his own recognizance.

Freddy Gonzales smiled and we shook hands. "You okay, really?" he asked.

"Yeah, fine." My head was still spinning and my knee ached but I would never give him the satisfaction of knowing. "Not so you guys would give a shit if I got killed."

"That's where you're wrong. You lost ten bucks to me on the Astros last week and I gotta collect. You punch out your ticket, I get nothing." Gonzie laughed again.

Cop humor is sardonic, dark and often downright crude, befitting the Chandlerian mean streets in which they ply their trade. Gonzie meant nothing personal and would have broken up the fight had it turned against me. At least I hoped so.

Frederico Gonzales is a longtime robbery cop and we are okay pals, having teamed up on other insurance cases. He's a thickset Hispanic man, perfect archetype of the TV cop. Today he wore unpressed slacks, blue shirt with bleach stains and an awful leaping bass fish tie that was new when Ronald Reagan was in the White House.

There was an informal poll going around the cop shop as to who was the worst dresser, Gonzie or my old buddy Lieutenant Joe Duggan in Homicide. It was a dead heat but I'd give Joe the edge for sentimentality's sake.

I consider Gonzie my friend but he is slowly sinking into a swamp of alcohol. Binge drinking, whether it's once a week or once a month, still works its devastation. And now that Gonzie had split with his wife, the drinking was even worse. It was just a matter of time before he showed up for duty with a load on or started carrying a flask with him. And that would get him suspended, fired maybe.

I'd broached the subject but he brushed me off. "Hey, you drink! Who the hell are you to criticize?"

Yes, I drink, but Gonzie would easily put down four whiskeys to my one. And he'd already been stopped twice for driving drunk. Because he was a cop, they arranged a ride home and no paperwork materialized, but I wondered whether they were actually doing him a favor. God help him if he cracked up while driving and hurt somebody.

This was of course disingenuous of me to be judgmental, considering my idiotic and legendary drunk driving performance last summer. But I'd learned my lesson the hard way and didn't want a pal to go through the same legal nightmare. Nevertheless, giving people unsolicited advice always sounds preachy and recommendations are rarely taken to heart. So lately I just kept my big mouth shut.

Chapter 10

All around us, the parking lot began to fill with cop cars. There were Houston Police, Harris County constables, even a contingent from Metro Transit. They hadn't been called but heard the arrest report over their radios and wanted to get in on the action. Cops on patrol are usually isolated, so they jump at any chance to get together and chat. That's the way it is, you need one cop and you get thirty. Other times you can't find them anywhere.

Taurean Williams walked over, stood next to his partner Gonzie and said nothing. He nodded slightly to me and I did the same. I don't think he liked me much but I'd get over it. What he had against me I didn't know and also didn't much care. Life's too short for me to play United Nations and try to get along with everybody.

Williams had just been promoted from uniformed street duty, so Gonzie was partnering to break him in. A black man with rugged even features, Williams has the build of a dedicated power lifter. I know him only slightly because he's new and is all business. He doesn't kid around, drink, smoke, or spend time goofing off. He comes to work, does his job in a quiet professional way then heads straight home to family, which is not my style. Me, I'll be hanging out at Alibis, a cop bar in downtown Houston, hustling the rookies at pool and generally making a nuisance of myself. I'd probably find Gonzie there later and pay off my bet.

Gonzales looked over to the pawnshop. "Stuff in there?"

"Yeah," I told him. "I've got the insurance papers and serial numbers. But first I gotta use the head. Been sitting in that damn SUV all day and my bladder's about to bust." I ducked into the pawnshop accompanied by Gonzie's laughter, relief nevertheless greatly appreciated and propriety be damned.

Nature served, I retrieved a clipboard from my 4Runner and began to check the stereos and other stuff stacked on the pawnshop floor. Gonzie and I verified some of the matching numbers then we walked over to the cop car and looked in at Shindler, who had already been Mirandized and was staring a hole through me. Guess he blamed me for the bust. Tough.

"Good news, Randy," Gonzie told him. "You're going down for receiving stolen merchandize." Shindler murmured some bullshit under his breath and grumbled about calling his lawyer but that was to be expected. "Your buddy

Carter here the same, Barnetski for grand theft too. Looks like felony jail time for all you sonsabitches."

Shindler glared out at me.

I'd gone boar hunting with Tony Vee once in Arkansas, and the guy who owned the property had a tusker in a pen for us to look at. The boar had the same eyes as Shindler, red and hot. "You dickheads," he growled. "I'm gonna rip all of you new assholes for this, don't forget."

I smiled broadly. "Fuck you very much."

Shindler hawked deep in his throat, ready to spit in my face. I quickly stood back, out of range. One of the uniformed cops named Ahmir Mohammed noticed this and moved to intercept. Mohammed is a huge black man, Bluto biceps and Popeye forearms, even larger than Taurean Williams.

Mohammed scowled down at Shindler. "You best listen to me, boy, 'cause I'm telling you this just once. You spit in my car and mess it up, your ride downtown's gonna be a long one." Their eyes met for a second, then Shindler swallowed his cud and looked away. The cop turned back to us. "He gonna behave. No trouble." Mohammed had a toothpick in his mouth and he shifted it back and forth as he grinned and winked. I couldn't tell whether he'd been blowing smoke or was serious, but I certainly didn't blame Shindler for taking him at his word. No sense tempting fate with a guy the size of Cleveland.

Taurean Williams got a listing of stolen property from his car and began to check out other things in the pawnshop. After a minute he found more items, guns mostly, so Gonzie radioed for an inventory team to tag the goods. A few pieces of this recent heist would be kept as evidence but the bulk of it could go back to my clients later next week.

Gonzie shook my hand again. "Thanks for helping out."

"Not to mention. Doing my job."

Gonzie let the perps stew in the back seat and hung around, shooting the breeze with the other cops. There were so many mirrored sunglasses you'd think that disco was back. The cops talked about sports and women and guns and checked out the stolen electronics, comparing prices on the better units. Some of it would end up at auction and the cops would keep their eyes open for bargains there. Cheers were raised when somebody produced a cold twelve-pack of Coke, liberated from Shindler's fridge. Carter's three leftover beers had long since vanished, I knew not where. I certainly didn't get one.

Finally, the inventory guys showed up and Gonzales headed downtown to book the perps. The sightseeing cops drifted away car by car, their conversation jones now satiated and the chill of air-conditioned cruisers beckoning.

The new arrivals were uniformed cops near retirement, filling in where they could. They helped me go through the shop's inventory, at least enough to make a good case. A complete records check would take several days, so they'd lock up and come back tomorrow.

After a while, I was finished. I signed the paperwork, then swung by Burger King for dinner. To celebrate my successful day, I supersized.

Chapter 11

Walter Albertson leaned back in his executive leather chair behind his executive mahogany desk and looked out his executive office window, perusing the Houston skyline. We were on the twenty-fifth floor and the view was substantial, meant to impress visitors and remind them of their lack of status compared to the man behind the desk.

Albertson's a poster boy for the dynamic and successful investment guru. He's trim, buff, in far better shape than most men in their fifties, tanned and coiffed, greying temples his only concession to age. He wore a rust tone monogrammed shirt with a deep blue silk tie, that color having recently supplanted red as the preeminent power color. I couldn't see his slacks or shoes from where I sat but I was certain everything he wore was handcrafted and exactly right.

I had been summoned to Frontline Investment Services, a headwater of Houston banking and finance, one of the few large money brokers that maintained a clean record during the recent downturn and scandals. Apparently, Frontline had negotiated difficult times by doing something quite unusual—they were honest and invested their clients' money diligently. If news got around it might signify a trend in the making.

Since Walter Albertson and his company still had requisite business cojones, I'd dressed appropriately, my best suit and shirt, neat rep tie, the works. I'd even foregone my habitual Nikes and wore polished loafers, the kind with little tassels. I did however defer putting pennies in the slots. I do have some pride remaining, after all.

I was no stylistic match for the man across the desk from me but he needed to find his wandering wife and was willing to pay me well for the job, which put us on equal status, temporary though it was. Besides, I had my fancy new Samsung man-toy and I'd practiced on it so I could show off. I figured that scored me some points.

Missing or wayward spouse cases are always a toss, which is why I don't particularly like them. I prefer to stick with stolen property and insurance deals because they're more predictable. Looking for stray jewelry is a hell of a lot easier than searching for stray humans anyway. I take a contract to find a disappearing wife, but after spending a chunk of time looking, she comes home under her own initiative. That means the client tries to back out of paying. Or I'm hired to discover whether hubby is fooling around while he's working those long weekends, I learn the straight stuff and have him by the short hairs and surprise, Mister Magnificent is forgiven his sins, which casts me as the wicked messenger. And since hubby wields the checkbook, I'm stiffed again.

As a result, investigators like me generally require a substantial advance for marital screw-ups. I usually ask a thousand up front, which quickly separates the tire-kickers from serious customers. Considering the surroundings, I didn't think Albertson would bat an eyelash, so I decided then and there to bump the advance to fifteen hundred. My mechanic told me last week the MGB needed yet another engine job, which lent an air of authenticity to my price schedule. Even so, I wasn't persuaded that I needed the headaches that were guaranteed to accompany this case, so I decided to see what came next and make up my mind. I'd been pretty busy lately so this job was optional.

Without turning his chair, Albertson addressed the city below. "I'm not sure I should even be talking to you, Mr. King."

I shrugged. He just helped me decide. And so much for my new fee structure. The MG would just have to smoke and cough a while longer. "That makes two of us," I replied and stood, picked up my attaché case.

Albertson turned around and tried to wave me back with a dismissive gesture. He was used to the exercise of authority and the signal was meant to put me in my place and keep me there. But I didn't work for him yet and therefore needed to assert my independence. So I pretended I hadn't seen anything and continued for the door.

"Sit down, Mr. King. Please?" He swung back to the window view.

Please. The magic word. I returned to my chair and joined him in assessing the city sprawl. We sat thus for a while, silence of the paneled office between us, barrier imposed by status and breached by need.

He swiveled to face me. "Normally I'd hire one of the larger Houston detective firms, K Griff maybe, Frontline's used them before. But this is strictly personal and I want it to remain on the QT. So I asked around. Larry McLaughlin says you're reliable."

I shrugged. I'd done some work for McLaughlin's law firm.

"Are you always this reticent?" he asked.

"Not really. It's my expected persona, the stoic private detective."

Albertson let out a sigh. "And the sarcasm?"

"Especially the sarcasm. But I don't charge extra for it."

There was a tweak of a smile on Albertson's face. He nodded. "I want you to find Valerie. My wife."

This I already knew. "The police are good at that sort of thing, finding missing persons."

"No. Not now. I'm sure she's okay."

"So you believe that she's staying away of her own volition."

"Our marriage hasn't, ah, been the best, I admit. Valerie has been known to, ah, take a break occasionally."

"But she's gone longer than usual this time," I guessed.

"Two weeks."

"No word?"

"Well, she phoned when she first left. She was staying with her friend Kathryn Morley." Albertson shut his eyes and rubbed his forehead in frustration. "Morley's a graphic artist down in the Montrose district, works out of her house. That's where Valerie goes."

When Albertson said Montrose he twitched his lips in faint distaste. I was amused at his slight regard for Houston's venerable arts and music neighborhood. People like Albertson would describe the Montrose as where those people live, meaning gays.

"But she's not at Morley's now," I prompted.

"It's been, ah, three days since she left Kathryn Morley. Kathryn insists she doesn't know Valerie's whereabouts."

"Mr. Albertson, my recommendation is to bring in the police. She may be in trouble. She may—"

He cut me off with another wave. "If you can't turn up anything quickly, then yes, I'll call them, but I'd prefer to keep it private until that time. That's why I phoned you."

"Okay," I said. "Deal." I recited my newly inflated rates and it was his turn to say okay. I pulled a contract from my attaché case, filled in some blanks, we both signed it and he gave me the advance check from his personal account. We shook hands as if we were longtime pals at a frat reunion.

Chapter 12

"Do you have any recent pictures of your wife?" I asked.

Albertson reached over to his credenza and swung a heavy silver picture frame around. A good photo of the happy couple, handsome and wealthy investment broker with his younger trophy wife. They were on the flying bridge of a cabin cruiser and dressed in casual sports clothes, the kind you see in yuppie catalogs or TV shows about rich people. Albertson standing at the helm, Valerie leaning alongside, his arm around and pulling her close. She was striking, raven haired and dark eyed, her face open and unlined, resembling a young Mary Tyler Moore. I took Valerie to be in her early thirties.

"When was this taken?"

"April, ah, May. We just refinished the boat."

"Okay if I snap a copy of this?" He nodded. I eased the print from the frame, laid it flat, grabbed a pic with my phone, slid the photo back into the frame.

I began my spiel. "We need to speak about some difficult topics, Mr. Albertson. You understand it's necessary. All will be in confidence." Another nod. "When did you first meet Valerie, what do you know about her?"

He spread his hands in acceptance and outlined the basics while I jotted notes into my handheld. "I first got acquainted with Valerie about four years ago. We, ah, hit it off from the beginning and were married right away. My first wife is, ah, deceased." He frowned deeply, perhaps reliving painful memories.

"Valerie previously married?"

"No," he said. "This is her first."

"And you both have daughters, I understand?"

"Yes. My Paula is eighteen, her daughter, ah, Cheryl just turned seventeen." Albertson furrowed his brow again. "Cheryl insists on keeping her original last name, Stern. Cheryl Stern. I don't know why."

I shrugged. "Who can figure out teenagers anyway?" Albertson nodded his assent. "How long has Valerie been, ah, running away?" I asked, mimicking his speech pattern just for personal grins. Many people are hesitant when nervous or uncomfortable and I'd picked up on it right away.

"Since last year. Things were fine until then."

"Always to Kate Morley's place? Or has she gone elsewhere?"

"Morley always."

"Why does Valerie leave? What does she tell you?"

"That I'm too demanding, too, ah, controlling, that sort of thing. Nothing specific. It's to recharge her batteries, take a break, she tells me." He smiled thinly. "I suppose I can be a bit overprotective at times. She probably has a valid point."

I caught a flicker in his eyes. He wasn't telling me everything, but few clients do and I'd find out more when necessary. "Mr. Albertson, do you have any indication whether another man is involved?"

"No, absolutely not!" His reply was terse. Then he looked away, out the window, as if to deflect my question and reinforce his executive status. His voice softened. "I suppose it's possible. But not as far as I know. I think she'd have given me some indication by now."

"Valerie and Kathryn. Their relationship strictly platonic?"

This made Albertson bristle. "Hell yes, it's platonic! They're just friends. Valerie's not a lesbian. Neither is Kathryn Morley for that matter."

I held up my palm in apology. "I had to ask." I next pressed on with more hard stuff. "Has Valerie ever suffered any mental or emotional problems?" Albertson shook his head. "Drugs besides an occasional toke on a joint?" No, not even that. "Excessive alcohol?" No.

I verified Albertson's home phone, cell phone and his address. He also gave me Morley's number. I clicked off my Samsung. "That about does it for now. I'll phone Kathryn Morley and try to see her today. And I'd like to stop by your house tonight and speak with both daughters, if possible."

"I don't want to bring them into this."

"Mr. Albertson, they're your family. They're already in this."

"They would have told me if they knew where Valerie was."

I let that hang in the air. Kids never tell their parents anything and we both knew it. I just looked at him, waiting for an answer. Finally, he relented. "All right, just don't pry too much. I don't want to trouble the girls more than necessary."

"I'll be circumspect." I was about to add that I wouldn't use the rubber hose but decided that bit of whimsy would be unappreciated. "I do need all the information I can gather if I'm to find your wife."

"I hope you find her, and soon. She's important to me."

Not I love her but she's important to me. But love comes in all flavors, and sometimes greed or possessiveness masquerade as love. Who am I to judge what really counts?

We agreed to meet at Albertson's house at seven so I could talk with the girls, then we shook hands again and I headed out.

In the elevator, my ears popped on the ride down. I wondered what effect it might have on your brain, doing it several times a day.

Chapter 13

I phoned Valerie's friend Kathryn Morley a few times but it went straight to voicemail so I gave up, grabbed a late lunch at Boston Market and went home to go through some recent invoices for my accountant.

I parked in my covered port and let myself in the back door, bypassing my small office at the front. Krazy Kat immediately ran to greet me, meowing a hello and crying for dinner in the same breath. Kraze is a little tuxedo-marked cat that my attorney friend Donna Boudreaux gave me to match my kitchen wall Kit-Kat clock, even though I've never been able to get my real cat to move his eyes and tail back and forth in sync with his mechanical cousin. Nevertheless, I love him. Kraze got a nice pouch of food and fresh water.

After a bit of obligatory accounting and number crunching, I worked out on my Bowflex, showered, reviewed my notes on the Albertson case before meeting the daughters.

The interview with Walter Albertson had been predictable, he being guarded but eventually divulging enough information for me to get started. I was certain there was more he wasn't telling. Was he abusive to Valerie? Perhaps, if only verbally. Did she have a lover? Likely. Did I actually care? Not really. All I wanted was to get her back home. Maybe I could steer them into some counseling or therapy, if only to better satisfy my client. A referral from Walter Albertson on my resume would bring plenty of work. I did some checking on the Internet but found only a few typical success-oriented stories on Walter and his firm. No dirt, sadly.

Still no reply from Kathryn Morley so I drove over to the Albertson house. It was early evening and the Houston temperature had plummeted to a chilly eighty-two. I passed pecan and oak trees along the way, cicadas buzzing angrily, complaining that their mates were too distant for their lustful song. Occasionally I'd hear the squeal of a cicada as it was snatched away by a bird, never to consummate its romance, instead stuffed into the maw of hungry nature. Reminded me of my own love life.

* * *

This was River Oaks, the most glam neighborhood in Houston. The sidewalks are clean and neat, hedges trimmed, lawns perfect. The homes have servant quarters larger than my own house. And better. River Oaks has its own rental cops, its own top-drawer country club and I'd swear its own private atmosphere to breathe.

I parked in front of one of the shabbier places, a modest little shack that would list for a million three. I'd driven the MGB and wondered whether it would get towed on general principle, not being a Lexus or Jag. But a private eye has to take risks.

As I strolled to the front door, I made sure my tie was straight. I couldn't check my shoeshine because I was wearing Nikes again, but I did make up for it by checking that my jeans were zipped. After all, this was high society.

I rang the bell and waited.

The door opened and I thought I was on the set of a vampire show. The pretty, elfin girl who stood before me was dressed in a ripped black sleeveless shirt, black micro skirt, artfully torn black net hose and huge black lace up combat boots. She had a bunch of rings through each ear and a stud in her right nostril. Her hair was dyed black with bright red streaks like Joan Jett once did, her eye shadow, lipstick and nails were black, and she had a smile to match the cheerfulness of the outfit. Which is to say none. She sucked in light like the massive black hole at galactic center.

Goth, they call it, a style that blends post-punk rock with an affectation for Gothic noir. It had gone dormant for a few years but the recent deluge of vampire TV and movies had launched another cycle. Think Winona Ryder in Beetlejuice, the clothing less studied, more cast-off, and you have it.

For most kids it's a harmless fad, rebellion against parents in the time-honored tradition of wearing the clothes that Mom and Dad hate most. A few of the less stable youth drift into a dangerous fringe environment of hard drugs and blood-sharing vampirism, but those are a distinct minority. This girl in particular would be known as a fairy, not in the homosexual slang sense, but because this subclass of petite, waiflike and attractive black-clad young Goth women resembled Tinkerbell's evil twin, minus wings and, far as I could tell, pixie dust.

"You are?" she asked, staring blankly straight through me, chewing gum all the while.

I smiled, hoping to counter her dour visage with my own exaggerated cheer. "I'm Mitchell King, a private investigator. Mr. Albertson asked me to stop by tonight. About Valerie."

She nodded. "I'm Cheryl Stern. Valerie's my mom. Walter said you'd be here. He wants you to help find her." A look of concern crossed her face, erasing the carefully planned insouciance. "He phoned, said he'd be late, another damned board meeting. Come on in."

She shut the door after me and I followed her down a corridor, passing obscure and vacant rooms until we reached a small library at the rear of the house. In the library with the candlestick by Professor Plum, I thought.

A strident beeping suddenly echoed through the house. "Shit!" Cheryl exclaimed. "Forgot to fucking turn off the alarm. Be back in a sec." And she scurried away.

Chapter 14

While she was gone, I looked around the room. Arranged on the walls were some abstract watercolors. I'm a fan of modern art so these gained my attention immediately. Most of the paintings were of a single mind and obviously on the same theme, whatever that might be. Each had a neutral backing with deep vertical color streaks in the foreground, slightly convex, the grouping reminiscent of the Georgia O'Keeffe Grey Line series. The art showed good command of form and a fine strong hand in color balance.

On another wall were three different pieces, excellent charcoal sketches that resembled a monochrome Leroy Neiman, except that the subject wasn't sports but strangely, offshore oil platforms. I could easily recognize the shape of the various rigs even though they were in the abstract. Why would Walter Albertson hang oilrig sketches? Far as I knew, he wasn't involved in the oil and gas business. Gifts, probably.

All the books on the shelves were in tidy rows and might have been that way since the place was built, the books lined up and framed in place like bricks in a wall to become load bearing structural members.

As Bill Gates once remarked, people don't read any more.

To support that axiom, a huge widescreen Sony digital TV was stuck against the far wall, sound muted, its picture snapping through dozens of channels like a kaleidoscope rolling downhill. The source of the channel surfing was a well built young man draped sidesaddle across the arms of an easy chair. He stared at the screen through half-lidded eyes as he flicked the remote, looking but not really watching, just twiddling his fingers.

He was costumed the same as Cheryl, all in black, except that his hair was dyed platinum blond and stuck straight up in tiny spikes like Billy Idol. That hairstyle is passé but I figured him for a traditionalist. His arms bore a considerable gallery of tattoos, some with indecipherable rock band logos formed from symbols that could be useful at an Albert Speer rally, some with rude and ostensibly clever slogans like Go Suck. The kid looked up and shot me a bored sneer.

"Hi," I said, waving like a loony and broadening my smile.

He sneered again, went back for more TV.

A moment later Cheryl returned. "That's Kenny," she said, nodding to her apparent boyfriend as though describing a piece of furniture.

"We've already met," I replied. "We were discussing the Uncle Charles principle in James Joyce's Ulysses. I feel it elucidates a derivative style borrowed from Flaubert, but Kenny disagrees. He maintains the technique is unique and wholly Joyce's." This was met with a blank look from Cheryl and a menacing glare from Kenny.

I knew the comment was insolent but I'd had a long day and I get cranky and petulant when I'm tired.

Cheryl continued to look at me openmouthed.

"Never mind," I said, handed her one of my cards. For the River Oaks visit I'd selected my conservative model, the one that simply read Mitchell King, Investigations, with my phone numbers, webpage and e-mail address beneath. Understatement is good. "Call me Mitch."

I reached out my hand in greeting and she took it tentatively like I'd passed her a dead lizard. Young people aren't used to the social custom of shaking hands but I was okay with this and didn't care. I could tell she was tense and it wasn't because she had just met the smartest private eye in Houston. There were small worry lines around the corners of her eyes, totally out of place for such a pretty girl. And she'd been crying.

Kenny looked at me narrowly. "You a real private eye?"

"Yep."

"You got a gun and everything?"

"Gun and everything."

"Fuck it," he said, then turned back to the TV, limited curiosity satisfied.

I suppressed an urge to put a bullet right through the big screen, just to test his reflexes.

"Don't mind Kenny," Cheryl told me. "He's so full of shit his eyes are brown."

So Kenny flipped her the bird without glancing away from the set. She returned the favor, adding the bonus of a wicked smirk. And they say today's youth aren't romantic.

I got to the subject of my visit. "I'm sorry about your mother," I said. "Her being missing."

Cheryl nodded again. "I'm sure she's okay, but I wish she'd at least call."

"Any idea where she might be?"

She lowered her head in denial. "No. She usually phones after a day or two, talks to me, then comes home. Not this time."

"I understand that she's gone off like this before. Walter told me. How often has it happened? Do you know why she does it?"

That brought Kenny out of his stupor. He'd taken an instant dislike of me and this was all the excuse he needed. He flicked the TV off, stood up and stalked over to confront me. He pulled himself to his best height and tried to stare me down. Kenny was a tall, solid kid, about six feet, muscular, and as used to getting his way as was Walter Albertson but for different reasons. Too bad. He didn't intimidate me any more than had Albertson.

"Don't fuck with her, okay?" He poked his finger into my chest, tough-guy style.

"Not to worry, Kenny. I'm trying to find her mother. We're all on the same team."

Kenny wrinkled his lip and increased his glower factor, making him look even more like Billy Idol. "Me and Cheryl aren't on your fucking team, or anybody's. We look after ourselves. And we don't need some private asshole pushing us around."

He poked me again and this time I'd had enough. I caught his wrist in a thumb lock with my right hand and twisted, pushing up on his elbow with my left hand, tilting my hip across his balance point and spinning him hard to the floor. I brought his arm up behind him and put my knee into the small of his back. He struggled and cursed but he wasn't going anywhere because I was better at this and knew the moves.

I glanced to see whether Cheryl was planning to spring across the room and land on my neck, but she simply stood there, taking it in.

"Look, Kenny," I said, keeping my voice even. "You will help or you will not, but either way, you will keep your hands off me." I twisted his arm again. "Do I make myself clear?"

He gave me a grunt of assent and I stepped back to let him up.

Kenny got to his feet quickly, thought about coming for me again, reconsidered. He looked at Cheryl. "I'm gettin' the fuck outa here. You coming?" Cheryl hesitated then moved to join him.

Fine with me. "You've got my card," I told her. "Phone me whenever you can."

She looked at me. "Sorry. We'll talk later. Paula's here now. She'll let you out."

"Paula?" I asked, but Cheryl was already gone.

"I'm not finished with you." Kenny's farewell.

"But I'm done with you, Kenny." Kenny gave me the finger and followed Cheryl. Nice kid, Kenny. Just the supportive type that Cheryl needs right now.

A female voice came from beyond the doorway. "I see you've met the grieving daughter and her ever-considerate boyfriend."

Chapter 15

The source of the comment was a lovely young woman, her appearance quite subdued in contrast to Cheryl. Her dark blonde hair was a conservative bob, makeup restrained, almost severe. She was dressed beyond her years in a well-tailored coffee brown suit, a pink silk blouse, low pumps and shade tint hose like the office assistant in a TV lawyer show. Slung over her shoulder was a wide flat canvas zipper bag, the type artists carry. She set the bag on the floor and walked to me, offering her hand. "Paula Albertson."

We shook. Her grip was cool and businesslike. "Mitchell King. I'm the investigator your father hired." I gave her a card and, unlike her stepsister, she actually read it.

"Walter's going to be late. A board meeting."

"Yes, I know." I guessed about the art folder she carried and motioned to the prints on the walls. "You're obviously studying art. These yours?"

She nodded, a bit shy.

Quite the detective, Mitch. "They're very good."

"Thank you. Walter likes them."

"If I may ask, why the oil rigs? Your father's not in the oil business, is he?"

"No. I just appreciate their linearity, their purposefulness. We can see them from the beach house and I often take the boat out to draw them. Walter has one of my sketches in his boardroom."

Twice she'd said that now. Not Dad, not my father, but Walter. Modern youth again, rearing its revisionary head. "Valerie, your stepmother. Any idea where she is?"

"No. Isn't she at Kate Morley's?"

"I don't think so. Your father tried to phone her, but she's elsewhere now."

Paula sighed. "Maybe it's best if she doesn't come back. I don't think she's good for Walter."

"Why?"

"I don't suppose I should tell you this," Paula said, a caveat always used just before someone was ready to spill a secret. I waited for her to fill the gap. "Valerie doesn't love Walter any more. Maybe she never did."

"Why do you think this?"

"She has no real connection with him. Nothing in common. Walter's so immersed in the arts, music. Valerie came from, well, another world."

"What's she like? How did they meet?"

She turned away and stared at her charcoals on the wall, perhaps to renew her strength for the gossip session. "She was a waitress. Just a goddamned cocktail waitress." She pivoted to face me. "And a whore."

I'd not expected such vociferous condemnation from this demure young woman. But with her in a talkative mood, I thought it best to soldier on. "Do you really mean she was a prostitute?"

Paula thought about this. "Maybe not exactly. Not for money. But she got her claws into Walter the second she had a chance. Fed him this sob story about being an abandoned woman raising a daughter on her own. Walter's a kind man, really. He has a sensitive side he doesn't reveal to everyone. It didn't take her long to dig her way into his life, into this house."

"How does your father feel about her?"

"He cares for her in a general sense, but I don't believe he actually loves her. Not when he thinks clearly, at least." She raised her arms in a protective arc around her father as though he was standing before her. "After Mother died, he was lonely. I tried to be there for him and offer support, but I couldn't do everything. I suppose Valerie came along at the right time."

"You don't think Valerie's good for your father."

Paula stared hard at me. "Not what he needs at all. Just look at the kind of people she brought here. Cheryl, and that loser Kenny Cramer." A sideways glance skewered me. "I think they've been stealing from Walter."

"What makes you say that?"

"A few dollars missing, here and there. A camera. Things like that. You'd think with all the money Walter gives Cheryl, she'd have enough. I bet it's going up Kenny's nose, too. I'd watch him if I were you. He's no good."

I would agree. Kenny was a rough one all right, but I didn't want to amplify Paula's opinion and provide more ammunition. After all, I'd been hired to get Valerie back, not drive a wedge into the family. Sibling rivalry would have to hoist its own petard without my assistance.

"If you don't mind talking about it, when did your mother pass away?"

Paula offered a small smile. "No, I don't mind. About six months before Walter met Valerie." She walked over to stand beneath her oil rigs. She looked up at them, receiving comfort from their bleak verticality. "I can understand why

Walter was taken with Valerie. She's attractive enough, in her own cheap way. And Walter blamed himself for Mother's death."

Really? I waited.

Another sigh, this one deeper. "Down at the beach house one day she, well, she swallowed a bottle of pills. She wanted to get away, that's what she told Walter the last time they argued. And I suppose she did. Get away, I mean."

Paula turned to me again. "Look. I don't want to sound uncaring about my mother. But she'd been ill a long time. Walter and I spent years taking care of her. Clinical depression. She was very much dependent on Walter but she was never there for him when he needed her in return. She slipped away so quickly, it was almost a relief when she died."

"Still, your father blames himself?"

"I don't know why. I'm sure he didn't love her at the end. But he still felt responsible."

"I need to ask. Was your mother's death ruled accidental?"

Paula nodded. "She didn't leave a note but nobody else was there. Walter was at work, I was in class. Everyone knew it was suicide but the coroner was very forgiving, said accidental overdose."

"I'm sorry for your loss," I told her. She gave a cursory nod. "But I need to focus on the present. Your father does want to find Valerie and that's why I'm here. Are you sure you can't think of where she might be?"

She shook her head. "It will come as no surprise to you or anyone else, Valerie and I aren't close. I don't think she'd tell me anything."

My turn to nod. Then my phone buzzed and the caller ID showed Albertson/Frontline. I answered.

"Mr. King? This is Walter Albertson."

"Yes, sir."

"Our meeting is running quite late and I don't think I'll be home for several more hours. The market took another down correction today and our stockholders are getting jumpy."

"Let's hope the jumpy doesn't apply to out of windows."

There was a pained silence. "Mr. King, I don't really appreciate your little jokes."

"Sorry" I replied, not really meaning it. "Cheryl had to leave unexpectedly. She and I will talk later, probably tomorrow. I'm here with Paula now. She's helping as much as she can, but she has no idea where Valerie may be."

"And Kathryn Morley?"

"I left messages but she hasn't called back. I'll drive by her place Monday if I don't hear from her before. She has her office in her home and I bet she'll be back at work then."

"Do you think she's ignoring you, protecting Valerie?"

"No way to tell. She may simply be out of town for the weekend. I'm guessing Valerie went with her on a whim and they're just enjoying some time off together, like Thelma and Louise, you know."

"Lord, I certainly hope not."

"Well, I don't mean the crime spree part of it." Did I have to explain everything to this man? I felt like Hamlet with the gravedigger, needing to be coldly literal. "I only meant that they may be getting out of town for a while. But regardless, I'll keep trying to contact Morley and I'll definitely go over to her house."

"I suppose that will have to do." His voice sounded tired. "They're waving me back into the meeting. I have to go. Please contact me as soon as you know something." He cut off.

"That was your father," I told Paula. "He's still in the meeting."

"Walter is driving himself too hard again. Friday night and he'll be in the office till ten at least."

"Perhaps he feels guilty about Valerie leaving and he's trying to push it away by working."

"He might be, but shouldn't. He's given her everything and she's thrown it back in his face."

I decided not to go down that road again. Instead, I tried to comfort Paula about her mother and her distracted father, complimented her again on the artwork, just to boost her morale.

She was such a sad young girl that I felt sympathy for her. She'd apparently assumed the role of surrogate mother, trying to make amends for the distress and disharmony in the family. But these things are never easy. Losing a spouse is a terrible blow to the partner, regardless of how shaky the relationship had been, and a daughter can only offer so much sympathy and solace.

I made my farewell, reminded Paula to reset the alarm and left her alone in that desolate and lifeless house.

Chapter 16

Homicide Detective David Meierhoff ladled slices of cantaloupe from the buffet onto his plate, turned away.

"That's it?" I asked. "That's all you're eating?" I frowned at his selection. Alongside the cantaloupe was a chunk of honeydew, a few fresh strawberries, a small piece of grilled chicken and a triangle of wheat toast.

"At least I won't need help carrying mine." He sniffed disdainfully at what I'd taken. "Or dragging my fat ass afterwards."

My plate was filled with a pile of TexMex scrambled eggs topped with fresh salsa, a mound of hash browns, several link sausages and two biscuits smothered by cream gravy. The gravy had run over most of the other stuff but that was okay by me because I had a couple flour tortillas on the side to mop it up. "Hey, we private eyes have to keep up our strength. You know how it is, solving locked room mysteries, fighting bad guys, rescuing maidens, doing the work that you cops won't."

Meierhoff tossed his head in disbelief. "More like sleeping till noon then driving around, checking out the high school girls during soccer practice."

"Just doing my job, surveillance. You never know what they're planning, those crazy kids."

Meierhoff nodded at my plate. "Keep eating like that, watching is all you'll be able to do. Some twentyish chicklet decides to toss you a freebie, you won't be able to bend over and pick it up, let alone put it to good use."

"Run my reputation into the ground, complain when I use comfort food to restore my energy then criticize my sex life?" I shook my head. "You cops are all alike, picking on law abiding citizens."

We both smiled. Insult trading was part of our normal time together.

David Meierhoff is younger than I, athletic build, open friendly face topped with dark curly hair, resembling a young Elliott Gould. David and I share several interests, including opera and art, so we double date a lot. And we both had squandered our considerable formal education by going into law enforcement, myself peripherally. That made us kindred spirits, I suppose. We had a falling out a while back, my fault entirely, but nevertheless David quickly forgave me and we patched things up. I consider him my best friend.

Meierhoff moved from Narcotics to Homicide a year ago and immediately established a class reputation with the more experienced investigators. Newbies often try to show off and are held in gentle disdain by the more experienced officers, but David segued perfectly into harness, not afraid to put in hard time and show expected deference to his senior investigators. My pal Lieutenant Joe Duggan took a shine to Meierhoff, brought him along quickly and he was now among the best new homicide investigators on the force.

Meierhoff and I had just finished our Sunday run in Memorial Park. As usual, he came through the ordeal easily, not even winded, while I nearly died a half dozen times.

Now we were having breakfast at Bubba's on Washington, and here at least I could hold my own. I can't outrun Meierhoff but I can surely out eat him. And out sweat him. With the morning temperature edging toward ninety, I was dripping like a snowman in the Sahara by the time we got back to my 4Runner. I cranked my AC up to high volume during the drive to Bubba's and now the bar's ceiling fans further cooled me down. Meierhoff however seemed ready for another two miles.

Bubba's is a big friendly sports bar with a no-frills but generous weekend breakfast buffet. Lots of runners gather here on Sunday mornings to relax and chat, and today the place was dotted with them. They mostly dress alike, skimpy tank tops and high cut running shorts, the men looking geeky and the women delicious. Meierhoff would wiggle his eyebrows Groucho style to signal whenever he spotted an exceptionally cute woman. I'd follow his gaze and nod in tacit agreement.

Four uniformed cops were having breakfast at the end of their shift. Meierhoff and I chatted briefly with them on our way to a table. It had been a quiet late night for a Saturday, Houston's recent decline in violent crime making for pleasant if somewhat boring duty.

Meierhoff and I took a seat near a window and David maneuvered himself so he could keep an eye on his dearly beloved, a used Porsche 911 on which he'd mortgaged the bulk of his salary, not to mention his immortal soul. But love is blind.

He spent all his spare time and disposable cash on the car, and the other cops in Homicide teased him unmercifully about it, especially when he was caught running over to the parking garage to buff the dust from its finish and make sure nobody backed into it. His colleagues plastered the Porsche with fake bullet hole decals, anti-cop bumper stickers and other garish items. It was a constant pas de deux, pranksters adding the decorations and Meierhoff meticulously removing them.

We got into our meal, David picking gingerly at his fruit like a dilettante while I scarfed down the eggs and hash browns. "Sausage any good?" Meierhoff asked, abruptly reached over with his fork, speared one of my links and began to nibble.

"You realize that pork isn't on the approved list of kosher foods," I told him, putting on a façade of stern disapproval.

"Oy. Report me to the local parve squad. I'll swear you said it was beef."

"Besides stealing my hard-earned food, what're you doing these days to make yourself useful? Any action lately at the cop shop?"

"Had a multiple Wednesday night over in the Heights, your neighborhood." He finished my sausage and began to suck on a big strawberry. "Usual thing. Guy shot his ex, their kids, then did himself." He turned serious for a moment. "God, I hate when it's kids."

I frowned, no reply necessary or appropriate. I'd seen it on the news and it made me cringe, tragedy just a few blocks from my house.

"And you?" he asked. "I heard about the Telephone Road shooting. How's that working out for you? Rough time sleeping?"

"For a while, sure. Things seem okay now."

"Don't get overconfident. Trauma like that can resurface when you least expect."

I nodded my assent. "I'm okay, I think."

"So what else is keeping you off the dole?" he asked.

"Some insurance deals, tracking down a skip check, plus a new client with a stray wife. She takes off from time to time, not sure why. Maybe a boyfriend on the side. I'm supposed to talk her back home." I shrugged. "The whole damn family is nuts anyway."

"Future customers for me?"

"Not unless you're starting up a sideline in divorce law or psychiatry."

Meierhoff pushed aside his heart-healthy breakfast and began to play around with his iPhone while I plowed steadily through my high cholesterol plateful. I sopped up the last of my eggs and hash browns with yet another flour tortilla, chuffed that down and was finally done. In the meantime, David, more bored than hungry, nibbled at the lonesome slice of cantaloupe that remained on his otherwise pristine plate.

We were both full—at least I was, and the warm September sunlight streaming through the windows made us lethargic after our Sunday run and breakfast. So we sat and chatted and sipped coffee, two rough beasts slouching nowhere in particular, certainly not to Jerusalem and definitely not to be born.

I was ready to suggest we head to Cue and Cushion for some nine ball when Meierhoff's phone chirped Beethoven's Ode to Joy. "Damn," he said, then expanded to "Double damn" when he saw the incoming number. He crooked the phone against his ear while he scribbled notes on a napkin. "Yeah? When? Damn... Shit... Okay... Yeah, he's here. Sure. Okay. Half hour."

Meierhoff put the phone away and drummed his fingers on the table, staring fixedly at the parking lot as though central truths of life were somehow revealed by interpreting a pattern in the way the cars were haphazardly parked.

"Problem?" I asked.

"Supposed to have the day off but y'know how that goes. We caught a felony one murder and Duggan apparently wants my little Hebrew self for the lead." Meierhoff squinted at me. "Wanna come for the ridealong? We can change in the john."

"Sure."

Meierhoff got up, brushed some invisible debris from his spotless sweatpants. "Besides, Duggan wants to talk to you."

"Any idea why?"

"Nope. You know Lieutenant Joe Duggan. Man of few words. But when he does deign to speak, we all perk up and pay attention." Meierhoff treated me to a cheery crocodile smile.

Joe Duggan. He'd shut me out since things had gone down badly last summer, scarcely acknowledging my existence. It was well deserved, though. I'd screwed him over. But why Joe wanted to see me now was anybody's guess.

I shrugged. "Whatever. Let's go."

Meierhoff looked disparagingly at the congealing mass of greasy leftovers on my plate. "Thing is, you maxed out at the food trough this morning."

"So?"

Meierhoff's mouth tightened into a narrow line and he looked at me with solemn dark eyes. "Might be a rough ride. This isn't just your garden variety homicide. They found another one."

"Another one?"

"It's the Slicer."

Chapter 17

"How many does this make?" I asked.

Meierhoff kept his eyes on the traffic and didn't immediately reply. When he did, his voice was flat and low. "Fourteen, far as we know."

I let that sit and didn't speak again.

Meierhoff drove briskly on I-45 into southern Houston, his 911 tooling along nicely. Any other time he'd be describing in stupefying detail how well the Porsche handled, how beautifully it was engineered. But today he was silent, befitting the anticipated carnage that awaited us.

Meierhoff consulted his TomTom, took the Monroe exit and headed west a while, turned north onto a side street. The apartment complex was one of those older U-shaped affairs, two levels of modest units overlooking a dirty, leaf-strewn swimming pool in the middle of a courtyard. A slew of cop cars and other cherrytops were parked everywhere. News helicopters were already circling and the KPRC remote unit was setting up a feed, with more crews sure to follow.

It was about eleven on an otherwise pleasant Sunday morning and there must have been fifty onlookers, some residents clustered along the second story balcony, some passersby just hanging around on the sidewalk outside the perimeter of yellow crime tape. Few knew what was up, but with this many cops it promised to be a fun day.

Meierhoff parked near the edge of the complex and popped his glovebox. "Here." He handed me a police lapel Visitor pass. "Stay out of the way. And don't touch anything." He swung his lean frame out of the Porsche. "Or step in anything."

We got out and walked toward a clump of cops. In the center was Homicide Lieutenant Joe Duggan and next to him, the newest rookie in Homicide, a quiet skinny kid named Jesus Ortiz. Ortiz had only been in the unit a month and I scarcely knew him, but everybody said he was a good addition to the squad.

Standing with the homicide crew was a man I didn't recognize but who looked vaguely familiar. He was middle age, average height and build, dressed casually in jeans and pullover Izod, but despite the mufti he may as well have worn a nametag that said Cop. We introduced ourselves and the mystery man resolved himself into FBI Special Agent Edward Scudder. He had a friendly face but it was sad and tired, a little like the cartoon dog Droopy. Then I realized why he seemed familiar. Agent Scudder bore a striking resemblance to the subversive cigarette smoking man from X-Files. I however decided it wasn't a good idea to bring up that point.

I was wary meeting Joe Duggan because of our past. I deserved it that night when he called me a weak bastard because I'd been precisely that, but hopefully Joe was ready to put it behind him. Joe had a right to be angry, though. He'd shared every detail of a case with me, yet when it was my turn, I held out on him. Not the best plan of action to cross a guy like Duggan. He's an original, a throwback to the old days, someone you certainly didn't want angry with you. Joe is a stocky muscular man in his fifties who could pass for Ned Beatty and was often mistaken for the actor. Like Freddy Gonzales in Burglary, Joe was no slave to fashion. He either wore the same shirt and tie each day or he bought them in bulk.

Duggan broke the ice as only he could. "Why the fuck you here?"

"Meierhoff," I replied, nodding at David. "Besides, didn't you ask me to come?"

Duggan glowered, then shrugged his acceptance. He wasn't much of a conversationalist in the best of circumstances, and this was not the best. "Just make sure not a fuckin' word gets out about what you see here," he warned. "And try the fuck not to shoot anybody, fer Pete's sake."

"Right. Not to worry."

"How's that little Springer?"

Joe's quick turn of topic stumped me for a moment then I realized he was asking about my new compact Springfield pistol. "Er, fine, Joe."

"Leave it to some pansy-ass private detective to buy a baby version of the real thing." Duggan patted his own gun, a full size Les Baer 1911 Custom Concept 5.

"I try, Uncle Joe, I try."

"That'll be the friggin' day." He smirked. "And I want to talk to you later, okay? Don't go running off to the nearest whorehouse like always." Everybody snickered, me being the butt of a cop joke. Par for the course when you hang with Houston's Finest.

I decided to act nice for a change. "Sure. I'll stick around." I didn't know why Joe Duggan needed to see me, but I could avail myself of the opportunity and go a ways toward patching up our dispute.

Meierhoff frowned at Joe. "You sure you want me primary on this? Thought Tameka was working today."

"She called in last night. Messed up her knee playing tennis with the boyfriend, or so she says." Joe grinned. "Probably playing some Tempurpedic tennis. Anyway, she had to go to the doc in the box, supposed to stay off the knee, so she asked me to sub for her. I said okay because Sunday afternoons are slow." Joe looked up at the open apartment door ringed by police. "Lucky me."

Joe Duggan now sent a devilish grin in Meierhoff's direction. "Unless you want to volunteer. You and Jesus get along pretty good." Joe pronounced Ortiz' name correctly, saying Hayzu instead of Anglo-mangling it. Ortiz perked up, happy to become the object of interest, however sidebar. "Besides, being HPD liaison for the Harris County Slicer unit, you're a natural."

Meierhoff knew he'd been bagged. Duggan was well aware of David's assertive reputation and was banking on it. "Okay. Primary it is," Meierhoff agreed. "Let's take a look."

So we all trooped upstairs in hesitant pilgrimage to apartment 14B where Rhonda Willett had lived.

And died.

Chapter 18

It was in that precise moment that the heat of the day seized me with renewed vigor.

The weather's effect on us is to a great degree psychological. Hot or cold, we acclimate ourselves, maintain equilibrium and don't give it much thought thereafter. But add some event, a word, a juncture acting as catalyst and the intensity of the climate is wholly experienced, fully impressed upon us in a single Gestalt. So it was with me. With each step up those shaky metal stairs, it seemed to gain ten degrees and ten percent humidity. By the time I reached the second floor, I was as drenched in sweat as when I'd finished my run.

It was quiet, too. Around me were cars, vans, traffic, cops, citizens. Hobby airport was nearby and planes roared overhead in concert with the circling news copters. Despite this clamor, all seemed to dwindle as I advanced, the sound reduced to a narrow well, rendered far less important than the object of our journey. The walkway was now a foreshortened tunnel, sucking me into a chasm with the Vertigo effect, like Jimmy Stewart trying to crawl up that mission bell tower stairway.

Just outside the apartment door was a cardboard box containing stacks of ugly blue disposable crime scene booties, plastic gloves and a trash bin for dumping them after you left. The trash receptacle was marked Biohazard and emblazoned with the warning symbol that has always reminded me of demonic scorpion claws. Nice thought that, just what I needed to enhance my digestion.

We all gloved up, stumbled around, leaning on each other, jerking on the booties and pulling the elastic tops around our cowboy boots, sneakers, or clunker cop shoes, one size fits all. These booties struck a chord in my jumbled mind, and then I remembered the supply of inexpensive slippers outside the door for Astronaut Tarah Jacoby's Shiva, at which the wearing of leather shoes is considered ostentatious by the Orthodox Jew. This of course triggered memories of Tarah's useless death, the sordid suicide of Pam Neely, and thoughts of Terrie Bartlett, provoking me quickly into a fugue state of remembered bad times. Thinking about Terrie always makes my guts ache, so I shook her away and tried to get back to the present.

Next to the bootie and glove box was a small pile of vomit, deposited by someone who'd already been inside. There was cat litter sprinkled on it, the half-empty bag nearby. Many cops carry cat litter in their cruiser trunks. It's a good cheap oil dry, fluid absorbent and general cleanup assist. Plus you can take the leftover litter home, assuming there exists the rare cop who owns a cat and not eight large barky dogs. If so, he'd absolutely need to keep his pals from finding out.

* * *

The stench of the spill wafted to me despite the deodorizing litter. I remembered Meierhoff's warning and immediately regretted the large breakfast. My nerves were already on edge, and trying to not think about Terrie Bartlett was like Tolstoy and his pals trying not to think of a white bear. I steeled myself, took a few deep breaths and sullenly filed into the apartment with everyone else.

We took our time because nobody was particularly eager to see what had been done to one Rhonda Willett, white female, divorced, age forty-six, now very much deceased.

Sadly, a great deal had been done to her.

Rhonda Willett lay on her back on the kitchen floor, she was naked and she had been methodically cut to shreds. Slashes upon slashes crisscrossed her breasts and pubic region, so many wounds that her skin in these areas had mostly been torn off to expose the muscle tissue and internal organs beneath, leaving little to indicate that a woman had once been there. Her lips had been cut away, her eyes bulged from the sockets because the eyelids were gone. Pieces of her were scattered across the tile floor and a puddle of black blood ran from beneath the body, not as much as I'd have thought, but certainly enough. The blood was mixed with a stain of urine and the stench of loosed bowels that added to the nightmare. Willett's arms were tightly bound behind her, legs spread wide. The parts of her face and head not bloodied bore evidence of numerous blows, and a thin white cord was twisted in a garrote around her neck. I could not look into what remained of the eyes.

Symbols were drawn in wide black marker pen across her torso. There were pentagrams and triangles and squiggly runics that were probably meant to be Satanic, but were in truth just the private and fevered machinations of a diseased brain.

Meierhoff and Ortiz squatted on either side of the corpse. They wore their requisite booties but still took care to step where there was no blood or body waste. Meierhoff looked up at Agent Scudder. "I'm gonna turn her a bit to verify the restraints." Scudder nodded approval. Meierhoff carefully lifted on one shoulder until her wrists were visible. White rope had been used. "Yeah. It's the same," he said. "Nylon. You can get it anywhere." Then he let her roll back and as he did, a slight sucking noise emerged from beneath the naked body.

Not thinking of the white bear came back with harshness renewed. A wave of nausea and dizziness swept over me and I fought down the aftertaste of breakfast. I turned away, the horrible image vivid in my mind.

I stumbled outside onto the walkway, went to the railing and gazed out across the treetops, trying to muster cooler thoughts. Behind me, the apartment began to flicker with strobes as photos were taken. I visualized the murder scene again and this time almost lost my breakfast, but finally my stomach settled due to the fresh air or maybe just willpower.

Nearby, a few uniformed cops were yukking it up, nervously laughing too loud for the jokes they shared. I knew some of them but declined to go over. I needed to practice breathing a while longer.

Chapter 19

A moment later and Agent Ed Scudder stood beside me. His strong resemblance to the cigarette smoking man made me smile. True to type, Scudder dug out a pack of Salems and offered me one. I shook my head. Cops everywhere were trying to get me smoking. A conspiracy, maybe? Only Jesse Ventura knew for sure.

Scudder lit up, glanced at me and noticed my pale face. "This your first bad one?"

"Yeah. I've seen murders before but nothing like..." I couldn't find the words.

"That's okay. Nobody ever gets used to it." He pulled an empty metal Altoids box from his pocket to use as an ashtray. "Don't want to compromise the crime scene," he explained.

"You with the Houston office?"

"Temporarily. On loan from Quantico."

I realized the FBI wouldn't be involved in a local homicide, no matter how gruesome, unless it was linked to other murders. "Behavioral Science?" I guessed.

"Yeah, BSU."

"So you travel around the country and help cops solve serial murders?" I was chagrined when I realized his job. "God, you see this all the time, don't you? How can you take it?"

Scudder regarded me with sad eyes. "I don't take it. I just endure. I proceed, day to day. I try not to become personally involved in the case but that's not always possible. Sometimes we catch the sons of bitches. That makes it bearable, almost. I have a lovely wife, three wonderful children and a grandbaby on the way. I think about them a lot."

"It would drive me nuts."

Scudder's eyes pooled deeper and he nodded as if considering the option. He inhaled his cigarette deeply and looked out across the treetops. "It does take its toll, that's for sure. God knows I've got more grey hair than when I started this unholy business. But what I do, I try to work at the case a piece at a time, concentrate on the immediate." He took another drag, sighed the smoke out. "Michelangelo. Somebody asked him how he managed to create a beautiful

work of art from a block of granite. He told them I just carve away everything—
"

"—everything that's not the sculpture." I finished the quote.

"Exactly," Scudder said, nodding. "And that's what I do, how I manage to keep my sanity. I chip away, a piece here, a piece there." He cupped his hands in front of him as if he were cradling a rare and delicate butterfly. "Eventually the turmoil dissipates and I'm holding a solution. I focus on that alone."

We stood in silence. I could hear cops in the apartment behind me gabbing about evidence, cops hanging around outside, gabbing about something else. The citizens had by now learned of the event and were staring up at us in their death vigil as though Scudder or I might suddenly begin to read a proclamation like Roman Senators in the Forum. Several more TV news crews had arrived and were pestering everyone. They hadn't been allowed up the stairs, a decision for which we were all thankful.

"How about this guy, the Slicer?" I asked. "Any good leads?"

Scudder shook his head. "Not so far." He pulled another drag. "You saw the rope he used to strangle and tie her?" I nodded. He peered at me sideways, a conspiratorial glint in his eyes. "Nylon rope, very ordinary stuff. But he always uses exactly the same brand and type. That's something we don't tell the press. Be sure you don't let that get out."

"No," I assured him. "Never."

Scudder shrugged, another drag. "We assume he's Anglo because all his victims are. As you know, serials mostly target their own race. And he's a lefty from the wound patterns. Aside from this, we're in the dark. He doesn't fit the mold. Difficult to characterize."

"Why is that?"

"Well, usually you have either of two types, the psychotic or the psychopath. Your psychotics are certifiable crazies like Jeffrey Dahmer. They hear voices and are not coherent in their crimes. They stick to a small geographic area and their killings are highly volatile. And being nut cases, they're unable to alter their modus operandi. This also makes them easier to find because they can't function properly in society between killings." He puffed again, deposited more ash into the box.

"Then there's the Ted Bundy category. Psychopath, well organized, intelligent, rarely impulsive. They move around the country freely because they can hold respectable jobs and fit into a normative mold on the surface. These guys keep track of what's going on, read the papers and such. They also have the mental capacity to control and adjust their patterns, fooling us sometimes. But they're still pressured by their insanity to kill and plan their attacks methodically and this gives us a way to track them."

He looked at me squarely. "Finally, you have the mixed types, like this guy. He's impulsive but he also has a predictable pattern, like the way he marks his victims with the drawings. Yet he's totally brutal and vicious in his mutilations. He seems to be centered in the Houston area, but his victims range from the lower Gulf Coast to as far north as Dallas. He behaves like a psychotic with his victims yet acts like a psychopath in his planning. It's like he's both. He's therefore tricky and extremely hard to pigeonhole."

Scudder took a final drag, snubbed his cigarette butt into the box, snapped it shut, tucked it away. "But we'll find him," he assured me, heading inside. He turned back, gave me a wan smile and again cupped his hands. "A solution."

I ventured into the apartment behind Agent Scudder. I didn't want to, but I'd already wormed my way into official police business today and I needed to show the flag.

The cops were finished taking photos for now. Meierhoff was still squatting beside Rhonda Willett's body, showing Jesus Ortiz the finer aspects of murder investigation while Duggan looked on. The Harris County pathologist was unpacking an evidence kit a few feet away, his gear spread out on a plastic tarp in a quiet corner of the adjoining breakfast room. Scudder hung back with the other cops, taking notes, cataloging each item in the apartment, getting ready to dust for fingerprints.

Meierhoff and Ortiz were bent low over the body. David gently pried Willett's eyes further open, instructing Ortiz, "See those little red blotches in the tissue surrounding the eye? That's petechial hemorrhage caused by strangulation. Most likely the cause of death."

"So she was dead when he—?" Ortiz asked.

"When he cut her? With the amount of bleeding, I'd say not yet dead, but probably brain dead from the head injuries and strangulation, and dying. Enough blood pressure to cause the small amount of bleeding we see here, not enough pressure to bleed her out completely." Meierhoff carefully rolled the body again. "Check the wrists. No abrasions. If she'd been struggling to escape or fighting to get loose while he used the knife, there would be marks. But there aren't any."

"I don't understand," Ortiz admitted. "Why tie her up if she's already dead?"

"Part of his ritual," Meierhoff answered. He looked over to Duggan, who nodded, then glanced at Scudder. Agent Scudder was leaning over the coffee table examining things, taking notes, and I first thought Meierhoff hadn't been heard. But Scudder turned to him as though he'd been paying rapt attention and confirmed it with a single word, "Ritual."

Meierhoff continued: "Ritual it is, otherwise there wouldn't be any of these symbols drawn on her. And he's a sexual compulsive. He beats them up or strangles them until they're unconscious, tries to rape them, but he can't get it up because he's not really a rapist. He's a psycho. So he flies into a rage, blames them for his lack of arousal, cuts them up. Defeminization, mutilating the breasts and pubic region. That's what gets him off and he finally ejaculates. Or we think he does, since he apparently uses a condom. Then he draws on them, marking them as spawn of the Devil, when in fact the Devil is in his own fucked up skull."

Meierhoff glanced up at the pathologist. "Jerry, we might find semen deposits on the external vaginal area. So far the guy's used a rubber but we could still get lucky. Be sure you look for male pubic hair, run tests for glycoprotein P30, have the DNA analyzed."

The pathologist nodded. "Roger. Got the kit right here."

"And Jerry, we're almost done with the prelim. You can start your sample collection. Let us know how we can help. We'll be out canvassing the neighbors." Another pathologist nod.

"Now, Detective Ortiz." David grinned. "Tell me how long she's been dead? And how do you know?"

Ortiz seemed reluctant to touch the body but overcame his trepidation. He moved the legs and arms slightly, inspected the blotches on her skin along her shoulders and buttocks. "The vic has been dead about thirty-six hours," he said, reciting with textbook phrasing. "Rigor is subsiding. Postmortem lividity indicates that blood has settled for that same approximate time. We won't know for sure until we get her liver temp. She's not been moved appreciably since the crime because the pooling of blood in the tissues matches her present position."

Meierhoff beamed with parental approval. "Grade A, Detective Ortiz. Right, Doc?" The pathologist gestured a thumbs up. Ortiz was again smiling. Serious as the situation was, I was happy for him. He was cool and knew his stuff pretty well for a Homicide rookie.

David looked over to me. "Mitch, I want to show you this. You were outside when we first talked about it."

I had been looking but not watching, and now I would be forced to actually see. My unwilling feet took me to Meierhoff and Ortiz. And to Rhonda Willett.

"Here." David pointed at something on the body. I stared where he indicated, between her legs. "See this?" A big chrome metal clamp of sorts had its jaws planted deep into her vagina, piercing the labia. "That's Slicer's special signature. It's a Pflaugher tissue clamp that's sometimes used in surgery and you can't buy them retail. He leaves this stuck into all his victims." Meierhoff stood up and flexed his knees. "And that's another little secret we keep from the news people."

The nausea returned, and all the blood and mutilation finally got to me. Without another word, I went out the doorway and redecorated the cat litter.

Chapter 20

"How have you been since we last met, Mr. King? Did you have time to think about what we discussed? Or would you prefer to talk about this recent shooting?"

Doctor Chen peered at me over the top of her half glasses. Her dark brown eyes were calm and mild, her face composed. She gave no hint of expectation, no reproach. She simply waited for my response.

I glanced around her office for the hundredth time, hoping to formulate a cogent reply. Dr. Carol Chen is precisely whom you might expect for a reform Jungian psychotherapist. There is the obligatory couch, two comfortable chairs where we now sat, an impressive array of books on the shelves, framed diplomas and awards dotted across her wall and flanked by photographs of Freud and Jung.

Sigmund was in his usual pensive mood, staring down as if gazing into a bowl of dark waters, while Carl Jung was posed in mountaineer outfit, all smiles, ready to scale new peaks. Doctor Chen's desk completed the decor with neatly aligned blotter, pen set, photos of smiling husband and kids.

These but the trappings and the suits of woe.

* * *

Lord, what had I fallen into? And why was Hamlet always intruding into my mind? Did he know something I didn't? Probably, but being Hamlet, he'd likely keep the secret to himself.

The problems started with my drunk driving arrest a few months ago. Conviction would mean a suspension of my driver's license and a possible loss of my investigator permit. But I had a clean record and therefore my lawyer, the ever-devious Donna Boudreaux, arranged a plea. Alcohol counseling was the get out of trouble tactic and I went for it. I couldn't abide group therapy so I opted for private sessions. My insurance would even cover part of it.

Surprisingly, it had gone well. Doctor Chen quickly surmised that booze wasn't really my problem. It was my pig-headed attitude. Of course she didn't use those words. In fact, she made no accusative remarks at all. She simply pointed out some things and let me form my own conclusions. Her perception was as sharp as that of a hawk circling a field mouse, the mouse being me.

In our second session I'd made a snide remark. "No Rorschach ink blots?"

"Well, Mr. King, if you think they will help us get on with it, I suppose I can dig the cards out of the storage cabinet and dust them off." Dr. Chen smiled.

"You don't use them?"

"If you go to the doctor for a broken arm, is she going to begin by X-raying your leg?"

"You use different tools for different situations, is what you're saying."

She nodded. "And different patients." She gestured to the portrait of old Sigmund. "Classic psychoanalysis…" Then she waved toward the picture of Jung. "…or psychotherapy, for that matter, have been reinterpreted and revised in the light of modern scientific medicine and contemporary therapeutic methods. Currently we work from varied perspectives and use the appropriate approach." She smiled benignly.

"And the approach for me?"

"You're an intelligent man, Mr. King. You are highly educated, articulate and fairly receptive to open communication. You are not profoundly ill, nor do I think that psychotropic medications are warranted. So we take the direct approach and simply talk. I'm here to help you gain insight into your personality. I don't possess miraculous cures and I'm not even persuaded that there is a cure per se. It's my objective to work with you to find those conflicting feelings within yourself so you can become aware of them, integrate those elements and thereby arrive at a more responsible and mature perception of your life. Agreed?"

"Agreed." She'd put me in my place and had done so with tact.

"If a patient is seriously disturbed, I would prescribe certain drugs, or even a brief stay in a clinic where we could work more directly with the problem. If I thought you were addicted to alcohol, I might send you to AA as part of a therapy profile. But I am of the opinion that we can get along nicely without these ancillary methods."

So we began. The requisite sessions were soon disposed of, my release signed and delivered to the court. I was off the hook legally, but those hours with Chen were a definite relief, much as my stubborn mindset tried to deny. So I decided to see her a while longer, clear up some things, allay some thoughts that nagged me.

I broke from my reverie. "I'm still not comfortable with this," I admitted.

"Few people are."

I waited for more but nothing was said. Doctor Chen leaned forward and adjusted her glasses. After several meetings I'd learned she did this whenever she was planning to make a point. "Just tell me what's on your mind. That's why we're here."

I hesitated, still embarrassed to let things go, to talk about my deepest fears.

She shrugged. "We can also discuss the latest movie you've seen, what's on TV, what you had for dinner last night. Or we can simply sit."

"It's my dime, right?"

"Your two hundred dollars, actually."

"What should I say?"

Chen just looked at me and smiled.

I sighed. Not what I'd figured when I signed up, but what the hell. In for a penny, in for a pound. When I opened my mouth, I would have sworn on a Kindle download of the King James Bible that I meant to talk about the Dutch LeBrock shooting, but something totally different came out. "I still blame myself for the failure of my marriage," I said. "Sandra, I miss her all the time. And my daughter Chrissie."

Chen glanced at her notes. "You were divorced three years ago. She moved to Arizona."

"Phoenix. Sandra went to live with her father. He's an architect, has his own firm."

"Nice man?"

"Sure. The best." I squirmed. I wasn't used to being asked hard questions. That was supposed to be my job. Having the tables turned wasn't fair.

"You told me that you once felt there was a chance for reconciliation."

"Yes, until she married Ted Forester last year."

"How did she meet him? What sort of person is he?"

"He consults with her father's firm. He's a structural engineer, designs high-rise buildings, arenas, that sort of thing."

"Is he a good husband to Sandra? Does he treat Chrissie well?"

"Yes, I guess," I admitted. "Yes."

"Isn't that what actually bothers you?"

Dr. Chen as usual hit the nail on the head. My head. If Ted Forester were abusive to Sandy, if he were only just cold to her, I would try to find a route to get inside, some ploy to work my way back into her heart. God help me, I had even hired my own kind, an investigator to look into Forester's life, but he came back clean. Cleaner than I was. I had to admit that Sandy had done well for herself, but actually letting that fact sink in was hard.

Chen and I talked some more but I was tired of Sandy and Ted. I hemmed and hawed, danced around the subject, yet eventually we'd gone as far as this day would take us. I shook Dr. Chen's hand and left the office, verifying my appointment for next month. I never even mentioned the murder scene I'd witnessed the day before. Thinking about it still made me dizzy.

In my car, I started the engine but just sat there, thinking. I considered my motives and purpose. The intellectual part of me knew that Chen was on my side and genuinely trying to help me. The emotional part resisted. I simply couldn't tell her how I felt. That I would keep inside, at least for now. Maybe forever.

Does it bother me about Sandy? Dr. Chen asked. Bother me? The guilt was debilitating. Bother isn't the word for it. I feel like Prometheus chained to his rock, feelings gnawing at my guts and chewing into my liver. Sometimes I get short of breath just thinking about it.

I hate Ted Forester. I hate him more each day, more than if he were a creep. I hate him for taking my place, for becoming what I had not been, a good husband and father. I hate him because I am a failure. I needed a drink but knew that wasn't a good idea either.

My life is total crap.

Chapter 21

Having witnessed the horror of the Willett murder, it took all the gumption I had to even make the Chen appointment the following morning. My stomach was still queasy and it fed on a resonance from the shooting of Dutch LeBrock just a few weeks prior. Overshadowing this, of course, was the killing of Victor Allison last summer. Both of these senseless deaths amplified the bloodbath of Rhonda Willett in my mind.

The day previous, after I tossed my cookies at the crime scene, I blew off waiting for Joe Duggan and phoned for a cab instead, picked up my car at Bubba's, went straight home and stayed there the rest of the day. Leave that terrible and brutal crime to the professionals, I decided. I wanted no part of it.

Therefore I was glad to get back to Valerie Albertson. I pulled up the photo of her standing beside Walter, zoomed in. She was a sensuous woman, dark lustrous hair and oval face. Valerie's smile bore a crinkle of complaint, as though she'd been pressed into this photo session against her will. Nevertheless, her eyes conveyed a passion for life that made me want to help her. So I drove down to the Montrose district to see Kathryn Morley.

* * *

I lived in Montrose when I first returned from college and love the area. It's an eclectic neighborhood a stone's throw from downtown, a wonderful mix of older folks, artists, musicians, singles, young families, gays of all persuasion, everything and everybody living right across the street from everybody else. There are small houses, apartments, townhomes, restaurants, bars, clubs, shops all over, typical for an artsy district in any major city. There has been a recent influx of empty nesters and upscale socialites, many of the fine old homes razed to make way for expensive condos to house the conspicuous consumptive habits of the yuppie, but for now the character of the neighborhood still holds true.

I cruised around the block, checking the side streets near Morley's house. I was looking for Valerie's car, a new canary yellow BMW 5-series, but it was nowhere.

Today I was driving the Stealthmobile. Stealth is a clean white Chevy minivan with a slightly faded paint job and a few small scratches here and there. I carefully cultivated the van's appearance until it was perfectly average and unrecognizable. Under the hood, another story. A mechanic I'd done a divorce job for paid for my services by transforming the car. He rebuilt the engine, transmission and all the other running gear until it was reliable, quiet and smooth. It's a terrific vehicle to scout from because nobody pays it a moment's attention.

I had the mechanic put two little portholes in back where I could sit and take videos. I hated doing this because the van quickly became an oven, but a resourceful private eye has to make sacrifices and having a cooler of beer helps.

A few accessories augment the surveillance scam and alter the deliberate blandness of the van. There are foil sunshades with advertising on them, assorted license plate covers and a big shiny detachable roof antenna that doesn't work. I have magnetic signs to stick on the doors depicting fictitious plumbing and remodeling firms. Another sign reads Texas Highway Department, one is University of Houston Traffic Survey and my favorite, Solid Waste Management.

I also keep clipboards with fake surveys for the door-to-door approach. These are backed up by assorted official-style plastic ID tags for my lapel, some generic uniform shirts with a utility company name embroidered on them and one hard hat I'd cumshawed from Reliant power. The energy business was in such flux with all the mergers these days that I was forced to snatch a new hardhat every six months or so when the providers changed their names and logos.

* * *

As I'd guessed, Kate Morley had been out of town when I phoned earlier, but she readily returned my call this morning and invited me over to chat. Valerie first stayed with Kate this recent escape, then she'd left after a few days and Kate Morley had no idea where Valerie had gone. Or so Morley had told Albertson.

I parked a half block down and walked to the house. Today it was predictably sunny and steaming. All around me, lawns were baked to a crispy brown with only a few green patches here and there, where the owners squandered their disposable incomes on elevated water bills by installing sprinkler systems. The sky was solid blue, hot and bright. I could feel the impact of the sun on my head and face, a manifest force that pressed down, tempting me back into the refuge of air conditioning.

Two old mixed breed dogs lay behind a fence, their tongues dangling from black lipped muzzles. They scanned me as I walked by and one of them ventured a low-toned sentinel gruff, but I could tell his heart wasn't really in it. Too hot for any serious guard duty.

Kate Morley lived in a Montrose original, a remodeled forties bungalow set back from the street, white stucco with brown trim and a slanted red tile roof. I could see new tiles where I guessed that some had been blown away by Hurricane Ike. The lawn was neatly cut and there were shrubs and flowerbeds planted all round.

In the front yard was a sign designed to resemble the house's paint scheme, white with brown edges. The sign proclaimed Neartown Design & Graphic Arts and was done up in a swoopy script that was hard to read.

I walked up, pushed the bell and after a minute Kathryn Morley opened the door.

Chapter 22

Kate Morley was tall and we stood nearly eye to eye. She was a honey blonde with longish hair and sparkling blue eyes. Her nose had a cute impish upturn and her lips were full and well shaped. I guessed her to be late thirties, maybe forty, but her radiant smile made her appear younger. She was wearing a flowery blue print dress, loose at the waist, a sort of ankle length artist's smock with not much on beneath. She was barefoot and there was pink polish on her toenails. "Mr. King?" Morley asked, offering her hand.

"Mitchell King. Call me Mitch." We shook. Her grip was brief, aloof. I handed her my card.

She glanced at it, squinted at me, sun in her eyes. "Come on in."

Morley had her office in the front of the house and apparently lived in back. I understood this because it was the same arrangement for me. Her place was pleasantly cool, languorous overhead fans pushing the chilled air about. There was a small entryway with a bright red wrought iron park bench and a little table holding some artistic magazines to read while you waited. A huge orange tabby was curled donutlike on the bench, artfully dozing and astutely ignoring my presence as I passed.

The office area was large and well lit by a multipane bay window and track lighting to fill the gaps. There were easels and poster boards and drawings pinned everywhere. One table held Macs and a large format color printer. There were high back roller chairs like you'd expect. Above one of the work desks was a small print of The Scream, the famous Edvard Munch painting of angst that always reminded me of Macaulay Culkin applying aftershave in Home Alone. A word balloon had been drawn on the image, complaining I'm over deadline and my brain hurts!

Along a side shelf was a row of modestly framed awards and some representative splashy graphics. One award was a star-topped crystal, an Addie from the Houston Advertising Council. I also recognized a few of Kate Morley's display graphics from recent newspaper and magazine ads touting the Galleria and assorted upscale enterprises.

Decorating the back wall were three large art prints, a Georgia O'Keeffe flanked by a Paul Klee and one subdued, murky print I couldn't quite recognize. The O'Keeffe was exactly the genre I'd remembered when seeing Paula

Albertson's charcoals, the strong vertical blues and reds framed by curved gray and white arches. Whether it was meant to suggest a vagina had always been subject to interpretation, Ms. O'Keeffe coy when quizzed about her inspiration. The Klee was Unterwasser Garten, a subsea panorama featuring a cheery and whimsical little orange fish that I'd always held a fondness for.

Morley gestured me to a modern chrome and leather sectional in the middle of the room and it proved surprisingly comfortable when I sat.

"Coffee?"

"Love some. Black."

Kate Morley went to a sidebar and filled two mugs from an electric urn. She dumped some artificial sweetener and creamer in one, stirred, brought the cups over. I watched her as she walked and liked what I saw. She had generous hips and moved with graceful ease. Her breasts were small, shapely. I got a whiff of delicate fragrance. Chanel? No, something more exotic, musky. Morley put the cups on a nearby table and sat on the other sectional across from me. She took a sip of coffee and lit a Marlboro.

I pointed to the back wall. "I know the Klee and O'Keeffe, but is that a Rothko on the left?"

She rewarded me with a brief look of wide-eyed appreciation. "Why, yes. Mark Rothko indeed."

"From his very depressed phase or from his really terribly depressed phase?" I asked.

She laughed aloud, giggling in a bubbly, rich tone. As she laughed she bobbed her head and shoulders back and forth in merriment, her eyes flashing. "Just the very depressed phase, I'm afraid. The really terribly depressed ones cost too much."

She frowned at me. "Surprised you know about art," she said. Meaning, how does a dumb private eye get beyond a Velvet Elvis.

"I graduated cum laude from UT Austin," I replied. "My degree is in American history and I have a minor in fine arts, music history, but I also know something about painting beyond ordering a landscape from the Thomas Kinkade online factory. My resume is available on my Website if you like, but if I knew there was going to be a test I'd have stayed up late and crammed."

Morley was chagrined. "I'm sorry. I was rude. I didn't mean to imply that you were—"

"—Nor did I infer," I said, partially rescuing the conversation and showing off my grammar as well. Then I smiled my best private investigator smile at her.

"I was being silly. I'm the one to apologize. I've always enjoyed art and music. My mother painted, an avocation. And my ex wife is in the same business you are, commercial art."

"I don't know of a King in graphics. Or does she use her maiden name?"

"She does, but in Phoenix. Scottsdale, actually. She's lived there a few years now. Remarried." Why I added remarried, I didn't know.

Kate Morley nodded. The sparring was over for now and it was time to get serious. She sat herself square and leaned forward, legs sprawled wide, her sharp eyes peering straight into my own, pressing with obvious directness. "Mr. King, I agreed to meet you because I'm concerned about Valerie and Cheryl. But I don't give a damn about Walter Albertson, his stuck-up daughter Paula, or his little financial kingdom. And right now I don't even know whether I should trust you."

She put it straight and I owed her the same courtesy. "Ms. Morley, I understand your concerns, so let me alleviate them. I can give you several personal references that attest to my character and work ethic. I agreed to find Valerie to ask that she remain in contact with her husband and hopefully persuade her to return home, mostly for her daughter's benefit. But she's an adult and can go where she chooses. I'm not a bounty hunter and I'm certainly not going to carry her back to Walter Albertson, kicking and screaming, slung over my shoulder like some Neanderthal's trophy. That would be illegal and I wouldn't do it even if it were okay. If she doesn't wish to get back with him, I'm not inclined to force her."

Long speeches weren't my style but recently I found myself on the soapbox a lot. I smiled. "And please call me Mitch."

Chapter 23

Kate Morley considered my request, gave her quiet acceptance. "Fine, Mitch. What can I do?" She grinned. "And I'm Kate." We shook again, this time with more zest.

"Any idea where Valerie might be?"

"Nope. She was here till Wednesday, then she left just before I went out of town. I was in San Antonio for an art fair."

"Did she leave with anyone? Tell you where she was headed?"

Kate shook her head but I sensed she wasn't forthcoming.

"You know that Cheryl is worried sick right now," I said, hoping to pry more information via the sympathy route. "If she were to get a phone call from Valerie, it would mean a lot."

"You think I know where she is, don't you?"

"I believe you know more than you're letting on." I held her eyes.

Kate pressed her lips together in thought. "Look, I'm no judge of conduct. I've sown my own wild oats." At that, she broke into a knowing smile and batted her eyes in a coquettish parody. "Of course, that was in my younger days." Her eyes locked back into mine.

Was she flirting, I wondered. If so, why? Was she attempting to distract me? Was she making a pass for the normal reasons? Or was I completely missing the point and seeing motives that didn't exist? After all, a few months ago I'd mistaken predatory behavior for genuine affection and could no longer trust my instincts when it came to personal relationships. I put these things from my mind and addressed the business at hand. "Tell me about Valerie," I asked. "Who is she seeing?"

Kate puffed again on the cigarette, snubbed it out in the ashtray. "Han Solo."

"Did he swoop down in the Millennium Falcon or is it in the shop again?"

Kate laughed aloud at this, giggles turning to guffaws. Her head nodded in a now familiar way. When the laughter subsided, she removed another cigarette from the pack, lit up and laughed again. "Han Solo's my name for him because he looks like a young Harrison Ford, but Pete Bally is who."

"And Pete Bally is?"

"An attorney friend. Guess I'm guilty of introducing him to Val."

"Don't think of it as guilt," I told her. "Because it's not. You have friends, you introduce them. What they do about it is their business."

"Even if I wanted it to happen?"

I shrugged. "My life isn't a moral compass so I have no room to criticize. And she's a client anyway. For me, it's just a job, trying to persuade her to stay in contact with her husband and her daughter, maybe return home should that be feasible. Regardless, I make no judgment either way."

Kate glanced up to the ceiling, perhaps for guidance, but all she had there was the track lighting, at which she blew smoke, and it proffered no response in its defense. Finally, "I guess you'll want to talk to Pete."

"I assume he's in the attorney listings. Lawyers aren't shy about proclaiming their existence."

"Pete works for a corporate firm. He doesn't have his own shingle hung out, so he won't be in the search lists." She stood up and walked over to a desk. "I'll get his card."

"How long has Valerie known Pete Bally?"

"Known as friends, or known in the biblical sense?" A sly grin cast over her shoulder as she thumbed through a card index.

"Whichever."

"Three, four months now," she said, coming back. She sat down and handed me a business card. Peter S. Bally worked for Jacobs and Pfeiffer. They were a midsize commercial firm with a classy reputation and if he was with them he would be a sharp cookie.

"So Valerie comes to your place as cover, then she and Pete get together."

"Does that make me a pimp?" Kate asked. "Or a hetero beard?" Another grin, this time broader.

"It makes you a friend, someone who wants the best for those whom she cares about."

"Still, she is married."

I shrugged again. "Not too married, apparently."

Kate sipped coffee, smoked some more, withheld comment.

"Is there anything else you can share with me?" I asked.

"Not much, really." Kate shifted on the sofa to a more relaxed posture. I liked the way she held herself, quiet but with a provocative hint beneath. "Call Pete, say I gave him your number and he'll let you talk to Val." Then she was upright, alert, her eyes narrowed. "But you screw her over, I'll find out about it and I'll dance on your grave. Okay?"

"Agreed. And when I talk to Valerie, I'll make sure she phones you." I sipped the last of my coffee and got up. "Believe me, I'm not trying to force anyone to do anything. I'm only working to facilitate communication between Valerie and her husband. And trying to get her back home. Her daughter cares deeply for her. That much is evident."

Kate ushered me to the door and there was a brief uncomfortable moment as we both lingered, near one another in the narrow entranceway, neither turning away nor advancing, two people waiting for a bubble to pop between them. Finally I broke the surface tension by reaching down and scratching her cat behind one ear. The cat uncurled and stretched its head out for more. I complied, going under the chin for a major coup. The cat writhed in pleasure.

"Twyla's a hog for affection," Kate admitted.

"Twyla Tharp?"

"Yep." She nodded, smiling. "Fine arts, you said. You'd know who she is, right?"

"Among other things," I said, straightening up and leaving Twyla to her dreams of interpretive dance. "It was nice meeting you, Kate."

"Interesting meeting you." She reached out her hand and gave me a surprisingly gentle, pleasant squeeze.

I was out the door and back in my van, trying to decide what she meant by interesting.

Chapter 24

Despite what Kate Morley thought, an attorney named Peter Bally was listed online after all and the number matched the one Kate gave me. It took me thirty seconds to get his home address.

I waited until evening so I could drop by unannounced rather than phone ahead and give Valerie Albertson time to scoot away. I took the 4Runner since I planned to get groceries on the way home and its AC was better than the Chevy Stealth anyway.

Bally lived in a new townhouse in West University Place, that small but exclusive area near Rice University. I figured he was home since there was a frog-green Lexus parked in a little driveway in front. Snuggled beside it, of course, was Valerie's Beemer. If I'd meant to hassle Bally I would have shown up at dawn, but I planned my arrival for dinnertime when he'd be most amenable to visitors, because I only wanted to chat with Valerie and make sure she was okay, not cause trouble.

I pushed the doorbell.

"Yes?" a man's voice queried through the speaker unit.

"Mr. Bally? I'm Officer Mrmnph of Grrmph Security." I tried to sound official. "There seems to be a problem with your car. Apparently someone tried to break into it."

"Okay, just a sec." That second later, Harrison Ford opened the front door. At least someone who looked like him from decades past. "I didn't hear the alarm go off. Is the window broken?" He then saw I wasn't a cop and tried to shut the door, but my foot was already in the gap.

"Mr. Bally? I'd like to talk. I'm Mitchell King, a private investigator." I held out my ID folder.

"Go away. I've had enough of your kind. Get lost or I'm calling the cops!"

I didn't know what he meant by "my kind", but his left eye was swollen and his cheek and ear were puffy. I assumed that Han Solo had run afoul of some Imperial Storm Troopers. "Mr. Bally, I don't know what happened to you but I didn't have anything to do with it. I'm not a thug and I'm not here to give you any trouble. I'm a licensed investigator and I only want to talk."

"Only want to talk? That's what the other guys said before they hit me. I'm calling the cops."

"Go ahead, call them. I'm out of here. I'll see you at your office tomorrow. You're with Jacobs and Pfeiffer, right? I'll phone your supervisor and make an appointment." I turned to go, but I was betting he didn't want me visiting him at work.

"Wait," he said. "You say you're not with the others?"

I offered him my card. "Mr. Bally, I don't even know who the others are. I've been hired by Walter Albertson to find Valerie. I just want to speak with her, make sure she's okay."

"You're too late," he said. "Valerie's gone. She left with the guys who beat me up."

Chapter 25

I sat in Pete Bally's kitchen and sipped a Coke. He was across from me, nursing his bruised ego and his matching bruised head. A scotch on the rocks was before him but he scarcely sampled it.

"I've never had a black eye before," he said. "Does it really help if you put a piece of steak on it?"

"They don't teach that subject in private eye school. Most likely it's a rumor promulgated by the beef marketing council."

This got a laugh from Bally despite his mood. "Sorry I was short with you."

"Hell, you were polite. Somebody pounded on me, I'd shoot the next guy who knocked on my door." And I was being honest. Peter Bally seemed like a reasonably decent fella who'd managed to fall into a relationship, maybe even in love, with a married woman. That might be questionable judgment but it didn't make him evil.

"Anyway," he said. "I don't know where Valerie is. No idea at all. These two guys came here last night, shoved me around, then she left with them."

"And you don't know who they are?"

"Never saw them before."

"Yet you didn't call the police about this. Why?"

He chuckled ruefully. "What the hell was I going to say? Well, officer, there's this married woman who's sleeping with me, except that we don't want her wealthy and influential husband to know, these two strangers came in and beat me up and she left with them, even though they didn't force her. And oh, by the way, don't mention this to the law firm I work for. They're very conservative and will probably fire me if they find out."

I'd have kept quiet too. "You said they were Hispanic?" He nodded. "Can you describe them?"

"One was short and pretty fat. He didn't do much, just stood there. The other guy, the one who hit me, was taller, about your height, slender. Both maybe forty years old. They spoke good English."

"How were they dressed? Neat or shabby?"

"Nothing special. Neat and clean, I guess. Ordinary street clothes, slacks, sport shirts. You know, like car salesmen." He grinned. "They wore jackets. I guess to hide their guns."

"Did you actually see a gun? Did they pull a gun on you?"

"The way they acted, I sort of assumed they were tough guys, maybe had guns, but no, I never saw one." Bally shrugged. "Hey, I'm no fighter. I tried to push them out the door, the taller guy hit me and I went over the sofa. I got up and he hit me again, so fast I didn't have time to blink. After that, I was pretty dizzy so I stayed down."

"Valerie went willingly with them?"

He nodded, adding a frustrated frown. "She was pissed that I got hit, but they didn't force her."

"She knew them."

Another nod. "She called the fat one Ricky. And they called her Valerie like they were old friends."

"You don't think they meant her any harm?"

"Not likely, I guess. They let her get her clothes and purse and all. If they were going to hurt her, they wouldn't do that, right?"

I wasn't sure but I told him they meant her no ill will, just to make him feel better. I took another tack. "What was Valerie's mood before they arrived? Was she acting different from the other times she visited you?"

Bally considered this a moment. "Come to think of it, yes. Absolutely. She was extremely nervous, apprehensive."

"What about? Did she say anything, give any indication?"

"Not specifically, but I guessed it was something about home. She wanted to tell me. I think she was trying to work up the courage."

"Maybe she was planning to leave Walter, be with you permanently."

Bally shook his head. "Sorry to say, no. We'd already talked that to death. She was determined to hang on until Cheryl finished high school next spring, then we'd make the move, maybe. But this was something else, something new and very serious."

"Bad, you say?"

"Bad. She didn't sleep well after she got here. I'd get up in the middle of the night and find her sitting in the kitchen. Just sitting."

"Any idea why? What she was so concerned about?"

"No. She tried to share with me, I think, but she was scared."

"You know I'm going to have to tell her husband about you. If she were here I might be able to stall, but with her gone, I've got no choice. It's in my contract, what I agreed to."

Bally looked resigned. "We were going to break the news to him anyway."

"I'll try to put it in the best light, but there's not much else I can do. I'm sorry this hasn't worked out. And don't worry—nobody at your firm will hear about this, at least not from me. I'll get her husband to keep it quiet, too. Bad publicity wouldn't help his business anyway." I finished my Coke and stood up. I'd heard all I wanted and said what I could. If I thought of something else, Bally would be available.

Pete Bally led me to the door and we shook hands. Then, like Columbo, I had one more question. "When these guys arrived, did Valerie seem particularly surprised to see them?"

That stopped Bally cold. "Now that you mention it, no. She just sat there when they came in."

"Thing is, I wonder how they knew she was here." And with that, I left Peter Bally standing on his front step, both mouth and door wide open.

Chapter 26

The night terrors.

In movies, the actor sits bolt upright in bed, a gasp of fear on his lips. This never happens in real life. The dream brain keeps you from moving, so waking is always a gradual paralytic awareness during which you learn anew that the real world is actually out there and every bit as insane as your dreams. That semi-dream state when you climb from the gloom can be the worst

I found myself awake, silently staring into the darkness beyond the bed and trying to catch my breath, focusing on nothing, inner turmoil having dragged me to sodden and dreary reality. I lay unmoving, droplets of sweat hanging in my hair and drizzling down my face. Presently my raging heartbeat slowed and I could breathe more easily.

The dream was a mix of enticing sex and graphic horror. Terrie Bartlett sat atop me and we were naked. She rocked rhythmically as I thrust into her, my excitement growing the deeper I penetrated. I reached up to massage her perfect breasts and it was then her face morphed into Victor Allison's ruined head, eye sockets dripping blood, torn mouth grinning.

He screeched in a high-pitched parody of Terrie's voice. "Having a good time, Mitch? Enjoy it while you can."

And even though the shattered visage hung there, transplanted onto Terrie's body, still I pushed my hips upward with desperate hunger. Vic cackled insanely while I tried again and again to climax, and it was with my last animal effort that I woke into the hollow and solitary prison of my bedroom.

There was silence for the space of about half an hour.

* * *

I rolled over and glanced at the clock glowing from my nightstand. Four am. I sighed, swung my feet to the floor, switched on the lamp. On his cushion by the bed, Krazy Kat raised his little head with a Mrrf? of complaint. He yawned, stretched, refolded his tuxedo body and went back to sleep.

I reached for my smartphone and once more called up the Chronicle news story I'd saved. I nearly had it memorized but I read the thing anyway.

911 Call Reveals Possible Homicide

EMT technicians arrived at the 11000 block of Mission Vista in Memorial late Wednesday evening, responding to a 911 call, but Houston police were soon dispatched as backup. The nude body of the homeowner, Theresa Bartlett, 24, was found in the outdoor whirlpool spa. She had apparently drowned after being thrown into the water unconscious. Indications were that she had been sexually assaulted and strangled.

Police arrested Bradley Chilton, 27, at the scene. Chilton identified himself as a fitness counselor and Bartlett's boyfriend and said that he lived with her. Chilton at first denied harming Bartlett but later admitted "grabbing" her and pushing her into the whirlpool after a bout of rough sex and an argument. Harris County prosecutors said that Chilton would be charged with homicide. A quantity of cocaine and marijuana was also seized at the residence.

This is not the first time that violence has visited this address. Last June, police found the body of homeowner Lawrence Trevillian at the same poolside, reportedly shot by an intruder. Theresa Bartlett, Trevillian's girlfriend at the time, was present at the shooting and briefly considered a suspect, then cleared.

In tabloid-style circumstances, Trevillian's alleged killer, Victor Allison, was later shot and killed by Houston private investigator Mitchell King. King had been hired to protect Bartlett during the investigation of the Trevillian murder and the two were rumored to be having an affair. Although initially detained for questioning about the Allison shooting, King was released and no charges were filed. When contacted regarding the death of Bartlett, King declined comment.

No matter how long I stared at the text the words didn't change. I hoped it would bring closure, provide whatever relief that trendy and overused word suggested, but thus far the knowledge only invoked feelings of guilt, anxiety, regret. And nightmares.

I put my phone aside, stumbled into the bathroom and swallowed two Tylenol, dry. I pulled on some cutoffs and went downstairs to the kitchen. I poured myself a glass of grapefruit juice and downed half in one gulp. I could still see Terrie's face mixed with Victor Allison's. Recalling Dutch LeBrock sprawled dead in that parking lot didn't help. Nor did the image of Rhonda Willett.

These visions were as vivid right now as if they'd been digital photos. In my mind's eye, Hamlet said. And yes, the mind's eye has perfect vision, perfect enough to twist my soul into knots.

Would I ever find peace, some small measure of contentment?

Leaning against the counter and sipping the juice, I tried to mitigate my depression by focusing on the present case. Chip away at it, Agent Scudder said. Valerie was still missing but there was also no evidence she'd fallen to harm. She simply found herself a deeper hiding place than previous. Tomorrow I'd check my contacts and locate fat Ricky and his thin companion. They would lead me to Valerie.

My reverie was interrupted by an impatient brushing at my ankle. Krazy Kat had tracked me to the kitchen, that place of wondrous treats. He emitted soft mews of supplication, begging for a snack. His sleek black white-tipped tail twitched in concert with his namesake hanging on the wall, ticking off the time.

I pulled some leftover Boston Market chicken from the fridge, nibbled a bit myself, broke up a chunk onto a paper plate and nuked it for a moment to take off the chill. All the while Kraze became more agitated about the upcoming food, and when I plunked the plate onto the floor he scurried to gobble, emitting a Gurrhr! of joy, just like Leopold Bloom's cat in that Dublin kitchen a century before.

How they depend on us, I thought. Each homecoming, each feeding, each rub of the head is cherished. Love unconditional. And how often we fail to comprehend that simple precept. We decorate our human affections instead with false ribbons of deceit and selfishness, cover our true feelings with layers of anger and past affront, conceal honest yearnings with a veneer of mistrust.

Myself included. The last coherent relationship I'd had was with my attorney friend Donna Boudreaux three years ago. It hadn't lasted. She soon pulled away from me, broke off the romance firmly but with good grace, ignored my surly attitude and continued to nurture our friendship until I put the sexual hang-ups behind me.

"You want too much," she said. "And you aren't prepared to give of yourself in return. Sometimes I think you haven't grown up at all and there's still this little Mitchell kid inside, calling all the shots, pulling the strings."

Which was why she made me a gift of Krazy Kat. "You need a real woman in your life, Mitch. Someone who will love you enough to throw the bullshit right back in your face, make you realize the truth of your screwy mindset."

Fine, except that Krazy was a male. Well, a putative male since he'd been fixed, but I got the point. I needed an honest relationship and Kraze would suffice until that time came. I reached down, gave Kraze a stroke on his flank as he finished the last of the chicken, then I switched off the light and went back upstairs to bed.

Feeling better now, I began to drift off.

No sooner had I laid my spirit into the arms of Morpheus, I was shaken back to the real world by the bounce of Krazy jumping onto my bed. He rarely ventured to this reserved plateau and his footsteps were tentative as he felt his way across the sheet. Emboldened, he tiptoed alongside my legs to snuggle his fuzzy little body solidly against my stomach. I meant to shoo him away but found myself rubbing his ears instead.

Soon his purring resonated through me and I sank into a welcome silent slumber.

Chapter 27

After sleeping late, I went out front to grab the paper. I waved to my neighbors, Ernie Banks and his son Malcolm across the street, trimming their lawn with shears. Or rather, Ernie doing the work and Malcolm criticizing harshly from his wheelchair.

Ernie Banks, namesake of the famed, late Cubs shortstop, is a widower, retired postman whose only son had come back from Afghanistan on a gurney. Malcolm lost the use of both legs and most of his willpower in some unpronounceable village in the mountains. Now he spends his days drinking and cursing God. I don't blame him much, though. A black man still has his share of prejudice to push through, even in a fairly cosmopolitan city like Houston. Add to that a major disability, stir in anger and you have the recipe for a traumatic condition. All that considered, Malcolm's ceaseless haranguing of his father was still difficult to countenance.

Ernie Banks had been a grunt in Vietnam, just a kid but twice promoted on the battlefield, three times decorated and had come through the Tet Offensive without so much as a paper cut. Malcolm had been the bright kid, a whiz at electronics who'd gone into the Army for the college tuition. He was stationed in country but assigned to brigade maintenance, a back marker position. His radio tent was hit by a mortar shell a few days after he arrived.

It was ironic, this juxtaposition of disparate fates. Yet such are the circumstances and vagaries of existence. Despite Einstein's admonition, God does indeed play at dice with the universe. And with us. Especially with us.

* * *

Ernie beckoned me over. He put down the lawn shears, wearily got up from his knees, pulled off his gardening gloves and we shook hands. He's a small man, weighing a hundred and change, with a thatch of white hair and stubbly goatee, his face and arms wrinkled and parched.

Malcolm is his father's opposite, massive shoulders and arms, a wide muscular chest and torso. His wheelchair is one of those zippy models with low rider seat and tilted wheels. I'd often see Malcolm tearing down the street, making great time and challenging trucks and cars to his place on the roadway. He'd spilled a few times, once breaking his wrist. But he was insistent on fighting the traffic, wheelchair be damned. Too bad he didn't feel the same way about other things in life. He's highly intelligent and could find a good tech job in a New York minute.

Ernie eased slowly onto his porch steps and took a long pull off an ice water jug sitting there. "How you been, Mitch?" he asked.

I sat next to him, feeling his son's glaring eyes boring between my shoulder blades. "I'm good," I said, in abject denial about my night tremors and the blood that filled my waking dreams.

"When we gonna take in another Astros game?"

Ernie Banks and I are big time baseball fans and go to as many games as we can. We try to get Malcolm to come along but he usually backs out at the last minute. In some way it's better though, giving Ernie a break from nursemaiding his son. The VA does its minimal governmental prescribed part and there were some veterans' groups that came calling, but Ernie nevertheless bears the brunt of caring for Malcolm. A father's loving concern notwithstanding, Ernie's simply too old to nurture each whim from Malcolm, each demand. It wears the old man out.

"Lemme check," I said. I pulled the Chron from its plastic bag and checked the baseball section. "They'll be back in town Friday, playing the Yanks. How about that?"

Ernie smiled and nodded. "We got a date."

"The edge isn't finished," Malcolm interrupted, complaining to his father. "Over on the left side by the driveway."

I looked where Malcolm was pointing. There wasn't so much as a blade of grass askew. In fact, the whole lawn appeared as though it had been transplanted from the Masters eighteenth green at Augusta. Ernie's as neat and careful about his front yard as he is about the remainder of his house and life, Malcolm the only dissonance.

Ernie sighed. "Just a minute, Son. After I talk with Mitch."

I heard Malcolm mutter under his breath, "Damn honky, fuck him."

Ernie heard it too. "Don't you worry with Malcolm," he told me. "On his pisspot today because his check ain't come."

I looked to Ernie. "I've said this before. Malcolm can have the money direct deposited."

"I told him, Mitch. Says he wants to hold the check in his hands."

I shrugged it off. These days you practically had to fight the VA to get checks mailed instead of deposited, but Malcolm was deliberately painting himself into a bind so he could play the victim game to the hilt, a classic passive-aggressive tactic.

So I changed the subject back to baseball. Ernie had religiously followed the career of his namesake and owned a small cache of the Ernie Banks memorabilia. My neighbor Ernie would cheer for the Astros too, so long as they weren't playing the Cubbies. "So we're on for Friday? We'll leave here at six."

"Sounds good, Mitch." Ernie took another pull on his water jug. "You drive, I'll pay parking."

I teased him about his name. "Hell," I said. "You shouldn't need me to take you to the game. A man of Ernie Banks' reputation would have a limousine come by to pick us up, skybox seats, catered food, free booze, everything."

Ernie laughed and clapped me on the shoulder. "Shit, Mitch, they was here yesterday! Where was you?" He nudged me. "Some fine women in that limo, too. Had to entertain them all by my lonesome."

"Limo my ass," Malcolm growled. He delighted in raining on his father's parade at every opportunity. "You spend all damn day preaching how great life is, how wonderful 'de Lawd' is. You want to kiss whitey's ass and suck his cock, you go ahead!" He jerked his wheelchair around and spun the wheels up the ramp to crunch through the open front door. He managed to scrape the woodwork on the way but that was payback for Ernie daring to speak with me.

Ernie watched his son roll into the house. "Mitch, I'm sorry." Deep ridges of pain ran across his aging face.

I stood up. "Nothing to be sorry for. Malcolm wants to blow off steam, let him. He doesn't bother me."

"Don't know what I'm gonna do about that boy."

"Keep the faith. Maybe we can still get him to that doctor I told you about."

"He ain't gonna want to see no shrink."

"Needs to, though. Dr. Chen could do him a world of good."

Ernie stood up wearily and pulled on his gloves. "Maybe, Mitch, maybe."

But it's futile and we both knew it. Malcolm didn't just hate whitey. He savaged Asians, Hispanics, all foreigners the same, his own people, too. When you hate that many around you, it means only one thing: you hate yourself. And it was unlikely that Malcolm would ever extricate himself from this cage of his own design and creation.

But Malcolm only needed a few years to engineer and build his self-restricting vault. Others work at it for a lifetime, like Jacob Marley's burden of chains. We all create our own customized shell, secreting it layer upon layer from the excesses of our soul. A few build towering ceilings and spires of promise and strength, but most of us only knock together hovels and lean-tos, pulling the dirt tightly around us for comfort. That's because we each create the dwelling for our soul and the residence for our being that best reflects the shape and boundary of the spirit within, expansive or shriveled as it may be.

I shook Ernie's hand and walked back across the street. Ernie again knelt to the task, trying not only to make his lawn attractive but also please his unyielding and demanding son. Obedient servant, placating his own flesh and blood, same as I. He to his son, I to my father. Dead or alive, it made no difference.

Chapter 28

I spent the rest of the morning finishing my insurance report for the pawn heist and closing out some other paperwork. I do most of my own bookkeeping and have a knack for computers, so it's easy. Occasionally I bring in a friend, Andrew Capshaw, to help with my other stuff, and my CPA cranks out the taxes, but otherwise I go it alone.

Andrew and I are partners in a little startup business, a dedicated site hosting service aimed principally toward small law firms. We supply all the software and maintenance for those too small to have their own IT department. Andrew is the computer whiz, I provide the financing and contact list. Thus far, we've just broken even, but we recently signed a top rate contract that should finally put us into the black for good. If not, I'll just have to dip deeper into my grandfather's trust. That's showbiz.

My fictional private eye Bugsy Binton doesn't belong in this modern world. Bugsy eschews cellphones, spends half his time searching for payphones then gripes because they no longer take dimes. He also chokes when confronted by technology, instead keeping his vital records on the back of bar napkins and matchbook covers from boxing gyms. He's too busy anyway, bedding all the dames that waltz into his squalid walkup. Myself, I hadn't had a date in months so there was plenty of time for computers in my life.

My office is at the front of the house and I mostly live upstairs. Back when prices were still sane in the Houston Heights, my wife and I bought a tidy brick colonial. When we split and she moved to Phoenix, I cashed in some bonds, bought out her equity and paid off the note. Since I own the place, I only pay property taxes, my middling income as an investigator works out well and granddad's fund helps fill in the cracks. I don't have extravagant tastes, my only concession to luxury being the nine-foot Brunswick-Balke pool table in the garage that I converted to a game room.

The office itself is modest. A sign by the front door proclaims Mitchell King, Investigations and the door opens into a foyer, leads to a small waiting room next to a half bath and my private office. The furniture is modern but cheap and comfortable. Ikea rules.

I added a false wall to divide the office from the kitchen and breakfast room in the rear. Upstairs are two bedrooms, full bath and a comfy study into which I cram my books, a good Bose sound system and every classical and jazz CD I can grab. The music, literature and my passion for pool are enough to keep me occupied and mostly out of trouble. Not long ago I sprang for a big HD-TV so now I'm now grudgingly phasing out my VCRs and DVDs in favor of Blu-ray. As soon as I get that done, they'll of course change from hi-def to ultra hi-def 3D, 4D, 5D and the cycle will continue unabated. Hopefully I'll be dead by then.

I saved my work, e-mailed my report to the client and I was done.

The desktop TV across the room was tuned to the Weather Channel, audio muted. Forecasters pegged this an active year for hurricanes and thus far they'd been right. People joke about inaccurate forecasts but satellites make predictions far more reliable these days. A big tropical disturbance was whirling around in the Gulf, probably headed for Brownsville and the lower coast, but sometimes these storms reject conventional wisdom and swing north.

In 2008, Hurricane Ike steamed straight up the Houston ship channel and dumped its load squarely into the Galveston-Houston corridor. Damage was immense, many drowned and some low coastal neighborhoods have still not recovered. On a personal note, a big pecan tree in my back yard blew over onto my vintage Dodge Charger, turning it to underinsured junk. Once bitten, I now took storm warnings seriously.

Krazy Kat was sleeping, curled up on my desk, generously volunteering himself as a fuzzy paperweight. Despite his groan of complaint, I gently slid him aside to get at my case folder, filed away the hard copy, opened my smartphone to notes on the Albertson fiasco.

I was pondering how to break the news to Walter Albertson about Valerie's boyfriend and subsequent disappearance with her two pals when Albertson himself phoned and rendered my dilemma moot. Talk about synchronicity, both Jung and Sting would be proud.

"I just talked to my wife," Albertson said. "She's okay and she'll be home soon."

"Did she say where she was?"

"Like you thought, she's not at Kathryn Morley's. She's staying with another girlfriend but wouldn't tell me where."

"And you're certain she's all right?"

"Yes. She sounded very upbeat and open."

Not open enough, I thought, considering that the new girlfriend was actually two Hispanic guys who whumped on lovesick attorneys.

"I should tell you what I've found out," I said.

"That she's been seeing someone else?" His voice was reserved. "I already know. I asked her directly and she told me."

"Did she tell you who?"

"I wouldn't let her. I don't even want to know. I just want her to come home so we can talk it over, hopefully work things out between us."

So much for my groundbreaking report. "What do you want me to do next?"

"Nothing. There's no more needed, I suppose."

Canned again, the runaway spousal syndrome holding true. "If you're terminating my services, I'll work up the invoice and send you a check for the balance of your advance."

"You needn't bother. The difference isn't worth the extra paperwork."

"Still—"

"I insist. For all we know, your investigation may have given her the incentive to phone me anyway. Keep it as a bonus, really."

Fine with me. Who was I to turn down some easy cash? "Nevertheless, I'll send you an account of my time. The state says I need to."

"Suit yourself." His imperious tone then turned conciliatory. "I want to thank you, Mr. King. Your presence did appear to set things in motion. And regarding Paula, I know that she's not fond of Valerie, but your talk with her may have done some good there as well. Paula's more amenable to Valerie coming home now."

"Glad to have helped," I told him, even though I scarcely believed it myself. "Does Cheryl know that her mom's all right?"

"Valerie phoned Cheryl before she called me."

"So that's it."

"That's it. Goodbye, Mr. King. Thank you." He hung up and that was it for sure.

Damn. I'd been fired from missing wife cases before, but only when the strays returned on their own. This time she was still missing, yet I'd been paid in full for not doing much of anything. Albertson hadn't even been curious about what I discovered, yet his dismissive manner had to be contrived. The concern for her at first seemed genuine, but after one quick phone call he was willing to toss the search aside and patiently wait for her to show up? Not in this world.

The situation was too pat and there were layers of deceit yet to be uncovered. Fired or not, I intended to see this case through. My curiosity was piqued and something was rotten in the state of Albertson.

I phoned Tony Villarreal a third time but he wasn't answering his page. Knowing Tony Vee, he was fishing, hunting, or in jail. I wanted to ask him about a pair of shady Hispanic guys, the fat one named Ricky.

Tony would know them. Tony knows lots of shady people because he is one.

Chapter 29

When the phone rang I thought it might be Tony Vee calling back, but it was Joe Duggan. "You ran out on me the other day, asshole." Joe is never one to engage in preliminary chitchat.

"Sorry. It got to me, all that blood."

"Shoulda stayed, pal. We need to talk."

"Yeah?"

"Yeah. You think I'd let you hang around a murder scene otherwise?"

"I did wonder about that, but I figured it was my scintillating personality."

"Screw that. I want personality, I'll go play with my golden retriever. Least he does what I tell him."

"I assume you're calling me because I'm forgiven, even if I won't fetch a stick for you?"

"Bullshit your getting forgiveness from me. Be a cold day in Hell or in Houston." Joe's kindness knows no bounds. "You busy right now? Or maybe you're all tied up, hustling pool, chasing cokehead pussy, shooting innocent citizens?"

"I leave that important work for the cops."

"Don't go anywhere. Me and Meierhoff are coming over. Fix some of that good coffee you got." He hung up. Joe never wastes time on goodbyes, either.

So I straightened up the house and put on some of that good coffee. I didn't have any donuts but they'd just have to make do. After all, my first name isn't Duncan.

I wondered why the esteemed Homicide Lieutenant Joseph Duggan and the somewhat esteemed Detective David Meierhoff were paying little old Mitch King a visit in the middle of the workday. Here I was, a PI, one of a breed who solves riddles in a flash, but it was certainly a mystery to me.

And the mystery became even more convoluted when Duggan and Meierhoff drove up and I saw they weren't alone. FBI Agent Ed Scudder, aka the Cigarette Smoking Man, was with them. And a fourth guy whom I didn't recognize at all, even though I knew in an instant what he did for a living.

The man had stylishly country-western length grey hair and a neatly trimmed mustache. He was tall, about six-one and slender, with the weathered visage of someone at peace in the outdoors. He wore a perfectly blocked white

Western hat, spotless white yoke shirt and carefully knotted tie in a soft tan color. The badge clipped to his belt was a silver Lone Star in a silver circle. He had Western cut dress khaki slacks bearing a razor crease and law enforcement stripe down the leg, with cowboy boots polished to a gleam. A 1911 .45 auto rode in a sharp looking open carry leather holster at his waist, worn with the same casual indifference that other men would display a cellphone. Only one person on the planet dresses that way. A Texas Ranger.

Joe Duggan walked into my house like he owned it.

I looked around at everybody and smiled. "What? Am I getting an intervention?"

Duggan stared at me for a second. "Will you for one goddamn time just shut the fuck up?" He shook his head in frustration. "And this is Ranger Arvis Danforth."

I stayed quiet after that, or tried to. We shook all around and soon were sitting at my kitchen table, sipping coffee. Meierhoff had brought a briefcase with him and I somehow knew that what was inside did not augur well for me.

Krazy Kat was delighted at the company, scooting from chair to chair, rubbing up against the legs of his visitors, each of whom reached down to pet him in turn. Stroked to satisfaction, Krazy found himself a nice perch on a nearby shelf from which to observe us, hoping that we'd soon begin to eat tuna straight from the can and invite him to join in.

"Mind if I smoke?" Scudder asked. His Droopy Dog face was too plaintive for me to say no, so I snagged my only ashtray from a cupboard and told him to go ahead. How could I refuse the FBI?

Meierhoff started the ball rolling, pulling a bulky manila envelope from his briefcase. "We need your help, Mitch."

"I dunno," I told him, grinning. "My fee structure is pretty high. Cop salaries and all, I don't think you can swing it."

Agent Scudder stared at me and time ground to a halt. His easy nature was cast aside and I saw the experienced FBI professional within, the hard flat stare of a lawman drilling into my skull. There was a coldness in him, a glimpse of the things he'd witnessed and I could not hold his gaze. I made the mistake of looking toward Ranger Danforth instead. He had intense bright blue eyes that darted like a laser, straight into me. Duggan was smirking and Meierhoff pretended not to notice my being skewered, looking down instead into his coffee cup. No help for me anywhere around the table.

Scudder sighed. "Special Agent Strahan spoke with me about the NASA case this past June, told me that you can be a jerk. Lieutenant Duggan says you're a wiseass and I tend to believe him." He took a drag, blew out smoke. "But this is not the time, so please play this straight, okay?"

I nodded, afraid to say anything. I'd been put in my place, low man at this confab and everyone knew it.

Meierhoff put the envelope on the table, continued. "You know that I'm HPD rep for the Slicer unit. Arvis is the same for the Rangers, and Agent Duggan is here on temporary assignment from BSU, coordinating the Slicer investigation."

I glanced to Duggan because he'd not been named. He grunted at me. "I'm just here to keep your ass in line."

We all grinned at that for a moment, and then the gravity of this meeting landed squarely, blew me away just thinking about it. I frowned at Meierhoff. "The Slicer, David? God, he's way out of my league. I do skip tracing, stolen jewelry, background checks, crap like that. Nothing major."

Meierhoff shook his head. "Let me outline what we have in mind. And I know you, Mitch. You bullshit around but you're also reliable as an investigator and can keep your mouth shut when necessary. Not to mention that you're my friend. I know this seems pretty ridiculous, a bunch of fairly high profile lawmen coming to you. But it makes sense if you think about it a while, based on what we already know."

"I gotta tell you, Mitch," Duggan said, "I didn't think you could handle this but I was outvoted by David and Scudder here. I want to be square with you and let you know." He shrugged. "But things have changed since, and maybe you've got yourself back on track." Joe nodded to David, giving him the go-ahead.

Meierhoff slid the manila envelope over to me. "This is a suspect in the Slicer murders. He fits the profile. Anglo, left-handed, works in the medical field, sort of an oddball but nothing that lights up the scoreboard."

I moved to open the thick envelope but Ranger Danforth's palm plunked down, holding it shut. "We need your word that what we say here goes nowhere else. We're breaking police procedure and about a dozen laws just showing you this."

Now I realized how significant this was and regretted my sarcastic remarks. "Absolutely. It goes no further. You have my word."

Danforth pulled his hand back and I looked inside the package. A guy named Raymond Burgess. Photo of a fortyish man, nondescript. A few pages of information, copies of newspaper clippings, some handwritten notes in the margins. I frowned. "I'll have to read this more carefully, but not a lot of incriminating stuff here, at first glance. I trust you guys, but you've got to have more on Burgess than this, to set you to thinking."

Meierhoff nodded. "We do, Mitch, just one thing. Check the white envelope." There was a legal size plain envelope marked letters and inside, three sheets of photocopy. "We've got the originals put away, of course. They were made on generic typing paper, each letter mailed to a different FBI office nearby, each from a different zip code. No fingerprints or DNA." Meierhoff pointed at the copies. "Typed on an old Smith-Corona manual. If we found the typewriter we'd match it in a heartbeat, but without the machine—" He shrugged.

I quickly scanned the letters. They were written in a deliberately illiterate style. Not even a marginally educated person actually writes like a 50s TV hillbilly. They said, "Raymen Bergess is gilty and the slicr" or "he kilt hur wit white rope frum eagel rope cumpny" and so on. Just enough information to tantalize. The offhand grammar and spelling, I decided, was to intentionally prevent matching the writing style with an existing suspect. "No idea in hell who wrote these, right?"

"Nope," Meierhoff replied. "For all we know, it's Ray Burgess himself, trying to confess in a sort-of subconscious mode. Besides naming Ray, all the letters actually do is to dangle tenuous clues before us. Understand that the FBI's received dozens of confession and accusation letters like these, most written by kooks. Those have been cleared but these letters mention the rope brand name. Also realize that the Slicer crime scene evidence is very thin. No DNA, no semen, no fingerprints. He's careful."

"Okay," I said. "But why come to me?"

Scudder took another drag. "We need a preliminary investigation that's completely sub rosa and separate from official police efforts. Nobody in law enforcement can know."

"We want you to look into this guy's personal life," Meierhoff said. "See if you can develop any indicators that he's a good bet for the Slicer. If you find something credible, we'll take it from there. But we can't risk using our people for the first phase."

"Because?"

"Because," Duggan said. "This guy's older brother is Captain George Burgess, head of Travis City Police internal affairs."

Chapter 30

I'd heard a lot about George Burgess but never met him. And like most people, I'd prefer not to meet him, either. Burgess had a fierce reputation throughout the area. Not only did he diligently pursue the dirty cop, but also ferreted out the small kickbacks and freebies, all the perks that many cops took for granted. His reputation was such that even though he was a Travis City cop, all the badges in larger Houston to the east knew him intimately. It helped that Travis City was an affluent satellite community with strong ties to the oil and gas business and subsequent area influence. Burgess also seemed to enjoy his job a little too much, arresting offenders with great zeal and showing up on the local news for each perp walk. He was therefore feared and hated by the rank and file, which helped explain why I was being brought into the mix. I was an outsider and had no axe to grind. Neither could he put my balls in a vise.

"Not the nicest guy around," I said.

"No, he's not," Danforth agreed. "But he's honest, at least on the surface, and has clout with top brass and in city hall, even here in Houston. Word gets out we're investigating his kid brother, shit hits the fan."

"But if you've got evidence?"

"Hard evidence is what we don't have," Meierhoff said reluctantly. "It's all in the notes for you to read. Just some hints around the edges, nothing specific. We've never had enough leads to interview Ray, even casually. He has no idea we've got a file on him. No one knows it exists, except us, others here and there, a very select few."

"So you want me to check him out on the sly, be careful not to let him know. And either clear him or bring you something definitive."

"Also," Duggan added, "if you find anything, it's got to be enough for us to take to a friendly judge and get a warrant, or at least to start a formal investigation. Something that can't be challenged legally."

Scudder stubbed out his cigarette. "Bring us evidence we can use, something concrete. Or enough to clear Ray Burgess for sure."

"Pardon for asking," I said, "but can't the FBI do this? They can certainly run surveillance and keep it from the Houston or Travis City police. So can the Texas Rangers, for that matter."

"Yes," Danforth agreed. "But our rules of conduct in the law are as restrictive as the local police. And we don't have a sliver of genuine evidence. That ties our hands. All we've got is a vague suspicion, rumors."

Scudder gave me his weary smile. "Besides, since nine-eleven, our resources are redirected. Serial murderers take a back seat to jihadists these days." He tapped the folder. "For me to activate a case file on Mr. Raymond Burgess, I'd have to make a lot of noise."

"And that's what we can't have," Joe concluded.

I looked at Joe. "There's a possibility that what I do might slide into, well, a gray area."

"We know that," Joe said. "But we never asked you directly to bend the law, either."

"Plausible deniability," Scudder added.

I nodded. "I'll do what I can. Is everything I need in the folder?"

"Should be," Meierhoff said. "If you have more questions, get with Joe or me. Out of the office and in private, of course."

"Of course."

Joe reached out, shook my hand. "About the money, we can all pitch in for your expenses, maybe more later on. But this has to be off the books."

"Forget it. It's on the house," I told him. "I just got paid a bunch for doing nothing on another case. I figure this balances things out."

"You got our thanks, that's for sure," Joe said.

"I appreciate you guys having trust in me. And I won't let you down."

"Just try to stay out of trouble this time," Joe said, adding his wry grin.

Business concluded, I escorted everyone out, then I poured myself another coffee and sat back down to learn more about my job, an assignment more serious than anything I'd ever imagined. When both the FBI and Texas Rangers show up at your front door, you pay attention. They even trumped Joe Duggan.

Chapter 31

Raymond Burgess worked for the Harris County hospital district in the clinical laboratory services group. He was a phlebotomist, which meant he went around all day drawing blood samples. Did we have a vampire on our hands? Too soon to say.

Burgess was forty-two, single, never married. He lived in Houston all his adult life, graduating Spring Branch High after moving from Richardson, a suburb of Dallas, as a teenager. He'd done a couple years of community college but no degree I could see. His employment history was sketchy, a mix of low-level jobs, mostly in the health services industry. Seemingly, he'd skated through life without making a dent or raising much dust. But that certainly didn't make him a murderer.

There were a few glitches. When he was thirteen, there'd been a terrible fire at the family home, both his parents dying. Ray himself was burned, apparently trying to save them. Older brother George had been out of town, staying in Nashville with friends, a secure alibi.

Ray spent time in the hospital but suffered no debilitating injury other than a rather nasty scar that required a minor skin graft. Circumstances of the blaze were undetermined and suspicious, nothing proven. Case therefore closed. Shortly afterward, George Burgess came to the Houston area to start a job at the cop shop in Travis City and brought Ray along as his legal ward.

Three years later Ray Burgess attempted suicide, overdosing on alcohol and sleeping pills. George found him, got him to the hospital in time. After this, Ray went through psychiatric counseling for depression. But lots of people went to shrinks. I could vouch for that.

Ray otherwise stayed clean. There were some traffic tickets, speeding and such but nothing that jumped out at me. One arrest for drunk and disorderly at a local tavern, charges dismissed as a result of brother George's influence. I flipped through the other info and studied the mug shot from the drunk arrest. I looked into Ray's eyes and tried to see a killer gazing out at me. There was nothing good or bad, just the emptiness of modern life.

After I read Meierhoff's notes, I retyped everything into the computer, using my own words. The three accusatory letters I typed verbatim, shredded the originals and flushed the confetti down the toilet. That effectively burned any bridges connecting me to my cop mentors. If I now got myself in trouble despite Duggan's warning, there would be no provable links back to the police. Plausible deniability, as Scudder reminded me. Which meant, of course, that it would be me and me alone twisting in the wind. But that's why I'm paid the big bucks.

Chapter 32

It was nearly two pm. Ray Burgess worked the day shift, which meant he'd get off at three. I figured no time like the present, so I fed Kraze and headed down to the hospital parking garage. I bluffed my way into the employee section by using one of my fake passes, took the Stealthmobile up the ramp and soon found Ray's aging brown Chevy Impala. It was parked just about where Meierhoff's notes said it would be. Parking was jammed so I doubled up a few slots over and waited.

Just after three, Ray sauntered out, along with his fellow staff members. Like many, he was wearing faded green scrubs. Ray got into his car, drove away and I followed, keeping one or two vehicles between us. We drove west on Holcombe and were soon in Sharpstown, an older mixed neighborhood with nice homes and apartments, tired old shopping centers, decent families and singles plus the usual crack dealers and petty criminals. Traffic was light.

I assumed Ray was headed home, but a few blocks from his address he turned off and parked in front of Woody's Tavern.

I'd been there a while back for an 8-ball tournament. Woody's is a decent neighborhood drinking spot, well managed, clean and as I remembered, featuring friendly barmaids. My kind of place.

I waited a few minutes then followed Ray inside. He was sitting at the end of the bar with other patrons, catching the tail end of an Astros game at Wrigley. As luck would have it, the stool next to him was empty, so I took it and ordered a Bud. The bartender was indeed cute, a pretty brunette with a nametag that read Jacqui and I fondly imagined that she'd sign her name by dotting the "i" with a little heart.

We all watched the game, groaning when the Cubs scored again, then again. I made the appropriate comments and blended with the group. We were all Astros fans and therefore instant lifelong pals, commiserating with each other when the Cubbies eventually took one from our beloved 'Stros.

Ray behaved much like everybody else, reacting at appropriate times, even saying "shit" when the Astros popped up for the final out. Nevertheless he was reserved in what I assumed was his home bar, not chatting with his bar mates or flirting with Jacqui. Even so, he didn't have a butcher knife on a cord around his neck or teeth filed to a point or otherwise offer any indications that he was a serial killer.

But neither had Ted Bundy.

* * *

After the game, several guys left the bar or wandered over to play pool, leaving Ray and me alone.

"Astros left too many on base," I said.

"Yeah, tell me about it."

"I'm Mike." I held out my hand.

"Ray."

We shook. His grip was soft and clammy, like meeting up with SpongeBob, but I smiled and played the part, Mister Friendly. I glanced over to the pool tables. "Game?"

"I'm not very good," he admitted.

"Me neither. We won't bet or anything, only for fun. I just find it relaxing."

It was of course anything but relaxing. Besides trying to be a new pal and get inside Ray Burgess' head, I had to play pool so far down my skill level that I briefly considered shooting with the butt end of the cue.

Ray wasn't kidding. He was probably the worst player in Houston, maybe all of Texas. So we batted the balls around the table without much success and managed to get through only three games in an hour. At least we saved our quarters.

But winning at pool wasn't my objective. Learning about Ray Burgess was. I studied him and chatted and made small talk. We bought each other beers but I only drank a third of mine while Ray drained his bottles each round. I counted six on his part, a bit stiff for ninety minutes but not unusual unless he intended to continue apace.

I gestured to his scrubs. "You a medic, or what?"

"X-ray tech."

Okay. So maybe he didn't think that admitting he drew blood was a keen way to meet folks.

"You?" he asked.

"Fed Ex. I work in the warehouse. Sit on my tail all day and track shipments."

Ray neither questioned my job nor inquired further. He was not an extravert by any means and certainly not a talker. So we just played pool badly and drank beer. Eventually I decided that little more would be served by an extended stay, so I excused myself. "Need to get going," I told him. "Gotta be at work early tomorrow."

"Me too. I start taking X-rays at seven."

"Good meeting you, Ray."

"Sure. Nice meeting you—?"

"Mike. See you around."

So I used the john, tipped Jacqui and left Woody's.

I moved Stealth away from the general line of sight and switched on sports talk radio to keep me company while I waited for Ray to show. Turned out that he was in no hurry, despite what he'd said. I was forced to resort to my trusty Gatorade bottle to relieve the old bladder before Ray finally emerged, wobbling on beer legs. It was nearly eleven.

I considered him fortunate to survive the five blocks to his house without hitting anything. He was all over the road before he eventually swung into his duplex parking lot. But lots of folks drive that way nearly every night, loading up on beer at the neighborhood bar, switch on autopilot to get home. Eventually the law of averages or the law in the cop car catches up with them and they're either crunched out or busted.

So what had I learned tonight? Raymond Burgess drank far too much on a Tuesday for someone who ostensibly had a responsible job early Wednesday morning, let alone driving drunk. He also lied about his profession, was nonassertive and uncommunicative, and was definitely not the brightest bulb in the chandelier. Otherwise, he seemed a reasonable sort, not at all someone who might be a crazed murderer.

But I'd only been on the job one day and it takes time to get into a new gig.

Chapter 33

The next day I turned my attention back to the Albertson case. I still wanted to find the two guys who took Valerie, but Tony Vee was still not returning my calls and my other sources were also out of touch, so I thought about asking Freddy Gonzales. He'd spent time on the Hispanic gang task force and might point me in the right direction. I called Gonzie but his cellphone wasn't answering. Nobody wanted to talk to me today.

Next I phoned Robbery division. "May I speak to Sergeant Gonzales? This is Mitch King."

"I'm sorry, Mr. King. He left early, said he's wasn't feeling well. Anything we can do?"

"No, nothing pressing. I'll catch him tomorrow."

Not feeling well, my ass. I knew where he was, Alibis.

Alibis is a classic cop bar, which means it's dark and private. Cops don't care much about ambiance as long as the drinks are cheap and there are other cops to hang with. Sure, there are teetotaler cops and social drinking cops who avoid such places. But the hard-core boozer will head straight for Alibis. So did I.

As I drove into the center of the city, I entered an immense cloud of haze hanging between the skyscrapers like some malevolent translucent beast crouching amid a forest of steel and concrete. Once I got there I couldn't really see it any more, but my watery eyes were witness to the junk I was breathing. These past few weeks, the pollution had been exacerbated by the hot and stagnant weather pattern and we needed another good rain to wash the air clean. But hopefully not a hurricane strength rain.

Lord, if you please, no hurricane. Ike was plenty.

Alibis is about five blocks from the cop shop, nestled between a bail bond agency and a shyster law office. I walked inside and the bartender had a Bud on the counter soon as he saw me. I guess that made me a regular.

The tavern is typical for an old style downtown place, long bar along the wall, a few narrow booths, pool table in the back. The place was nearly empty. Two vice cops whom I knew were sitting at the bar, watching Dirty Harry blow away creeps on TV, the sound turned down. Alibis has an extensive collection of cop movie DVDs for their discerning clientele.

Aside from the action flicks, the local news was always shown each evening and the cops watching would play a game among themselves called Guess Who. If a robbery or shooting was being reported, one of the cops would comically cover his eyes as the photo of the perp was shown on screen. The other cops would yell "Guess Who?" and the hand-blindfolded cop would describe the suspect's age, general appearance, and angry stare. And he'd usually be right.

Next to the vice cops was a guy named Tom Parks who sold office furniture or something. Parks was buying a round for the bar and he motioned my wallet back into my pocket. In cop slang, Parks was a buffer, a serious cop groupie. Had he been a woman, he'd be passed around like a joint at a Deadhead reunion. Being a guy, he was useful for buying drinks and borrowing a few bucks from.

Buffers are not the normal citizens who simply appreciate cops and the work they do. Instead, they're cop wannabes who hang on every vestige of law enforcement and endure ridicule to stay the scene. Why is anybody's guess. They aren't necessarily bad people, maybe just lonely and unfulfilled.

In the back, several cops were at the pool table playing three ball, or as I call it, three ball fuck your buddy. Ordinarily I would wander over and methodically take their money, but today I was on the clock. Okay, it was pro bono, but I was working a case nonetheless.

Gonzie was at the bar, as I figured. He was sitting by himself, playing a touchscreen video trivia game. I stood behind him for a minute, silently kibitzing and resisting the temptation to reach over his shoulder and punch an answer. The subject he'd selected was sex and each time he picked a correct answer, a video of a woman would appear and she'd lose another piece of clothing. At the rate Gonzie was going, however, he could have bought a dozen stroke mags and received a faster and cheaper glance at naked women. I suppose it was the thrill of victory that kept him at it.

Gonzie guessed wrong again and lost. He reached for his drink and spotted me. "Hey, Mitch, nice surprise. You come all the way down here to pay me that ten?"

I knew he'd ask me about it so I already had the bill in my shirt pocket. I put it into his outstretched palm and looked into his eyes. He was already blitzed.

Gonzie flipped the money onto the bar and downed the last of his drink, rattling the ice in his glass. "Hey, Bobby!" he called. "Gimme another one. Double. You ready, Mitch?"

I shook my head. I'd barely sipped my beer and that's where I intended to keep it. After my drunk driving idiocy a while back, I'd gone on the wagon. Sufficiently dried out, I found that I really didn't need to guzzle beer all evening. Two or three were plenty, a couple times a week at most, and I hadn't drifted over the line since. I kept telling myself that I'd learned better and maybe I had.

"You here just to pay off?" Gonzie asked. "Or you kissing up for a favor?"

"Well—"

"Okay, what?"

"I'm looking for two Hispanic guys, probably in the business. One is slender, one is a fat guy named Ricky."

Gonzie nodded. "Yeah. Mid level bad boys, Ricardo Perdon is the fat one, his cousin is Angel Perdon." He pronounced the name Anhel. Gonzie frowned. "Last I knew though, Angel was up in Huntsville, doing two to four. Could be out by now."

The bartender brought Gonzie's whiskey and Gonzie siphoned off half before the glass had time to frost.

"Know where I might find them?" I asked.

"Don't recommend you try. Rough dudes. Shooters. You get in their way, you're in total shit without a shovel." Gonzie's voice was slurred and his eyes were unfocused. "They work for Julie Cards. I could check for you."

I'd heard the name Julie Cards somewhere and meant to ask more, but Gonzie was swaying now. "You okay, Gonzie? What say we head over to Kim Son for dinner? My treat. I'll get you a cab home."

He shook his head. "Nope." He pushed a dollar bill into the game slot. "Got to beat this fucker and I'm not leavin' till I get this bitch's clothes clean off."

I wheedled and cajoled but it was useless. He was deep into his cups and would not be otherwise dissuaded. Eventually I gave up, sat my nearly full beer on the counter and slipped the bartender a few bucks to ensure that Gonzie got a taxi home. I left for Kim Son anyway. I was hungry.

* * *

My cell cheeped as I was starting the 4Runner. It was a surprise, Cheryl Stern. Except for Valerie, I'd nearly forgotten about the crazy Albertsons. Why Cheryl was calling me, I had no idea. But chatting more with her might give me insight into Valerie's problems. Hungry would have to wait.

"Mom called! She's okay!" Cheryl was clearly happy.

"I know. I talked to Walter earlier."

"Fuck Walter."

119

"Maybe so, but he is your mom's husband." There was no reply. "Cheryl, I'd like us to talk. We didn't have much of a chance earlier." She hadn't mentioned my being fired so I figured she didn't yet know. It gave me an opening.

More hesitation, and I could imagine her mulling over options. "Okay. You know where the Raven is?"

"Yes. On Washington, just past Shepherd."

"Meet you in an hour," she said, clicked off.

I was committed to the prospect of closing this case to my own satisfaction even though I'd been canceled out by Walter Albertson. This dedication to follow up was motivated by my determination to prove that I could fulfill my father's high standards of excellence. I may not have chosen the legal profession but I could make my point elsewhere. Therefore I took it as a challenge and was reluctant to let the case go. I wanted to see Valerie safely home and, if possible, discover what baleful spirit pursued her soul.

Chapter 34

The Raven is like a sixties beatnik coffee house gone upscale, hangout for underage punk kids. It's on Washington Avenue in a low rent portion of town dotted with auto parts outlets, discount clothiers and liquor stores, the type of neighborhood where you not only lock your car but keep an eye on it all night. The area is however rapidly going upscale, places like the Raven being shoved aside for trendy bistros where lawyers sip designer martinis, but like all transition zones, each block along Washington still has its unique flavor and the Raven was holding its own for now.

The club is in a little strip shopping center and looked like it had once been a shoe store. Its plate glass windows are painted over and decorated with a large mural of a cartoon blackbird playing a chopped Stratocaster, Marshall stack behind. The guitarist bird has avian sidemen on drums and bass and features an especially nice vulture on Korg keyboards.

The Raven itself is one large room with chipped tile floors and whitewashed walls, awful hip-hop pseudo-music playing too loud. There are intentionally badly painted and mismatched restaurant-style chairs and tables, magazine and bookracks and a standup bar along the back wall where they sell soft drinks, millennial approved bottled water and coffee. Above the bar a big sign: No Drugs! No Booze! Not Now! Not No Time! The barman looked about sixteen but he had a cheerful grin and was polite to an old geezer like me. I ordered espresso, looked the place over.

It was full of teenage kids, most of whom were texting, tweeting, or otherwise glomming onto the free Wi-Fi the Raven offered. Few of the kids were actually speaking directly to one another, but for all I knew, those sitting across the tables were texting each other via synchronous satellite to achieve a communications gap of two feet. Grown people do that these days too, not just kids. I guess I was either born too soon or too late to want in on the excitement.

Some of the youngsters dressed punk, some like hippies, some like whores and pimps. I was easily twice the age of anyone else and got plenty of stares. I'm sure I looked like an undercover vice cop. Or a father searching for his wayward daughter. Or more likely, a dirty old man searching for someone else's wayward daughter. Regardless, I wasn't very welcome and I could feel harsh eyes on me as I stood there sipping the hot bitter liquid.

One feature of the Raven I'd heard about was their graffiti collection. Each table has a small jar with felt tip pens of various colors. Patrons are encouraged to write on the walls, fill them with poetry, jokes, wisdom of the ages or rude commentary, the principal difference between wisdom and rudeness being the advance of time and use of the word fuck. I looked at a few of the offerings on a nearby wall but didn't learn much. The jokes I already knew and many of the more difficult words like your or its were misspelled.

* * *

Cheryl came in as I finished my coffee. Some of the other kids called her name and she waved to them. There were smiles throughout, so I guessed she was popular with her peers. I bought her a Diet Dr. Pepper, God only knew what that tastes like. We sat at a table a bit removed from the others.

Tonight she was out of goth uniform, this time wearing pricey designer jeans with even more pricey designer holes artfully worn through the knees, Day-Glo pink sneakers and an oversize pink sweatshirt that nearly swallowed up her small frame. Her black hair had been freshly red-streaked, she wore a bunch of tiny jeweled studs in a row around the top of her ear and enough eyeliner to make her resemble a lonesome raccoon. Despite this, I thought she looked sort of cute and felt slightly guilty for thinking so.

"Thanks for being here, Cheryl."

"Anything that'll help get my mom home to stay, Mr. King."

I glanced around, hunched over in a joking conspiratorial posture. "You realize the damage you're doing to your reputation, talking to an old guy like me in front of your pals?"

"They probably think you're hitting on me."

"More likely they figure me a nark. You'll need to come up with a good cover story later."

"If I tell them you're a cop asking about Kenny, they'll believe that. He got kicked out of here, trying to sell blotter."

"It's none of my business, but I think you could find a more agreeable boyfriend."

She rolled her eyes with well-practiced theatrics. "Now you sound like my mom. Or Walter or Paula. And you're right. It isn't any of your fucking business."

I raised my palms in supplication. "Sorry. Won't mention it again." And I meant it. She had enough turmoil in her life without any more volunteer referees.

Cheryl took a swig from her Doc, frowned. "Look, maybe you're right. I dunno. Kenny's a pain in the rear. He's always on my ass, giving me a hard time. When I was worried about Mom, he was a real shit, acting jealous like I was taking my time away from him."

She obviously didn't have anyone to talk with about these things and there was pent up frustration inside. "Maybe you should spend more time here," I suggested. "It's a nice place and you obviously have lots of friends."

Cheryl nodded, sipped, smiled broadly. And that was the first authentic smile I'd seen from her. I found myself plotting romance, racking my brains for some friend who had a deserving teenage son. Ah, that old matchmaker Mitch.

But I was here for another reason. "I need help, Cheryl. I need to know why your mom keeps running off. It's not just a marriage gone sour, is it? There's something else behind all this, right? Something deeper?"

She nodded. "She won't tell me." Tears began to brim in her eyes. "I've tried, Mr. King. I've asked."

"Any ideas?"

"No. Things get worse and worse between her and Walter, then she heads over to Kate's. She comes back after a couple days and it starts all over."

"From what you say, it sounds like abuse. Does he ever hit her?"

She shook her head. "I never saw him hit her or anything, never even start to. Walter's a turd but he's not got a hot streak, not violent, that much I'm pretty sure about. And I don't think Mom would let him do anything to her regardless. Least I hope she wouldn't. She's never been the type to take that kind of shit off anybody."

"Good for her, but there are other types of abuse. Mental, psychological. No marks on the outside, plenty within."

Cheryl thought about this, shrugged. "Maybe. Maybe that makes her run off. I really don't know."

"And this time she stayed away longer."

"I'm worried fuckin' sick." More tears now and she wiped them with a sleeve of her big sweatshirt, smudging her eyeliner. "I miss her. She's all I got."

"I'm sure she'll be home soon," I told her, not half believing it. Cheryl smiled through the trickle of tears and I once more thought she was an okay kid, someone who hadn't received all the breaks she needed but was hanging on nonetheless. "Tell me about you and your mom before she met Walter. Where did you live?"

She frowned a moment at my change of pace, gathered herself. "Apartment down near the old Astrodome, on Braeswood."

"Nice place?"

"It was okay. The AC never worked worth shit." She smiled at that, raised her eyebrows. "Wasn't like the fuckin' palace we got now, but I'd be happy to just go back to the way things were before."

So would we all, I thought. But Stephen Hawking says that time's inevitable arrow presses us forward. Always forward, never back, irreversible entropy our eternal nemesis. And Thomas Wolfe presaged Hawking when he told us that we can't go home again. Both of them were right, too.

"Where did Valerie work?" I asked.

"A place called Club Caliente. They tore it down. That's where she met Walter." With that, a disdainful sneer.

I remembered the place, down on South Main. It was a popular Mexican restaurant, dance club, hangout for the fast crowd during the thankfully brief revival of disco. Now there was a dollar store in its place.

"Your mom tended bar, or what?"

"Yeah, bar, waited tables. I'd get home from school, she'd sit with me and make sure I did my homework. Then I'd go over to the neighbors till she got back from work. Sometimes it would be real late, three, four in the morning, I'd be asleep, she'd carry me to bed. But she would be up anyway at seven, making my breakfast and all. She was great."

"Keeping an apartment, working long hours, sending a daughter through school isn't an easy thing to do. Did your mom get any child support that you know of?"

Cheryl's head dropped. "My father," her voice failed. "I don't know who my father is."

"I'm sorry. You don't need to say any more if you don't want to."

"No, that's okay. I got used to it. Mom won't tell me who my dad is, she said he's dead. I about died myself when I saw my birth certificate. It says Father Unknown."

The tears began again and I started to reach out and put my arm around her in comfort, then hesitated. I didn't want to be misunderstood so I opted instead for a perfunctory pat on her shoulder.

"A lot of people go through life that way, not knowing their parents," I advised. "It doesn't make them less valuable individuals. And I'm sure your mom loves you enough to make up for a dozen fathers."

She nodded and wiped away the tears. Her sleeve was getting soaked and the makeup was everywhere on her narrow face.

A flickering thought came to me. Missing parents, wayward child. My father sliding into his grave, still waiting for his petulant son to return to the fold. But the prodigal did not, and now it was too late. Again, time's arrow, its inexorable drive and our inability to deter its direction.

God, how I'd royally screwed up my own life.

"Cheryl," I began carefully. "I need to ask about something else. Please understand I'm not trying to upset you with these questions, but I need to find out things."

"It's okay. Go ahead."

"Was your mom seeing anyone special, back before she met Walter? Did she have a steady boyfriend?"

Cheryl screwed up her nose and frowned. "I'm sure Princess Paula has told you that my mom was sleeping with half of Houston, but it's not true. She's never been that way. Honest."

"I'm not accusing Valerie of sleeping around and frankly I don't think she did," I said, my voice as placating as I could make it. "But I'm trying to help her and it would go a long ways if I could locate any former boyfriends."

Cheryl launched into a pensive stare, reconstructing pieces of her past. "I was a kid then, but not that little. I knew enough about what was going on. She went out sometimes, but never overnight. I guess she wasn't dating anybody regular that I remember."

"Any close friends? Besides Kate Morley?"

"This guy she knew. They weren't, you know, dating, just friends. I called him Uncle Ricky."

I'd been a fan of mystery novelist Robert Parker for ages and this was what his Boston private eye Spenser called a clue. My heart swelled with joy abundant. A real clue.

"What sort of guy was Ricky?"

"He was pretty chill, nice to me. He'd bring me toys and cookies and stuff when I was little."

I nodded. "But he wasn't dating your mom. They were just friends?"

"Yeah. He was a nice guy but, well, he was pretty fat. Like huge." Cheryl pantomimed a big stomach with her hands. "I don't think Mom went for his type. She always liked the tall ones, like Walter." Again the sneer.

"You see Uncle Ricky any more?"

She shook her head. "Not for a long time." Cheryl looked at the ceiling, counting back. "Several years, I guess." Then she glanced at her watch. "Jesus. I've got to go now. School tomorrow and there's this fuckin' history test and I haven't studied at all." She smiled again and stood up.

"Phone me if you hear anything," I told her. "And good luck on your fuckin' history test."

That got a laugh. As we walked to the door, she said, "I hope Kenny isn't too pissed."

"Why would Kenny be pissed?" I opened the door for her.

"He's been out here waiting for me all this time," she said, about two seconds before Kenny hit me with a brick!

The blow caught me upside my head and I was immediately stunned. My vision twisted but I still managed to see him swinging again. I ducked and the impact glanced off my shoulder but it still hurt. Next a slam from the other side and I felt my breath go. Kenny had a helper. They hit me again and I sank. I got in one good uppercut but was slammed to the pavement for my efforts.

I heard Cheryl scream, "Kenny, no!" but the attack continued.

Kenny and his pal bore in, beating me across the head and shoulders. I curled into a fetal position to protect myself from the kicks that were bouncing off me and I tried to reach for my pistol but I was already drifting away.

Suddenly it was over. There was yelling and cursing and somebody new was leaning over me. "Mister, you all right? You okay? We run them assholes off." I tried to get up but my legs were still rubbery.

Cheryl was crying.

I just lay there and made incoherent mumbles until the ambulance arrived.

Chapter 35

Meierhoff was leaning casually against the wall in the ER of Twelve Oaks Hospital, watching while a surgical resident stitched my head. The doc had already put in a couple of teeny staples and now he was adding a row of nearly invisible stitches, using a gadget that resembled one of those twenty buck handheld sewing machines they sell on late night TV. I could only hope the hospital had a higher quality model.

The stitching didn't hurt because the doc had already zapped me with a local but it was still disconcerting, having to sit still while somebody used a Singer on your forehead.

As always, David Meierhoff was splendidly dressed. He wore a cream-colored sport coat, trim and tapered beige slacks, blue shirt with French cuffs and a silvery tie, his lapel cop badge being the only discordant fashion accessory. Meierhoff obviously had his evening spoiled by my call to him.

Meierhoff stepped forward for a better look and offered a suggestion to the resident, a stocky, tired looking guy named Bashir. "While you're at it, can you spell out something with the stitches?"

"Sure. What should I put?" Bashir immediately picked up on the joke and seemed eager to help.

"He's always had the hots for Madonna. How about that?"

"Consider it done." The stitching continued.

"On second thought, you could make it say Fuck You and that way he won't waste time insulting people like he usually does. The stitches can speak for themselves."

"Too late," Bashir frowned. "I already put Madonna." He pursed his lips thoughtfully and looked over to Meierhoff. "I could pull them out and start over."

"Naw. He'll just complain and I'm tired of listening to him bitch. I'm bored already anyway."

Naturally I was studiously ignored throughout this interchange. It was my skin but their joke. And I knew it was meant to cheer me up but I wasn't very cheery right now. No concussion but a headache, one partially cracked rib, bruises.

Bashir was cleaning up, pasting a nice bandage on my forehead. "Try to keep it dry," he told me. "Come back in a few days and we'll take the butterfly stitches and staples out. Don't pick at it. I don't think there'll be a scar, except for the Madonna thing."

He smiled, then got serious. "You get dizzy, feel faint, you get to us asap. Also if you have a bad headache or nausea, it starts bleeding. Head injuries can come back on you, so be careful, okay? And no alcohol." He handed me a bottle of painkillers, the good prescription kind that really work.

I tried to thank Bashir but he was already off and dealing with another case he'd been alerted about that had just come in. Night call at the ER is usually one trauma after the other.

* * *

Meierhoff helped me down the hall, to the parking lot, into his Porsche and we drove out. "We got a pickup order for old Kenny. We'll find him quick. He's not a master criminal, you know."

"Mastermind enough to blindside me," I groaned.

"Shit, that's not much of a challenge." Meierhoff upshifted as we sailed along through the night, scooting up Kirby, switching over to Heights Boulevard. He drove smoothly but every bump sent twitches through my ribs and made my head rattle.

I tried to come back on his wisecracks but felt too shabby. I just wanted to get home and hit the bed. Tomorrow I'd look for Kenny and hit him. A lot.

"Monique took your car. She dropped Cheryl at her place and drove up to your house, took a cab back to my apartment." Meierhoff was dating a motorcycle cop, Monique Devereaux, a tall Nordic blonde who looked exactly like a James Bond girl.

"Thanks," I told him. I dug a twenty out of my wallet and tucked it into a crease in the dashboard. "Should take care of the cab fare."

"Glad we could help, pal." Meierhoff switched on the CD player and some opera came out. Verdi I thought but didn't know for sure. I gestured to the speaker and grunted.

"Il Trovatore," he told me. "I hate this crap but I'm trying to impress Monique with my cultured side." That was a hoot. Meierhoff is probably the only beat cop on the force who has season tickets to Houston Grand Opera.

We drove up to my house in the Heights and sure enough, there was my 4Runner. "Monique put the keys through the mail slot," Meierhoff said. "I kept the house key." Which he handed to me. Always the thoughtful friend, a treasure. I wish I'd been nicer to him. How could I ever make it up? Yet another challenge for the future that I'd probably toss thoughtlessly aside.

Meierhoff made sure I was steady enough to get along, then dumped me. Monique would be waiting.

When I got inside, I closed the door on a harsh world, fed Krazy Kat, set the alarm and went upstairs. Before I crashed out, I went into the bathroom and checked myself in the mirror. I looked like hell but that would pass. My ribs hurt the worst and I knew that they would nag me for the next couple weeks.

The bandage on my head was still fresh, no leaks. Nevertheless, I gingerly peeled back the tape and examined the stitches. I halfway expected to see annodaM but there was only a neat professional row of surgical thread.

Strangely disappointed, I went to bed.

Chapter 36

"What happened to you?"

Kate Morley was staring at my face. We were meeting for lunch at El Tiempo, an upscale Mexican restaurant on Richmond that's owned by the famous Laurenzo family. I'd just swung around in my seat at the bar when she arrived and I was sporting a small stylish bandage and some bruising on my cheek. The stitches had come out earlier, but signs of Kenny's brick love still lingered.

"I ran into a door?" I smiled my patented all-knowing private detective smile.

"Door be damned. You got beat up."

"You should have seen the other guy. I'm supposed to say that."

She rolled her eyes at me. I suppose my acerbic wit wasn't appreciated.

I was rescued from further embarrassment by our waiter, Benny. He figured we were now ready to eat. "May I show you to your table?"

Kate said yes, I said yes, and we followed Benny to our spot. Kate asked for a table on the patio because she wanted to smoke and I tried not to wince. At least the patio was nicely decorated in villa mode and festooned with potted ferns and hanging stringy things, plenty of greenery. This was fine with me even though I can't tell one plant from another and have to trust gardeners for such. There were two big grackles sitting on the perimeter fence, waiting for leftovers. Those guys I knew.

Kate ordered a margarita, up, and I had a Dos Equis. Kate lit up, perused the menu while I perused her.

Today she was in gypsy mode, a bold print skirt, long and billowy, brown lace up leather boots with matching belt and a crisp white peasant blouse open at the throat where hung a finely worked cloisonné necklace. Her hair was brilliant, deep blonde with reddish highlights, offsetting her fine blue eyes.

"So you've heard from Valerie," I said.

"Yes. After I talked with Pete Bally I was really getting worried, but she sounds okay."

Kate Morley's voice was troubled and I don't think she believed that her friend was as well off as she let on. But if Valerie was in a serious situation, she still managed to phone everyone and tell them hello. Everyone except me. I'd been looking for Valerie and I was the last one to know. My usual luck.

Morley looked at me. "So Walter canned you?"

I made a dismissive gesture. "Valerie's okay, services therefore no longer required."

"But you don't really think so, do you? You think there's still trouble."

"And I'm still trying to find her. Any idea at all where she is?"

"Nope. I asked. She wouldn't say."

"Cheryl is pretty upset. Misses her mom."

"I know. I told Val that she needed to get back home, even if things aren't going well with Walter."

"Even if he's abusing her?"

"I don't know that he is. She's never said so to me and I never picked up any vibes in that direction."

"Something's wrong in that house for certain," I said. "Abuse wears many masks. There's a reason she's so skittish about returning home and I'll bet that abuse is the root of it."

Kate nodded. "I'll push her on it next time we talk. If there's a problem with Walter, I'll try to get them to counseling."

"Good idea. Better for the kids too."

Benny brought our drinks. Kate and I decided to split some ceviche for starters, then she chose the chicken fajitas, I picked the blackened redfish. Fresh Gulf seafood was again readily available and everyone was happy to see that. Except of course the fish.

We nibbled on tortilla chips, sampling the varieties of sauce. Everything was tasty without being so spicy as to bring on the fire rescue team. I did get some green sauce into a cut in my lip, which made me grab for the cold beer, but those are the breaks.

Kate looked at me again and frowned. "Does this sort of thing happen to you all the time?" she asked. "Getting beat up."

"Not usually. I'm averse to being hit, same as everyone."

"Anyone I know do the hitting?"

"Cheryl's loving and considerate significant other."

"The charming Kenny Cramer?"

I nodded. "A pal of his pitched in to help." I told her about the incident and my conversation with Cheryl. "Cops have a warrant out."

"Couldn't happen to a nicer guy," she began, smiled. "The warrant, I mean. Not you."

"For this relief, much thanks."

Kate raised her eyebrow at my comment, quizzical.

"That's what the guard says at the beginning of Hamlet. Francisco or Bernardo, I forget who."

"Do you go around quoting Shakespeare all the time?"

"'Brush up your Shakespeare, and the ladies you will wow.'"

"Wow?" she smiled.

"That's from the musical Kiss Me Kate," I blurted before realizing the entendre.

"Do you always flirt so shamelessly with your clients?"

"Often. It helps pass the time. It also works that you're not really my client."

She smiled wryly at this and again Benny saved me and my smart mouth by bringing us a dish of ceviche the size of a rowboat. She snubbed out her smoke, thank God for small favors.

We dug in, savoring the delicate flavors of the chilled fresh fish, shrimp and shellfish. For a while it was quiet, except for the childish groans of pleasure we both made. Sharing good food is a true delight, particularly with someone as cute as Kate Morley.

I could even overlook the smoking, maybe.

* * *

"No, I'm serious," Kate said, backtracking. "I don't know anything about real private detectives. Do you get in fights a lot, trouble and all, same as TV? You certainly don't look like one of them."

"Like I don't wear a Burberry trench coat and slouch hat, pint of rye in the back pocket, hot and cold running dames, blazing gat in each hand?"

She laughed and nodded, wiping her lips with a napkin. "Yeah, exactly."

"Sorry to disappoint. This sort of thing happens only once in a great while." I was stretching the truth but I didn't want her to think ill of me.

"Do you carry a gun, though?"

"I do. It's part of the deal." She frowned and for a moment I felt uncomfortable, knowing there was always a pistol under my arm.

"I can't stand violence. Or guns." When Kate said guns she quivered like an old maid hearing the word breast.

I deferred. "What I normally do is quite mundane, actually. I spend hours on the net, searching databases and checking information. I interview people, verify eyewitness accounts of traffic accidents and I vet for insurance companies and law firms. Most of the time it's exceptionally boring."

"Just promise you won't shoot anyone while I'm around, okay?"

"Cross my heart." Maybe she'd think kindly of me and not Google my name. If she did, I was toast.

Kate smiled at me again and I immediately felt better. More food came, she ordered another margarita and I switched to iced tea.

"You've known Valerie how long?" I asked.

"Quite a while. Seven, eight years."

"Before she met Walter."

"Yeah. She was taking some business courses at community college and I was teaching an art class. We met in the coffee shop."

I cut off a chunk of my broiled fish and sidled it onto her plate. She reciprocated by plopping a huge slice of chicken on mine. We had enough food for a squad of hungry soldiers but were nonetheless determined to make a major dent in it.

"Was Valerie seeing anyone steady at the time?"

Kate gave this some thought. "Not that I remember. Of course, we didn't become close till later."

"How about Ricky?" I asked. "Big overweight Hispanic fella."

"Yeah. There was Ricky. How do you know him?"

"He's one of the men who pushed Peter Bally around. Valerie went with him and another guy when she left Pete's place."

Kate was surprised to hear this. "Ricky never seemed to be the rough type. He was very nice to Val and Cheryl, always bringing toys and gifts."

"Any possibility that he's Cheryl's father?" I asked.

"No." She shook her head. "I even asked Val about it once. She said Ricky was an old family friend and they were never physically involved. Time or two I met him, I didn't get the idea he was the boyfriend type."

Being a glutton for punishment, I dribbled some salsa verde on the chicken Kate had given me. "Maybe he was a go-between," I surmised. "Keeping an eye on Valerie and Cheryl on behalf of the real father."

She shrugged. "It's possible, but it seems odd that Cheryl's father would care enough to have someone look in on her and yet not visit himself."

"Maybe the father is some big shot, had to keep a low profile. Or married. But that's not important now. What we need to focus on is Valerie, for Cheryl's sake at least."

"Do you think she's going to be all right?" she asked. "Cheryl I mean."

"Can't say. If she manages to dump Kenny, maybe. But you know how it is with young people. They seem to diligently search out what irritates their parents, then do precisely that. Her being with Kenny is a way of challenging the status quo at home. Tit for tat."

"Tell me about it. My nephew is the same way."

I brightened. "Your nephew the same age as Cheryl? Maybe we could fix them up." I was pulling for Cheryl and hoped there might be some chance.

"Sorry. He lives in Michigan." Kate started for more chicken and decided against it. She pushed her plate away with a small flourish. "God, I'm stuffed. This is delicious but I can't eat another bite." She gestured at her plate. "You?"

I shook my head. "I'm done." I nodded at the alert Benny and he began to clear our table. Kate and I both asked for doggy bags. Kate lit another Marlboro.

"Actually," she told me, "it's more of a kitty bag."

"For Twyla?" I replied. "I've got one at home, too. Mine is named Krazy Kat."

"Cute."

"A few years ago my daughter gave me a Krazy Kat clock. You know, the kitschy black and white wall clock with the eyes and tail?"

"Back and forth?" Kate smiled, mimicking the action with her eyes and fingers.

"Yep. My real cat's a ringer for the clock. And I've got him trained to wave his tail on cue, but no matter how much I plead, he won't do the thing with his eyes."

She laughed again. "Tried bribery?"

"Bribery, threats, prayer. He's even more stubborn than I am."

"I may just have to hire you," she said, grinning mischievously. "I sort of like stubborn. In its place, of course."

"You have my number." And I meant this both ways.

Later, outside the restaurant, we waited for the valet to bring our cars. "I'd like to see you sometime," I said.

Kate looked sharply. "You mean, other than about Valerie."

"Yes. Maybe dinner, whatever?"

"Okay, sure. Call me." Then her Mustang came and she was away.

Be still my heart.

Chapter 37

"Jesus, Mitch, you got a life of your own?" It was the next morning and Tony Vee was calling back.

"Why?"

"You left four, five damn calls on my phone. Go on a big drunk or get laid or something. Why waste time hassling me?"

"Actually, I've got better things going on in my life, but I consider it my mission to give you grief."

"I know that you idolize me, but did'ya actually have a reason to call?"

"Other than to make your day?"

"Yeah. Other than fuckin' that."

"I'm looking for two bad guys, cousins I think. Ricky and Angel Perdon."

"Better meet somewhere. We can talk."

I smiled at Tony Vee's paranoia. He was under the impression that a half dozen law enforcement organizations were continually monitoring his every move, recording each second of his phone conversations, reading his mail. Hell, maybe they were.

I suggested Rudyard's Pub. First, we could grab some food. Second, I could wax Tony in eight ball.

* * *

Rudyard's Pub is in the Montrose district. It's a British-style bar with good import beers on draft, music most nights and tasty pub grub. I walked in, sat at the bar and ordered a St. Arnold's Elissa IPA.

I was reading the Public News and sipping my beer when Tony Villarreal came in. Everyone at the bar turned to glance at the newcomer, stared openly. Tony Vee is a huge guy, six-five and over three hundred, his muscular bulk augmented by a dark brooding face topped with a thick black head of curly silver shot hair and fronted by a dense but greying beard. Visualize a demonic Santa Claus.

Tony has olive skin, his rugged face made even more distinctive by having endured the busted noses and lacerations indigenous to NFL interior linemen. He comes from interesting roots, his father a wild Salvadoran dockworker out of San Diego, his mom a feisty Samoan gal. Together they'd turned out quite a product. Tony played left guard for the Oilers until he'd blown out his knees, made a brief run at pro wrestling, then took up more challenging occupations. He's a bouncer, enforcer and freelance persuasion provider. Yet he operates under a quixotic ethical code, refusing jobs that bring trouble to innocent people. His credo: Only those who got it coming.

Tony ordered a 24-ounce can of Fosters, looked to me. "You want another beer?" I shook my head. Tony paid and sat next to me, taking about forty seconds to drink his beer and get a refill. We chatted for a minute, went to the back room to play pool and talk business. I shoved some coins into the pool table and let the balls fall.

As I began to rack, Tony pointed at my forehead. "What happened there?"

"I ran into a door."

"Fuck you did."

"What about these two Perdon guys?" I asked, ignoring his taunt.

"You looking to buy into the tit bar scene, old salt?"

"Hadn't planned on it. That's what the Perdons do?" I rolled the cue ball up the table where Tony stood. "You break."

Tony nodded, smiling his huge wide grin, just like King Kong when he first met Fay Wray. "The Perdon cousins do whatever Julie Cards asks. Julie's the boss." His white teeth shone like bright new tombstones in his swarthy face, small black eyes glittering with wicked humor. He set the can down and reached out a big paw, taking up a cue stick. He chalked, bent over and broke the rack with a mighty blow, sending the balls rocketing all round the table and the cue ball bouncing onto the floor. As usual, Tony Vee overdid it.

"Costs an extra quarter to play on the floor."

"Fuck it. Your shot," he said, laughing at his mistake.

I retrieved the cue ball and stroked in a few, one by one. My ribs were bothering me but I could still shoot okay. Halfway through the rack, I missed. I didn't really want to bear down and blow Tony off the table. He was my friend and there was no purpose in it. I could beat him flat, he knew it, so why not just have fun, goof around?

Tony sucked on his beer, leaned over for another shot.

"So who's this Julie Cards?" I asked. "A lady mobster?"

I said this just as Tony was ready to shoot. His stroke sent the cue ball soaring high over the table, sailing across the room to rebound off the far wall.

Tony was bent over, laughing. "Christ on a crutch, Mitch! Some goddamn private eye you are. Lady mobster my ass! You mean you fuckin' never heard of Julio Cardozo? Where the fuck you been?"

Tony was right. Julio Cardozo was well known in the Houston crime scene. Why I hadn't connected him to the slang name Julie Cards, I was clueless. I tried to tell myself it was because his real name was pronounced Hoolio compared with the hard J of the Anglo slang derivative Julie, but that was no excuse. I wrote it off as a senior moment.

Tony was laughing so much he had to sit down. To hide my embarrassment I slunk out to the bar and ordered two more beers.

The bartender was a tall stocky guy with a quiet smile. "You and your friend okay? We could hear you guys way out here."

"We're fine. Just a slip of the cue."

When I got back, Tony was still giggling.

"Okay, okay," I told him. "Enough." But his laughter was infectious and it set me off. We both sat there a while, snickering like little boys. Eventually we quieted down.

"Could you arrange for me to meet the Perdons?" I asked.

Tony shook his head with wonderment. "You sure got a way of getting in trouble, Mitch. First, you don't even know who the fuck you're talking about, next thing you want to dive into a crap hole with them."

"That bad?"

"Bad enough. Julie Cards has his fingers into lots of the action on the north side, plus liquor stores in Mid City, gambling, hookers. He's got a bunch of legit restaurants and bars all over the place. He owns Fred Danson on city council, a judge or two, plus some cops. You know how it goes, whatever pays the rent."

"Drugs?" I asked.

Tony shrugged. "Sure." Then he screwed up his well-used face. "Not as much as the Colombians, but hey, everybody's got some white dust up his nose these days. But Julie Cards mostly stays away from the hard trade." He nodded to himself as if checking an imaginary notebook. "Cardozo always said that hard drugs are too risky, even though the profit is high. He likes to make his money the old fashioned way, safer, keeps Federals off your tail. Kind of like the Godfather wanted."

"Government bonds versus day trading?" I asked.

"Yeah, kind of."

We began to play pool again, taking turns showing off while I told Tony about Valerie Albertson, her boyfriend Peter Bally, how Ricky and Angel Perdon showed up and took her away.

"You just want to talk to her?" Tony asked.

"Just talk."

"Is hubby gonna be okay with that?"

"To be honest, Walter Albertson is already pleased. He closed my contract after she pulled an ET and phoned home."

"Hold on. You've been canned?"

"Canned. Fired. Shown the proverbial door. Not renewed for next season."

"But you still want to stick your head into the hornet's nest?"

"Yes. I still want to talk to the Perdons and to Valerie Albertson."

"Why do you give a shit?"

I sat down and leaned the cue against the wall. "I promised her daughter. The kid's got nobody else and she needs her mom."

What I didn't add was, because I'm such a fuckup and I want to set something straight for a change. Because I need to please my dead father. Because I regret the way I treated my own wife and daughter. Because I've been a jerk.

Tony shrugged. "It's your head. And you got lots more room for bandages there. I'll make some calls, see what I can turn up."

We shook on it, my normal size hand disappearing within his catcher's mitt grasp.

Tony and I played more pool and drank more beer, grabbed some food. I got the fish and chips and, being the gentleman, Tony announced that I would pay, got three large orders of deluxe nachos. The nachos were piled high but Tony was undeterred. He slammed down two platefuls, then sampled the third before wrapping the leftovers. Everyone in the bar watched while he ate, tracked him as he strolled out to his Caddy.

Tony always made waves.

Chapter 38

Saturday near midnight. I was watching my remastered Blu-ray of Taxi Driver when Meierhoff called. "Gonzie's been in a bad wreck. He's down at Hermann in the Med Center."

"What happened?"

"Nobody knows for sure. Allen Parkway, went off the road and hit an overpass. By himself, probably on the way home. No damn seat belt."

"How is he?"

"Busted up, worst is his head injury. They just brought him out of surgery. Touch and go."

"Had he just got off work?" I asked. My true question, Was he drunk? went unspoken.

"He signed out at seven. The wreck was after eleven." There was silence while we both tallied the doubles he'd downed at Alibis in those four hours.

"You at the hospital now?" I asked.

"Still at the shop. Caught a stabbing, need to finish up. I'll see you soon as I can."

I checked the latest weather on the drive over. A storm in the Gulf had grown into a minimal Category One hurricane named Ellie. The hurricane had come ashore southwest of the Houston-Galveston area. We were receiving a sizeable bunch of rain from its fringes, the temperature dropping a good fifteen degrees. Further down the Gulf coast, Ellie was giving the folks a time of it, spawning tornadoes and washing out beachfront property along with the occasional bridge. Still, it was modest as hurricanes go, and the residents had been given plenty of time to prepare. They'd be okay.

In 1900, a monster storm caught Galveston by surprise and flattened the city, killing over six thousand, more than the Johnstown flood and San Francisco earthquake combined. By comparison a mild storm, the 1983 Alicia had drowned several dozen people and caused a billion in damages.

Of course there was Katrina but it hit New Orleans and many Houstonians got complacent. Three years later, that all changed when Ike savaged the entire Houston-Galveston area in 2008. Nobody ignored weather forecasts again. It was always wise to keep an eye open for the whims of Mother Nature during hurricane season.

* * *

Hospitals are the most insane place to be, especially if you're sick. They're noisy, hectic, disorganized, bureaucratic and frustrating. You surely can't get any rest there. Yet when people get sick or hurt, they're rushed pell-mell to the nearest medical center, the larger the better. And the Houston medical complex is one of the biggest, something like thirty hospitals and clinics, providing both the best medical care and the most tumult per acre you could ever wish for.

Because of my work I'm in hospitals a lot, so I thought I knew my way around Hermann. But it's a monster sprawl with dozens of wings and dead ends. I got lost and finally had to ask. Most people didn't know what Green Six even was, let alone where. Finally, I collared a tired old white-haired black guy who was meticulously mopping every square inch of a long corridor. He gave me crisp and accurate directions.

Five minutes later I stood in a crowded anteroom and peeked through the open doorway into neurological intensive care, where Freddy Gonzales lay amid a nest of tubes and breathing hoses. The side of his head was swathed in wrappings and that, together with his shaved, antiseptic-painted scalp and the respirator nozzle taped into his mouth, rendered him unrecognizable. There were splints on both legs, pins running to tensioning devices, one arm suspended in a space age framework and very little of his actual body visible. Gonzie resembled a Star Trek Borg undergoing recharge.

He was also hooked up to several drip bags and every conceivable type of monitor, each beeping its own discordant rhythm, like a Philip Glass quintet.

Cops were all around, some I knew, most I didn't. I spotted Gonzie's partner Taurean Williams. He was in deep conversation with a woman whom I remembered as Gonzie's wife.

When Meierhoff arrived, he immediately commandeered one of the staff neurosurgeons, a short round-faced black guy who spoke with a precise British accent and whose nametag read Endawbe. Meierhoff flashed his Homicide credentials and gained a private audience. He waved me over, grabbed a female cop from the accident team and the four of us found a small niche off the main hallway where we could talk.

"What's the prognosis?" Meierhoff asked.

Endawbe frowned. "His condition is guarded. There has been some cerebral trauma but we cannot tell how much. We do not think we will lose him and we have good indications that he has no permanent damage, but we cannot tell for certain. Life Flight got him here quickly and we relieved the cranial pressure straight away. After he is stable, we will go back in and finish things. He may recover completely. We have induced coma until the cerebral problems lessen. We will know more after that."

"Other injuries?" I wanted to know.

"Bad, but treatable. Broken left humerus, both femurs, internal injuries but not too serious, considering he was not wearing a seatbelt. He should regain use of his limbs and do quite well. If he survives the head trauma, that is."

A beeper went off and we all pawed at our waists to discover who had drawn the short straw. Endawbe was the chosen one, so he hunched over his phone and talked, clicked off. "So sorry, but I must attend a new admittance, a bad motorcycle wreck, likely brain dead. I will talk with you later." Endawbe gave us all his business card and hurried away, probably to secure some donor organs. Motorbikes provide a steady and reliable source of replacement hearts and kidneys these days, especially after Texas repealed its helmet law.

Meierhoff turned to the cop, a specialist who investigated car crashes, a dark-haired woman of about forty. "Betty Zaiteno," Meierhoff introduced me.

"You do the write-up?" I asked.

She nodded. "Soon as we knew he was law enforcement, we expedited things. Got there just before the Life Flight copter. Paramedics used Jaws of Life, getting him out of his car onto a body board."

"Anyone see the wreck actually happen?"

"Nope. At least nobody who stayed around. We do have two wits who came on the scene right after." There was a quizzical tone in her voice.

"You mean somebody else might have been involved in the crash?" I asked.

"Not necessarily. By late Saturday night, lots of drivers are drunk. So other people might have seen the wreck but were afraid to stop and end up in jail themselves."

"Toxicology come back?" Meierhoff asked.

Zaiteno winced because she knew the real deal. She glanced at her e-book. "Blood alcohol zero point two-three."

Meierhoff and I sighed in unison. Nearly triple legal. What we all dreaded and it could easily cost Gonzie his job. If he lived.

"What happened, exactly?" I asked.

Another glance at the report. "He was headed west on Allen Parkway. His car left the road just before the Waugh Drive overpass. He crossed the median, struck the overpass support, flipped over once." She shook her head in sympathy. "This guy and his wife were driving down the ramp right after it happened, saw the wheels spinning and dust kicked up. They were smart enough not to move him and called 911 instead. Probably saved his life, not playing heroes and trying to drag him out of the wreckage like people do on TV."

"Anything else?" I asked her.

"There is one thing." Zaiteno frowned. "His service pistol, Beretta nine mil. It wasn't in his holster. He had it in his hand, held onto it all the time, even though he was slipping in and out of consciousness and the medics were scared it would discharge. They practically had to pry his finger off the trigger."

Chapter 39

The thunderstorm bore in at dawn, pulling me from a shaky dream into an equally shaky reality. Unable to sleep, I sat at my kitchen table, sipping coffee and musing in disjointed segments of worry and discomfort.

Eventually I showered, got dressed and drove downtown. The city isn't exactly crowded on Sunday mornings and the steady rain kept all but the most determined crazies off the street, so the 4Runner and I had the road mostly to ourselves. I took it easy, the rain sluicing off my windows, flickers of lightning like a laser show on the skyscrapers.

I cruised into the covered garage next to the cop shop and took the skywalk over to police headquarters.

Homicide had recently moved into their new digs, a renovated office building on Travis. It was a welcome change. The air conditioning actually functioned and there was finally enough room for each homicide cop to have an office and computer. And even if they were small, the offices were private, granting the cops a more relaxed venue to make personal calls and surf the net for suspicious porno sites.

We were meeting in a sparsely furnished conference room. Sheets of rain thrashed against the windows, filtering the morning light and forming moiré patterns on the gray sheetrock walls and dull carpeting. I set my chair against the wall, back from the table in deference to the actual police officers who ringed it, discussing what to do about Sergeant Frederico Enrico Gonzales. Despite our relative coolness toward one another, Gonzie's partner Taurean Williams had surprisingly asked me to be here, since I'd worked closely on several of Gonzie's more recent cases. I was happy to assist and felt better about Taurean in the balance.

The fix was in, at least for now. Because of his overall good record, Gonzie's dynamite blood alcohol level would be kept quiet, damning portions of his medical profile sealed and subject to review by the Chief or county attorney alone. If he recovered and was able to return to the force, he'd be required to undergo counseling. The therapy would nicely dovetail into his physical rehab and everyone would win. Houston would regain a dedicated and effective cop and Gonzie would hopefully kick the bottle, drunk charges being the Sword of Damocles to keep him in line. After all, he'd harmed no one but himself.

If he were deemed unable to come back to work, he'd get early retirement and full disability. And if he didn't make it at all, the insurance would go to his wife and kids. Hanging him out to dry for his probable drunken crash would favor nobody except the insurance company and who gave a damn about them?

The latest from the doctors was that the inflammation in his brain had subsided, the EEG showed a normal pattern and he was expected to regain consciousness soon. Despite terrible injuries, Gonzie may have lucked out.

Prognosis out of the way, discussion turned to the principal agenda. Was Sergeant Gonzales intentionally run off the road? Yes, he was drunk, but was he also attacked?

Gonzie's boss was Captain Bill Dean, Deputy Chief of Robbery. He's a conservative, highly intelligent career cop who allows no bullshit but has a reputation for fairness and integrity. Dean's a handsome black man who sports a shiny shaved head and a little goatee, reminding me of Avery Brooks from Deep Space Nine.

I'm thankful for the positive changes that Houston police has undergone in recent years. For the main, promotions and rank advancement have become increasingly merit based. That, together with the weeding out of the old black glovers, those rancid and abusive cops who delighted in throwing their weight around, has brought the city's police reputation into higher esteem. And Captain Dean is an example.

Dean leaned forward, tapped his finger on the forensic report, looked up at those around him. "New deposits of blue paint, scratches, fresh dents on the left rear bumper and fender that weren't part of the crash itself," he said, leaned back in his chair, swiveled side to side. "Not that it proves anything, but it may be something to work with."

The crime scene technician interjected her bit. "Sergeant Gonzales' car left the road very abruptly, not in a gradual way consistent with the driver being impaired or asleep. There are skid marks indicative of a second vehicle but not enough for a make on the tires. We sent the paint scrapings to the lab for a match, should be hearing something right away. We went through the scene with a fine tooth comb, didn't find anything else. Checked his cellphone and office message board too, nothing unusual."

Meierhoff glanced to Joe Duggan. Duggan nodded and Meierhoff took the floor. Although not directly involved, he was a pal of Gonzie's and because of his superb camera presence he had gained the ear of the news media.

"I talked to Cynthia Moreno at Channel Eleven. She's going to run a special segment tomorrow, asking for witnesses to come forward, no questions asked. The folks at KPRC will do the same. And the Chronicle will print a box on page one. Everyone's putting it on their website, of course. Hopefully we'll hear something. We also sent a notice to all the Crime Watch body shops to track repair on the other car, but there are so many small places, we can't rely on that to be successful."

Dean looked at me. "Any ideas who might be trying to get to Gonzie? We've run our list dry."

"One contender. A few weeks back we nabbed these guys connected to a pawnshop job." I briefly explained the situation. "The pawnshop owner, Randy Shindler, threatened us when he was arrested. Of course, that happens all the time."

Dean nodded. "Still, it's a possible." He turned to an assistant. "Carrie, you run the file, find out where Shindler is, where he was last night. And what he drives."

I raised my hand. "We might check one other guy." I consulted my notepad. "Rudy Barnetski. Barnetski was in on the scam, actually did the burglary. He's probably bailed out by now." Carrie scribbled in the margin of the report and nodded to me.

"Anyone have more to add?" Dean asked.

Nobody did, so we broke up the meeting.

Duggan and Meierhoff pulled me aside and we convened in the coffee room just off Homicide. Somebody had brought a box of Krispy Kremes and there was one donut left. I made a run for it but Duggan cut me off and snatched it up.

"I'm an old married fart," he said, eating. "You single guys need to keep your girlish figures."

I told myself I really didn't want that lone donut anyway but couldn't actually persuade my growling stomach to believe it.

Meierhoff looked around to verify that we were alone. "Any more news on Ray Burgess?"

"Nothing other than what I told you before. I'm going to have a look-see inside his house soon as I get the chance. Getting thumped on by Kenny Cramer put me off my feed for a bit."

Meierhoff nodded. "We'll find your friend Kenny. He's got paper out on him and he'll show up eventually."

Duggan finished the donut, damn him. "Take care of yourself. And Meierhoff and me didn't hear you say anything about an illegal break-in."

"What break-in?"

* * *

It was still raining steadily as I drove home. Just to fix it in my mind, I took Allen Parkway and slowed as I approached the accident scene. The landscape was plowed into a long irregular furrow where Gonzie's car had spun off. I pulled over, grabbed a big golf umbrella from my back seat, got out to survey the scene.

Nothing. The cops had already searched every blade of grass and bagged each possible clue. I stood for a while, taking in the lay of the land. Had Gonzie done a solo? Maybe. There was nothing definitive to show otherwise. But the paint ding and pistol in his hand pointed in another direction. I shook my head and splashed my way back to the car.

What had really happened? Likely we'd never know.

Chapter 40

Tony Vee was still working on the Perdon visit, so Monday I went back to our Slicer suspect Ray Burgess. I wanted to know more about Ray and brother George before their move to Houston.

I fired up my computer and ran an archives search on the Dallas Morning News but their online files only went back a few years. I tried Nexis but it only retrieved the same clippings that Meierhoff had copied for me. So I checked my phonebook and called Irving Bernstein, a pal in Dallas. Irv and I had worked together at the Houston office of Jarrett Investigations when we were both new at the PI game. Later, Irv relocated to manage their Dallas branch.

"Jarrett Investigative Services." A pleasant voice. "How may I help you?"

"Is Irv Bernstein in?"

"Whom shall I say is calling?"

"Tell him Marlowe. Philip Marlowe."

A snicker. "Philip Marlowe you say? From Los Angeles, right?"

"Houston, actually. Irv and I are old friends."

A moment later and Irv was on the line. "I thought you were still hanging out in the City of Angels, Phil."

"Just moved to Houston, absorbed all the noir they had in L.A., wanted to expand into new territory."

He laughed. "How the hell are you, Mitch? What's up?"

"I'm okay, staying out of trouble."

"That's not like you."

"I've been a good boy lately. Honest. At least I work at it."

"So if you don't need to be bailed out of jail, why call to pester me?"

"I need some research, Irv. A fatal house fire in Richardson some years ago."

"Sure. What can I get you?"

"The police and fire investigation files, hopefully. Who worked the case, what they found out. Maybe I can talk to them."

"You ask a lot of questions for a guy from Houston."

"Can you fix me up, Irv? I'm in a hurry."

"Important case?"

"You could say that. Highly confidential, though, and no joke. Eyes only stuff."

"You can tell Uncle Irv."

"Not this time, except that it involves a murder."

"Murder's bad."

"Murder most foul, as in the best it is," I quoted from Hamlet.

"Quit showin' off and gimme the details. I'll keep it quiet."

So we talked about old times while I emailed him the names and dates, rang off. It would take a while for Irv to get back to me, so the next thing on my list was Ray's house.

* * *

Ten am and the Stealthmobile was parked just down the street from Ray Burgess' duplex, preparatory to my forced entry into his life. I first phoned the hospital lab and asked for Ray, taking a chance he would answer and I'd have to hang up abruptly.

"I'm sorry, Ray's making rounds." A female voice. "May I take a message?"

"That's okay. I'll catch him later." So I got out of the van and strolled over to his place.

I wore my gas company shirt, name tag and ID, clipboard and equipment at the ready, Canon camera in my pocket. I'd bought an old bulb type leak detector at a junk shop and built the big red LED display from a cheap calculator into the top of the unit to make it look operational. The sniffer itself didn't work but that wasn't its purpose anyway. I consulted my clipboard, studied a nonexistent work order, looked around.

Playing utility guy is a lot more risky than it used to be. Thieves and rapists have begun using this ploy with greater frequency, so neighbors are far more watchful these days and the utility companies are also better about identifying their workers. I had to counterfeit a whole new series of ID badges this year. Thank heaven for Photoshop, a color LaserJet and laminate kit.

The street was deserted. It was hot this morning and everybody was inside or at work, hiding behind the air conditioning. Good for me, fewer witnesses. Ray lived in a group of duplexes, six older wood-frame units in a semicircle surrounding a small asphalt parking lot. The property was well maintained, grass trimmed, buildings neatly painted and in fine shape for their age. There was a small sign out front that read Sharp City Properties, a phone number for emergencies and No Vacancy.

I walked purposefully up to Ray's front door and knocked, hoping that a girlfriend whom none of us knew about wouldn't open the door. She didn't. I waited a respectful interval in case a neighbor was watching, took another glance at my clipboard and walked around to the rear of the building. I was shaky today because I normally had a backup like Tony Vee to watch my ass, but here I had to go it alone.

I pretended operating the sniffer a minute while I scoped out the surroundings. A shaggy privacy hedge blocked me from view of the adjacent duplex, so I quickly took a shim from my tools and slipped the casement window latch. The place had no alarm system and I was inside in ten seconds. I slid the window shut and locked it behind me.

Now I was really on my own. There was no way that Duggan or Meierhoff would cover for me if I got caught. As with Mission Impossible, they'd disavow all knowledge and I'd be a goner. But you pays your money, you takes your chances.

The place was quiet, only the hum and rattle of a window air conditioner set on low to challenge the silence. I stood in a small utility room just off the kitchen. There were some boxes stacked, an old busted chair and two big cardboard clothes storage units, everything covered with dust. I stuck the clipboard into the back of my belt to keep my hands free, slipped on some surgical gloves and started my tour, snapping the occasional photo as I walked.

The kitchen was a mess, dirty dishes in the sink, smelly overflowing trash bags, roaches skittering to and fro in merriment at the picnic Ray provided. The fridge had lots of beer, the cheaper generic brands, plus packages of lunch meat already edging into greenish rot. Kitchen cabinets yielded little more, off brand microwave soup and cans of cheap chili.

The living room wasn't a lot better but at least it didn't stink. Clothes were draped over the sofa and chairs, dirty socks on the floor, empty and crumpled beer cans stacked on a table, a ratty old recliner scooted up to the TV. There was a shabby discount stereo and some CDs of pop groups I'd never heard of. I checked the cabinets and closets but no surprises. Just more junk. Nowhere was there a Smith-Corona typewriter. Or any other mode of civilized communication, for that matter.

Upstairs were two bedrooms, one on each side of the bathroom. One of the rooms was closed and oddly, locked with a padlock. I assumed it was the spare bedroom because this is the way older duplexes are built, but I couldn't know for sure.

The bathroom was just as filthy as the kitchen but otherwise unexceptional. The open bedroom featured an old bed that sagged as much as his recliner downstairs, apparently using the same vintage springs. The sheets had once been white but now were stained to yellow scum. I guess Ray didn't bring too many chicks home. At least not more than once.

I was ready to pick the padlock to the other room when I was interrupted by a rapid knocking at Ray's front door.

Chapter 41

"Hello? Hello?" A woman's voice, loud and demanding. "Mr. Burgess? Hello? Mr. Gas Man?"

I figured if I held off, she'd either arouse the neighbors or phone the real gas company, neither of which promised a desirable outcome. So I ran downstairs, took off my gloves, put on a professional face and approached the front door. Ray, thank God, had a spring latch lock and not a deadbolt. I opened it, clipboard at the ready.

An elderly black woman stood there, wearing a sunny yellow housedress patterned with blue flowers. They call them patio dresses these days but it was a housedress, pure and simple. The woman had gently wavy white hair, a bit too much makeup and a generous grandmotherly smile.

"Oh, hello. I'm Mrs. Viola Winton. I live in the unit next door. Are you with the gas company?"

"Yes ma'am." I thought it best to switch to the offense, so I checked the clipboard. "Were you the person who phoned about a leak?"

"We got a gas leak?"

I gave her a big grin and patted my detector. "I'm happy to say no, ma'am. Everything's okay. It must have been a mistaken call. All clear."

She was relieved and so was I. But crisis past, she got into nosy neighbor mode and tried to peer beyond me into Ray's shabby apartment. "Is Mr. Burgess home?"

"No, I understand he's at work. The management folks gave me the key. I detected some vapor around his back door and thought it best to check inside. But it must have been a false reading. Nothing at all." I knew she might tell Ray later but there was no way to stop her.

"Thank you." She peered at my nametag. "Mr. Cole."

"Glad to be of service, Mrs. Winton. I'll lock up and call in my report."

"Mr. Cole, as long as you're here, do you suppose you could test my kitchen? I get the oddest smells sometimes."

I was trapped. I couldn't refuse, because I'd already declared Ray's place safe and now my time was hers. So I dutifully followed her, locking Ray's front door behind me.

* * *

I did a fine job as gasman, the task made easier because Mrs. Winton's kitchen was as spotless as the clean room where they assemble Mars probes. I ran my sniffer around her stove and sink drain and even her refrigerator. All the while, the red display continued to read zero, a fact I cheerfully pointed out. Unlike Ray's crappy home, Viola's half of the duplex was scrubbed clean within an inch of its life. The floors had been carefully stripped and polished, and the furniture, although old, was well kept, everything in its place.

I soon learned that Viola's dear husband Jimmy had passed away some years previous, bless his soul, don't you know, and that her daughter and son didn't call as much as they should, even though they could afford to because long distance was free these days, don't you know. And after she and Jimmy had worked their fingers to the bone to put the kids through college they could show a little gratitude, couldn't they? She would also be happy to hear from her grandchildren too, and their living in El Paso didn't mean they can't pick up the phone and call now and then, don't you know.

But at least the church came by in the van every Friday for a day out so she could see a movie and go shopping with her lady friends. And the duplex was very nice, even though the air conditioners didn't work as well as they should. And that Mr. Burgess was a nice neighbor and very polite and quiet, and even though he was a messy housekeeper, he didn't have those loud parties like that young couple in unit three and they weren't even married, don't you know.

Viola tried to get me to sit down with her and have some tea or coffee but I pleaded a busy schedule. I knew she was a lonely widow who yearned for company so I was extra polite. I let her give me some homemade cookies to take back to the shop with me. I should eat more and I was too thin, don't you know.

I wondered about her later phoning CenterPoint Energy to say how nice that Mr. E. Cole had been and they shouldn't work him so hard. I hoped not, because that might start an investigation, but there wasn't much I could do about it now.

Funny how this happens. Spies and crooks and people like me devise elaborate ruses and intricate plans to move beneath the radar, but it can come crashing down at the slightest push from an unexpected and benign source. At least I didn't have any hollow coins with microfilm inside.

Eventually I extricated myself from Viola Winton's gentle clutches, but I was still screwed. I couldn't very well let myself back into Ray's place since I'd pronounced it clear from gas and I knew she'd be watching. I was forced to leave so I could phone in my report to the supervisors at CenterPoint, even though I ceased to work for them as soon as I got to the Stealth, changing into a regular shirt and normal civvies. I'd have to check out Ray's locked bedroom when Viola was away.

Don't you know.

Chapter 42

It was a little past three and on the way home I got hit with yet another small thunderstorm. This pattern had persisted for nearly a month now, the land cooled temporarily by the rain then warming up again toward steam bath zone soon thereafter, another storm following right behind.

As I turned into my driveway I noticed a bright red Lincoln Town Car sitting across the street, so I assumed that Ernie Banks and Son had company. I parked under the carport and slid through the rain toward the back door, my key out and mind fixated on that leftover slice of Star pizza in the fridge.

A tall slender Hispanic guy was standing under the back edge of the overhang, just out of the rain, and as I saw him, I reacted, reaching for my pistol. There was a blur and somehow he was holding a big chrome automatic in his hand where he had none a microsecond earlier.

"Don't," he said quietly. "I ain't gonna pop you, ese. If I was, you be dead already."

Persuaded by his superior logic, I held my arms away from my side.

A moment later and a rotund shape appeared from the shelter of my 4Runner parked nearby. "We ain't looking to give you any trouble, Mr. King."

The fat man and his partner spoke with an Hispanic accent and being the always alert and highly deductive private investigator, I concluded I was in the presence of Ricky and Angel Perdon. Both men were casually dressed, slacks, shirts, light sports coats. Pete Bally was spot on. They looked just like car salesmen, even if they were a Mutt and Jeff pair of mid-level tough guys.

Angel held his pistol on me as his cousin gently but thoroughly frisked me, relieving me of my gun, spare magazine and cellphone. Ricky held my small but potent auto between two chubby fingers like it was a teacup at a social gathering. "Springfield Armory Loaded Micro-compact 1911 .45 ACP, six round magazine plus one in the chamber. Nice gun. Shoot okay?"

"Yeah. Shoots fine," I said, decided to play the good guy. "Look, I know you're the Perdons. You want to talk, let's go inside out of the rain, okay?"

Ricky smiled in a condescending manner like I was some unruly child to be tolerated. He was an overweight and paunchy man, but he held himself with ease and I had the impression he was all business and could move faster than his girth implied.

Cousin Angel stepped closer and took my gun from Ricky, slipping it into a pocket of his jacket. He still held his pistol on me, unwavering like some radar targeting mechanism was guiding it. The hammer was back and I decided that confrontation was not an option.

Ricky smiled again. "It's not us that you need to talk to, Mr. King. You asked to see Valerie and we're gonna take you."

* * *

Ricky Perdon smoothly piloted the big Lincoln while Angel and I sat in the back. Angel held the pistol across his lap, muzzle pointed my way. I couldn't tell whether he'd put the safety on and I didn't want to find out.

We headed down Heights to White Oak, then east, skirting the city towers and turning north on Fulton. After a bit we cut through some side streets until we arrived at a rambling warehouse, heavy cyclone fence surrounding the property, concertina wire atop the perimeter. A crudely lettered sign said Pease Trucking. Another sign read Closed but I had my doubts, because the metal gate was opened for us by a big man wearing a long dark cowboy-style duster. When we drove through to a building in the center of the property, the guard was joined by another guy who wore the same style coat. Maybe there was a sale someplace.

Ricky leaned back and looked at me. "You gonna behave? We got cuffs if we need 'em."

"I'm not here to cause trouble."

Ricky nodded somberly as if I'd signed a lifelong contract. Maybe I had.

He got out and opened my door for me. I followed him into the building, Angel trailing behind. My fear had passed now. If they meant to punch my ticket, they'd have done it right away and left me dead in my driveway. But their orders were to bring me to see Valerie Albertson and they were performing their assignment with grace and efficiency.

Just inside the warehouse I was stopped and frisked again, this time by Angel while the two guards tried to frighten me with their fierce stares. I was more scared of the easygoing Angel.

"Wait here," Ricky said, as if I could do otherwise. He walked to the rear of the place and went through a door. The two guards wandered off, presumably to glower malevolently at something else, maybe each other.

I smiled nervously at Angel like I would my dentist and Angel smiled back, except that his smile was the kind you might expect from a velociraptor about to pounce on a primitive and very helpless mammal. His pistol had disappeared but

I'd seen how quickly it could materialize, so I entertained no thought of dissent. Instead, I strolled forward a few steps and looked around while Angel simply stood there and watched me.

The warehouse was empty except for a big sailboat, propped up on braces and surrounded by scaffolding. There were men working on the hull, applying wax and buffing with small electric handheld units. I don't know much about boats but I do appreciate beauty and this one had it to the nines.

The boat was what they call a motor sailer. There were real sails and masts and all, plus a propeller for calm conditions or just lazy touring. The boat's lines were graceful, even while sitting high and dry in a dumpy old building. I could see some of the features, how the keel was hinged to swing sideways and fold flat during transport or in shallow water, how the masts pivoted down to the deck. Even so, getting it to the water would be a real job, requiring a big flatbed truck. I played out my invisible leash a bit, Angel permitting, and walked to the bow. The boat was named Val.

Ricky appeared and motioned for me.

Angel and I joined him and we filed into the back. There was a small reception area and a modest private office beyond.

Chapter 43

I'd never been in a gangster's lair before. There were no Tommy-guns lying around the place or stacks of gold bars in the corner. It looked instead like the office of an Allstate agent, except that the guy sitting behind the desk was probably someone you didn't want the good hands treatment from.

He was a young Hispanic dressed in clean pressed jeans and western shirt, and he leaned back, ostrich boots propped on the desk. He was reading the Spanish language edition of People. When he glanced up at me, his eyes were heavy lidded, flat and lifeless, like a crocodile's. The eyes didn't so much look at me as regard me as some insignificant object. I got the feeling he'd kill me with scarcely a measure of breath drawn. Being neatly scissored between Angel's smile and this guy's glare put me on my very best behavior.

We all passed him and walked into the back office where Valerie Albertson sat behind a desk, more lovely in person than her photo. Her hair was dark and richly shining, her emerald eyes sparkled and she was an elemental and lithe cat on the prowl.

Next to her was obviously Julio Cardozo, whom I thought bore a fair resemblance to the old character actor Victor Jory. Cardozo was handsome, slender and postured and he carried himself in a stately manner, as befits nobility. He wore a green polo shirt and light colored slacks. There was a Rolex on one wrist, a gold tennis bracelet on the other.

"Mr. King," he said, standing and gesturing to Valerie beside him. "I would like to introduce you to Valerie Albertson. She has agreed to speak with you." His accent was slight and English perfect, although the grammar was stilted and forced, characteristic of someone who learned by rote rather than absorbing the language from birth.

"Thank you," I said. I turned to Valerie. I decided the straightforward approach was best. "Mrs. Albertson, I don't know the details of your decision to be here and it's none of my business. But I should tell you that Cheryl misses you a great deal and that she needs you to come home."

Valerie nodded, looked to Cardozo. I could sense a passion between them and perceived the depth to it.

Cardozo glanced to Ricky and Angel, moving his head slightly, dismissing them. Without a word the two men turned and left, closing the door behind them.

Cardozo motioned me to a chair and we both sat down.

* * *

I thought it good to start on an up beat. "I respect your privacy, Mr. Cardozo. I have no intention of letting anyone know where Valerie is, or who she is with."

"That is a wise decision," he said pleasantly. But I caught his glance and knew that for me to do otherwise would not only be foolish but likely fatal.

"What do you want me to tell Cheryl?" I asked Valerie.

"That I love her."

"She'll ask when you're coming home."

The brightness went out of her visage and Valerie's head sunk. "I... I can't say. Not yet."

"Things are rough for Cheryl right now," I told her. "She feels lonely, abandoned."

A tear glistened in the corner of Valerie's eye.

Cardozo stood up again and moved beside her, putting his arm around her, offering support. He looked at me, then to Valerie. "My dear, would you let Mr. King and me speak for a moment, privately?" She nodded, got up and went into the receptionist's office. Before she closed the door, I saw Ricky hand her a can of Sprite and pat her shoulder. Cardozo looked after her with great concern, turned to me.

The intensity of his gaze and strength of his personality were palpable. "This is very difficult for all of us," he said.

"You've known Valerie a long time?"

"Yes. She came to Houston about twenty years ago, from a small town in Oklahoma. Her mother had remarried and her stepfather—" He went silent a moment. "Her stepfather took... liberties with her. She was nine when it began, thirteen when she ran away." Cardozo smiled at me. "You consider her a lovely woman, yes?"

"A lovely woman. I noticed her name on the sailboat. A fitting tribute."

"A tribute, yes." He sighed. "But you should have seen Valerie Stern in her youth, Mr. King. I think I have never seen such beauty as when I first saw Valerie. The name Stern means star in German, you know. And she is certainly such a star as to dazzle the heavens."

"How did you meet?"

"I am responsible for a great many business ventures, Mr. King. Among them are gentlemen's clubs."

"Topless bars."

"As you wish," he said. "When I take on the management of an enterprise, I make certain that it is run properly. Some of these clubs have a bad image. Drugs between the employees and customers. Prostitution. But not at my places. I made my way by being faithful to my promises and I keep my promises to those who work for me. At my clubs, the girls dance, the customers watch them dance, the girls talk with the customers and the customers drink. This is all."

I nodded. I didn't really care, but he was going out of the way to let me know how things were for him and if it was important to him, fine by me.

"Valerie had been dancing at the Golden Girl when I met her. The manager discovered she was underage and even though she worked hard, he would be forced to let her go. He telephoned me, asking whether there was some work for her elsewhere because she was so sweet. I came to the club to interview her."

"And you fell in love with her."

"From that very moment." A look of pathos came over his face. "Love, Mr. King. Love is not easy for someone in my position. There have been women, of course. But love? Not in many years. It is difficult to gain trust, enjoy privacy, things interfere." He opened his hands, showing his palms like a penitent. "And of course the nature of my business is also a barrier."

"How long were you together?"

"Three years." He smiled. "Three wonderful years."

"And you are Cheryl's father."

"Something known only to Ricky, Angel and to Carlo, who you met out there." He pointed to the office. "Mr. King, I would not be very pleased if that information became available to others. You can understand a person like me, the possibility for kidnapping, for revenge or blackmail."

"Mr. Cardozo, you have my word. No one will ever know."

"Another good decision on your part, Mr. King." I could detect the sarcasm but I also knew he was dead serious, the dead part being me.

"Does Cheryl know?"

He shook his head. "She does not. When Valerie became pregnant, I knew what was best for the child. My life would not be appropriate for her. I was reluctant even to visit after Cheryl was born. I relied on Ricky to tell me of her, take care of her."

I sat watching this man who was up to his neck in crime, who lived outside the law all his life, who certainly had men killed, and yet I felt sympathy for him. I did not doubt that he loved Valerie and it was apparent that she had strong feelings for him. Whether she actually loved him in return or had come back to him from loyalty and friendship alone did not matter. The bond between them was what counted. The fact that she was married or had Pete Bally on the side wasn't pertinent. After all, she had called Julio Cardozo and asked him for help, no one else.

"It must have been a stressful time for both of you."

"Very. I stayed away, we agreed it was best. Valerie obtained her high school certificate, some college. She wanted to sell real estate. I was going to set her up in a small business, but she insisted on working while she was in school. She wanted to be self-sufficient so I gave her a job at a restaurant I owned."

"Where she met Walter Albertson."

"Yes. Again, it was difficult." He shrugged. "But I hoped for the best. He could provide for Valerie and Cheryl as I could not."

"He says he cares for her," I offered.

Cardozo sneered at this and his voice was harsh. "He does not! She is mere property to him, a possession to display to his friends. There is no love in his heart for her, Mr. King. Believe this."

I nodded, not certain whether I agreed, but halfway persuaded. Albertson hadn't shown any genuine compassion when I met him and his curious detached attitude toward Valerie was evident. Perhaps he was incapable of genuine affection. Some people are.

Now it was time for the question that had plagued me from the start. "Mr. Cardozo, do you know what is wrong with their marriage? I've not had any chance to speak with Valerie but everyone whom she loves feels that there's a serious problem, something she's reluctant to discuss, something beyond simple marital discord. Do you have any idea? Abuse, perhaps?"

"She will not tell me. But if it were abuse, if he were to strike her, I would learn of it and take steps to prevent it from ever happening again."

Another territory where I feared to tread, so I changed the point. "You do know that she must return to her husband, to her home, if only for Cheryl's sake."

"Yes, I know." His expression turned dour and the regret was apparent. Then a thin smile came to his face. "Shall we speak with Valerie now?"

Cardozo rose and went to the door, beckoning Valerie in, escorting her to a chair. As she entered, her natural loveliness again brightened the room. "My dear," he said. "I have told Mr. King everything about us and about our daughter."

"Cheryl doesn't know," Valerie said.

"I realize that," I told her. "Your secret is safe. But we're agreed that you need to get back to Cheryl soon."

She nodded. "I know. Julio and I already talked." Her resolve was firm but her reticence was also clear.

I spoke gently to her. "I understand that things aren't the best between you and Walter. But I also know something else is bothering you, some situation at home. Can you tell us?"

There was apprehension in her eyes. "Not now. Maybe later. And maybe I can work things out on my own."

I nodded. "All right. But I have many contacts in the legal and paralegal professions. If you should ever need help, you can phone me any time and I'll do what I can." I gave her my card, passed one to Cardozo as well.

I looked to Cardozo. "Unless there's something else I can do, I don't think there's anything more," I told him. "I appreciate your bringing me here. And you both have my confidence. Nothing of what we say will get out." He nodded. I turned to Valerie. "Shall I phone Walter and Cheryl, tell them you'll be home soon?"

"No," she said. "I'll call them myself. Or I might just go back to the house today."

I stood up and shook hands with Cardozo and Valerie.

"Mr. King," he said. "You have helped. Thank you."

"I was only a witness," I said. "I didn't do anything."

Cardozo smiled at me. "Perhaps it was necessary to speak with someone on the outside, someone who could listen. You did help, Mr. King. Thank you again."

I accepted the accolade, made my goodbyes and left the star-crossed lovers to themselves.

Ricky drove me home, Angel remaining behind. Halfway to my house, Ricky handed me my gun, ammo and phone. I guess I was family now.

Chapter 44

After Ricky let me out, I ran to Fiesta for some groceries. By the time I got back it was evening and I realized my cell was shut off, thanks to Angel, and a bunch of messages were stacked. There were calls from Meierhoff, Walter Albertson, Taurean Williams, Tony Vee, Pete Bally and Kate Morley. Guess whose I returned first.

"Valerie called. She's coming home tonight!" Kate's voice bubbled with happiness for her friend. "She said you met, talked her into getting back with Walter. I don't know how to thank you." I had a couple of ideas but thought better of hinting thus. We chatted and agreed to get together later in the week, maybe for dinner.

Pete Bally didn't need a return call. Valerie had phoned him to break things off for good and I guess he blamed me. The voicemail said I was an asshole for sticking my nose where it didn't belong. Though the anatomical references were mixed, the sentiment was clear. Tough.

Tony Villarreal simply laughed, asking whether I'd finally met that famous female crime lord Julie Cards. I knew he'd rib me about this for weeks.

A bit of good news from Taurean. Gonzie had regained consciousness briefly and was beginning to return to reality. Thus far he was too weak to speak much, but that would come.

Albertson I simply blew off, despite his pleas for my return call. Instead, I connected with Meierhoff because he promised me a surprise if I called him back at the cop shop before seven. I made it with fifteen minutes to spare.

"Want to take a ride?" he asked.

"Last time we did that, it was the Slicer. I'm not doing that again." But Meierhoff said nothing and eventually I had to bite. "Okay, where?"

"Pay a visit to your old pal Kenneth Cramer. We dragged a fifty dollar bill through some doper bars and found out where he's hiding."

"What does Homicide have to do with it?"

Meierhoff laughed. "Not a damn thing. I invited myself in. Wanna come?"

"Hell yes. With bells on."

Chapter 45

I was in the back seat of a patrol car next to a uniformed cop named Franchetti whom I knew slightly. Franchetti has the annoying habit of talking all the time and making bad jokes, but it's better than sitting beside Angel. Maybe.

Another uniformed officer drove while Meierhoff rode shotgun, literally, holding a nasty looking short-barreled Ithaca twelve gauge. Another car with a couple more cops was behind us.

What Kenny Cramer had done to me didn't merit all the attention, even though I'd have personally mustered half of HPD to find him. What made Cramer a person of immediate interest was that he'd also skipped three court appearances and now had multiple warrants for an array of offenses. Kenny also caught the attention of the felony people because of his recent strong-arm mugging of a valued police snitch. An informant in the hospital isn't much help, so the cops were loaded for bear. Equal protection of the average citizen, me, never even figured into the equation.

The day had turned delightful and weather perfect, mild temperatures and fine breezes following the storm. We ran our windows down as we drove west on I-10, turned north onto Silber up toward Long Point and the Spring Branch area. All the way, Franchetti gave us a running commentary about cops he knew, guns he owned, women he'd screwed, perps of every variety he'd arrested, whatever crossed his mind. I guess he was a good cop in his own way, but the nonstop chatter set my teeth on edge. If I were his partner, an unidentified body would soon be found floating in Buffalo Bayou. I preferred Angel Perdon after all.

Spring Branch has undergone extraordinary social change during the past few decades. In the seventies it was a quiet residential area with middle class homes and unassuming schools. Then the exodus to the deep suburbs began and Spring Branch was soon populated by working-class immigrant Hispanics. You could go blocks without seeing a sign in English. Another change and this time Asians. Many of the street signs now have Vietnamese or Korean subtitles. Meierhoff and I often met for lunch at a great Korean buffet just a few blocks down the street. Most recently, a return to the general Caucasian middle class. Like much of Houston, Spring Branch is in continual flux.

We cut west again and stopped a hundred yards short of a large apartment complex. Meierhoff looked back over the seat. "Mr. Kenneth Cramer is staying with two other guys on probation, all with outstanding warrants. Three for the price of one, we hope."

"Probably all fucked up and doing coke too," Franchetti had to chip in.

A Harris county sheriff's unit pulled up across the narrow street from us. He flashed his headlights and it was a go.

We drove through the gate of the complex. "They're in unit fourteen," Franchetti said. "At the back."

We chunked over speed bumps and rolled toward the final row of buildings.

As we came around the corner, I saw Kenny and another guy getting out of a jacked-up yellow Dodge pickup, the kind with huge off-road tires. "That's Kramer," I said.

Our driver whooped his siren and we all piled out.

Kenny's pal ran down the driveway, pursued by the two cops from the second car. Kenny jumped back into his truck, goosed the engine and peeled out.

"Shit!" We all yelled the same word in unison, dashed back to the cop cruiser to follow. Cramer's truck glanced off a parked car and swung toward the exit gate. We were a little behind him with his head start, but the truck tires didn't have proper traction for pavement, we made up time and our car was soon right on his bumper.

The chase was enthusiastically joined by several more cops who picked up the radio message and eventually we were all parading through the suburbs in a snake dance of flashing lights and sirens. Franchetti announced the chase for us like a NASCAR event. "Kenny's taken the lead, fans, but Denny Hamlin is closing fast, Dale Junior is coming up on the outside and Franchetti and company are ready to kick butt!" I considered asking him to put a cork in it, but knew I was guest dog in this hunt and kept my mouth shut.

We switched back and forth on residential streets, sped east on Long Point, dodging slower traffic and pissing off all the citizens.

Kenny swung into a Walgreen parking lot, spun onto another side street, doubled onto Long Point once more, this time headed west. At a busy intersection his way was blocked by cars stopped for the red, so he dodged through a Texaco station, ricocheted off one of the pumps and took off down Bingle. We all followed, heading south toward I-10. We weren't going too fast considering it was a police chase, about sixty.

As Meierhoff was casually checking the shotgun, he began to hum a familiar tune. It was picked up by the driver, then Franchetti, and soon we were all singing the Cops theme song, Bad boy, Bad boy, What 'cha gonna do? None of us could remember the verses but we were hell on the chorus.

The radio squawked. The dispatcher announced that Harris County constables had set out spike strips at the intersection with the Interstate a half mile ahead. Other cops blocked off side streets to keep Cramer away from the residences and funnel him into the trap.

Our instructions were to drop back so the spikes could be yanked away before we hit them ourselves. We came around a gentle bend in the road and I could see the assembled cars ahead, lights flashing, blocking entrance to the freeway. There were so many of them it looked like a Christmas display. Kenny saw them too, his brake lights flashed and we had to jam our brakes to avoid rear-ending him. He was caught between us and the blockade.

He screeched away again and for a second I thought he was going to ram the barricaded cars. Then abruptly he jerked the truck to the right and cut across the curb. He almost rolled but recovered and tore off through the grass. Ahead was a little wooded glen and he ripped into it like a grizzly in heat. I could see gouts of dirt and sod tossed up by each of his four knobby tires. There was a huge spray of crushed rock and he was away toward the west.

We immediately realized where he fled. The old Santa Fe railroad line once ran parallel to the freeway but the tracks and ties were pulled up and recycled not long ago, leaving a gravel thoroughfare that would soon become a widened Interstate. Having nowhere to go, Kenny took this cutoff in desperation and now he had the off-road advantage. We tagged along but he was losing us. The heavy cop car slewed back and forth and the noise of the rocks churning beneath us was deafening.

Still, we kept up pursuit, first place in the caravan of flashing lights and sirens behind our intended prey. A string of cops also sped along the access road to our left, blocking Cramer from diving off the disused rail bed and back onto the roadway.

Quickly the radio beeped with the command "Break off! Break off!"

I heard the message and snapped to the situation. Santa Fe not only tore up the tracks, they'd also removed the bridges!

We slowed and Kenny zoomed ahead.

A second later, the inevitable. Kenny smashed through a small guardrail and launched himself across a wide ditch, but this wasn't the movies where you magically levitate over empty space. His truck flashed straight through the gap and slammed head-on into the earthen wash beyond. It was a terrific crash, pieces flying everywhere. The momentum flipped the truck up and over and it came to rest upside down on the far bank.

We all got out, scrambled down the embankment and hauled ourselves up the other side. The cops brandished their weapons until they discovered it was unnecessary. We stood there listening to the tick of hot metal and staring at what was left of the truck and its driver.

Franchetti stooped to look inside the smashed cab, faced us and spoke deadpan. "Oh my God," he said. "We killed Kenny."

Chapter 46

Today at the Burgess duplex I was the cable TV guy, different nametag and new ball cap.

Viola had just left her house, pulling a little wheeled grocery cart. She was apparently going Krogering and I guessed I had an hour, don't you know.

I was just about to get out of my car when a Travis City police cruiser drove past me, turned into the property and parked in front of Ray's. An athletic man in full uniform got out. I recognized Ray's brother, Captain George Burgess, from his many TV interviews.

George had a big plastic Best Hardware bag in his hand. He walked to Ray's front door and promptly let himself in. Five minutes later, he came back out, minus the bag, got into his car and drove off. I sat for a long while, thanking fate or Odin or whomever that I'd not been inside the duplex at the time.

Clipboard in hand, I strode to the building, walked around to the side and slipped the window latch again. This time I headed straight upstairs. The lock on the second bedroom was a cheapie affair that my autopick defeated a fast as using the key. I opened the door and stepped straight into a bad dream, a nightmare of aberrant sexuality.

A world of loneliness and pain lay before me. I'd read about people like Ray Burgess, but to see it close up was still a shock. The room was dark because the window had been taped over with foil, leaving just enough room for the air conditioner vent. I flicked on the overhead and saw it all more clearly, despite my strong urge to turn away and leave this discovery to those with stronger stomachs.

Nearly filling the small room was a metal framework, cobbled together from parts of home gyms, drilled and bolted into a complex arrangement of uprights and crossbars. Each vertical and horizontal piece had leather straps attached, wrist and ankle restraints, sliding nooses and halters, even what looked like a horse's bit, for God's sake.

Hanging from magnetic tabs in orderly rows along the horizontal bars, ready for use, were various hooks and clamps and other sharp implements that Ray used on himself, self-asphyxiation apparently not being enough torture. Some of the tools were studded with brads or little needles in the jaws and seemed to be crudely made, like you might find in S&M catalogs. But a few were professional, chrome and very medical. None resembled the Pflaugher style clamp I'd seen jammed inside Rhonda Willett, but I'd done my best to erase that scene from my memory, so I couldn't tell for certain. Nevertheless I took pictures and noted the model numbers of the medical clamps displayed there, ready for what use I didn't even want to guess. Some things are better to remain unknown.

All the cuffs and harnesses on the frame were arranged with nylon cords and pulleys to allow personalized operation. This was a one-man show and private, as is common with most who follow this fetish. As if the word "common" could be applied to this sordid nightmare of autoerotic asphyxiation. Ray was, in street lingo, a gasper or space monkey. Ray's brand of self- torture is also known as scarfing, which seems a handy and safe-sounding excuse word. In truth, it's a sad, sick and often dangerous practice. Nearly every day some poor kid or drugged-up celebrity is featured in the headlines, having pulled the knots a bit too tight or let the release cord fall out of reach.

Just ask Grasshopper.

On the walls were various photos and posters. Most were nude men clipped from male porn mags, oiled bodies hard with inviting, huge erections that made my head ache. There were also pictures of women clad in perverted variants of wedding dresses, chambermaids and of course that old standby, nurse costumes. Surrounding all the pictures were the cryptic symbols of the Slicer, triangles and diamonds and pentagrams, the black marker runics filling every available space.

Incongruous to this twisted gallery but taking center spot was a normal color photo of an older man and woman posed before a Christmas tree, smiling uncomfortably, side by side as if they were two strangers dragged in from the street for a photo op. The picture was faded, the hairstyle and dress of the couple told me that the image was from years past.

Regardless of its age, to see a mundane family snapshot amidst all this sickness somehow increased the surrounding nastiness. Ray had drawn a large black circle around the man's face and several crude arrows pointing inward toward him. Maybe this was a focal point for the mystical symbolism that Ray used elsewhere, but I had no real idea what the photo meant. It made about as much sense as anything else here.

What got to me the most and made the least sense, however, was the very normal Best Hardware bag sitting on the bedroom floor.

Inside the bag were several hanks of nylon rope, same as that on the asphyxiation frame. The rope was Eagle brand, the type mentioned in the oddball letters the FBI received and identical to what the Slicer used. There were also some new pulleys, a package of assorted bolts and nuts and a small socket wrench set.

So Captain Burgess was the ever-helpful older brother, aiding his self-strangling and murderous sibling. And he apparently had his own key to the secret room so he could augment the system. What the hell was going on, anyway? This made the bizarre workings of the Albertson clan seem as bland as a Hi & Lois cartoon.

Ray's murder gear must be stored in the closet, I thought. There wasn't a door proper, just a hanging curtain on a rod. The closet had racks of leather bondage gear, all for a man. There were hoods with various openings and buckles, corsets of a sort with numerous leather straps and a box of what I assumed to be cock restraints. I used the tip of my flashlight to move them around. No touchy for me. Creepy, but nothing surprised me now. I took more photos.

I locked the bedroom door behind me and quickly swept the remainder of the house, looking in all the closets and other storage spaces. Trash, dead roaches, filth galore, but no antique typewriter. No knives that could be used in the killings, either. Apparently, Ray didn't want any such evidence at home and simply acquired himself a new supply each time. He wouldn't be the first serial killer to use newly purchased knives. Some wanted the cutlery as symbols and trophies to keep, but to others they were simply tools and were easily discarded in the next trash dumpster or storm drain. I figured Ray of the latter variety.

Or so I assumed. Right now, I was confused and not a little sick to my stomach. I closed up the house and drove over to the West Alabama Ice House for a beer and some fresh air. I needed both to help me think.

I sat there, watching the traffic stream by, sipping a Bud and trying to put a case together.

Ray was deeply disturbed and apparently used his torture rig to absolve himself from the guilt of his murders, brother George the enabler. What I couldn't countenance was George Burgess allowing Ray to commit murders. Self-abuse, yes, but not killing the innocent. And he was certainly a professional cop and smart enough to see the indicators, even if he wasn't privy to the private details of the Slicer's calling cards. All I could assume was that brotherly loyalty ran deep between them and with the parents dead, possibly even murdered by Ray, George not only assumed care but subsumed all guilt for Ray, too, allowing the murders to proceed through his misguided and warped sibling loyalty.

One beer certainly didn't solve the dilemma and one beer was my limit, so I gave up and called Joe Duggan.

Chapter 47

Joe Duggan and I cruised the Burger King drive-through and parked in their lot. Eating a hasty and environmentally unfriendly lunch, we talked about Crazy Ray Burgess and his weirdly supportive brother.

Joe had already glanced at my photos but he waved them off as if swatting a fly. "I'm enjoyin' my burger here. Gimme some slack." Still, Duggan was incredulous. "So Ray is a perv and a killer, and his brother knows about it?"

"Not only does he know, he's helping. Like I said, George brought a goodie bag of ropes and other stuff for Ray, put it in the playroom. I'm as amazed as you are."

"Why would he buy the stuff for his brother?"

"I don't know. If he's the facilitator, it could be some sort of goofy protectionism, trying to keep his younger brother out of trouble by making him happy."

"That's bullshit," Duggan said. "He's a fucking police professional, fer chrissakes. He knows these sicko types don't go away or get well. If he was actually bein' helpful he'd get his brother some therapy. You got any more ketchup?"

I had to laugh, Duggan tacking on a condiment request to his clinical analysis.

I rummaged deep into my food bag, found a packet, handed it over. "Bon appetit."

Joe grunted his thanks.

"Consider this," I said. "George is afraid that if it comes out his brother is a sexual pervert, it will ruin his career."

"That's for sure," Duggan agreed. "He wouldn't want to jeopardize that. He's up for deputy chief soon and everybody will be gunning for his ass 'cause of his ramrod attitude. Any slip-up, they'll pounce. Nobody really likes the guy. They just tolerate him."

"Regardless of the motive, it's inexcusable," I said. "And even so, sickness accepted, George must also know that Ray is killing people, that he's the Slicer. There's just too much incidental evidence for a trained cop like George to ignore. George must think he's helping Ray with his erotic games and that will keep him preoccupied enough to not kill anybody. Thinking that is bull crap but he must be blinded by brotherly love."

"Agreed," Joe said. "And now that George knows the truth, if he let it come out, he'd be accessory to murder. That has to be what's keeping him quiet." Duggan sucked his straw till the cup rattled noisily. "But enough about goddamn George. You didn't find anything else that points to Ray being the Slicer, right?"

"Nope. Other than the symbols and some of those clamps being the same basic style the Slicer uses. But there was no actual Pflaugher clamp and gear wasn't in a special place, either. The clamps were lumped in with the other S&M gear so Ray could use them on himself. It's as though he grabbed this stuff at random from a storage locker at the hospital and improvised."

"Don't let me think about that," Duggan said. "I'm still eating."

"Anyway, I didn't find knives. Not the big kind used in the murders. I searched the house but I still think Ray's got a secret place for his goodies, if only to hide them from his brother. Or maybe he buys them new each time."

"Nothing we can get a warrant on?"

"Nope. His special room is locked, so there's no way I would be able to find out what's there without breaking both the lock and the law. That renders the evidence inadmissible and any judge will see that."

"Shit."

"I'll keep at it," I told him. "There are two possibilities. Either he's keeping the stuff in his car, or he's got some special hidey-hole that I didn't have time to uncover. I only searched the cabinets, but I didn't have time to look for a false baseboard and such."

"How much time would you need for that?"

"An hour. Two would be better. But I'd need to distract the nosy neighbor."

"Thanks for what you're doing," Duggan told me. "Keep us posted but don't make any more moves on his house unless you hear from me or David first. I'll call Scudder and see what he wants to do."

"Okay."

"And Mitch?"

"Yeah?"

"Sure you don't got any more ketchup?"

Chapter 48

I sat in the stiffback chair and watched Raj Patel run out the rack. He left the seven ball just outside the triangle, stood back to admire his work while the porter racked the balls for the next frame. I checked the score. Patel had run off twenty-three straight, passing me, and I was getting antsy. I'd whumped him easily last year but he'd improved measurably since, while my skill level had remained about the same. Now I might pay dearly for my slacker attitude and my custom Richard Black cue might not be used again today.

We were at Cue and Cushion on North Shepherd, playing in their straight pool revival tournament. Most tourneys these days are 9-ball. I do pretty well at that game but my favorite is traditional call shot, also known as 14.1 continuous. It is the essence of pocket billiards. You call the ball and pocket, shoot until you miss, one point per ball. When you've made all the numbered balls except the last, you rack up the other fourteen balls in the triangle leaving the head spot open, and keep shooting. The object is to pocket that lone ball from the previous frame, then send the cue ball crashing into the rack, scattering the balls for more shots to keep you going. First player to a hundred twenty-five wins. It's elegant, simple and maddening. Maddening because you have to sit quietly and watch your opponent run ball after ball, his score mounting while yours stagnates. Check out the match between Paul Newman and Jackie Gleason in The Hustler and you'll get the idea.

But sitting was what I did a lot and I was good at it, so I bided my time and watched Patel chalk his cue, preparing for his break shot on the seven. Patel is a tall skinny guy with thick black hair. He's quiet-spoken, polite, but possessed with the persistence of a snapping turtle. Twice now, I'd slipped up and missed, leaving Patel a good shot. He seized each chance and now he was ahead, 95 to 89. Two more racks and he'd beat me, knocking me out the running. The winner of our match would face Arturo Munoz from Fort Worth for the championship. The chance of either of us whipping Arturo was roughly equivalent to that of a Snickers bar surviving in the parking lot after a Weight Watchers meeting, but second place would still pay a cool thousand bucks.

I looked at Tony Vee. He'd come with me, not because he wanted to be a pal and keep me company, but to make side bets. He was standing amid a group of gamblers and they were exchanging little betting slips between themselves like kids passing notes in class. Tony was so big that he looked out of place with the others, a head taller and several gamblers wider. He glanced over, frowned at my predicament, nudged one of his comrades and mumbled something. Another slip, another bet. I wondered whether it was for or against me. Probably against.

Patel leaned down, his stance and grip picture perfect, patterned after the greatest pool player ever, Willie Mosconi. "Seven ball, corner," Patel said calmly. He aimed, took a practice stroke, then drove the cue ball forward into the seven. The cue ball kicked sideways into the rack, breaking up the object balls as planned. But what wasn't planned was the seven ball's obstinacy. It caught in the jaws of the corner pocket, rattled around a moment, then simply sat there, defying both gravity and its presumptive master.

Patel had missed!

He spun on his heel and grimaced, muttering to himself, the strongest display of emotion I'd seen him reveal.

I sat there a few seconds, letting it all sink in, then I stood up and walked to the table. The balls were everywhere, asking to be nailed.

"Six in the side," I called and popped it in, using draw English to halt the cue ball in place, ready for the eight ball opposite. Next came the ten, the nine, the one. I was excited at first but that quickly passed. Now I was in my element and the cue seemed to have its own mind and direction. I was only pointing it. Balls dropped quickly and cleanly and I stopped with the five ball remaining. Fourteen balls were racked and I began on them, the five in the side, the cue ball tapping the rack and dislodging enough of the four ball for my next shot. That broke up the remainder and I zipped through them, too.

Patel sagged visibly when I broke the next rack, because it was over. I ran the final balls without glancing back and the game was mine.

* * *

After the tournament, Tony Vee and I sat in Poison Girl, a tavern on the Westheimer curve with probably the best name for a bar, ever. The place is a smallish dive, artistically shabby yet friendly. They feature premium mixed drinks and a row of well-maintained classic pinball machines along a far wall. Spider-Man is my favorite.

Tony tipped his glass of Shiner Bock toward me, took a swig, grinned. "You did okay, pal."

"Arturo waxed my ass."

"That mighta been expected. He's maybe the best pool shot in Texas."

"I tried."

"Hey, don't feel bad. You made me three large."

"You won three thousand bucks on me? I played the damn game and only made one! And by the way, were you betting for or against me?"

"Division of labor," Tony chuckled. "Somebody has to do the work and somebody has to relieve Austin Joe Barnes of his bankroll." Tony laughed again, "And I ain't saying where I laid the money." He waved to the bartender for another round.

I checked my cellphone for messages because I'd shut the thing off during the tournament. David Meierhoff had called twice and I buzzed him at Homicide.

"Got good news and bad news," he told me. "Which do you want first?"

"Give me the good for a change."

"Freddie Gonzales is fully conscious and he's going to be okay. At least the doctors think so."

"Glad to hear." I'd stopped by the hospital nearly every day and Gonzie was showing signs of recovery, but when he would fully come out of the coma had been a crapshoot. "Does he have any memory of the accident?"

"None yet. But we got email from the FBI lab. That's the bad news. Those paint scrapings from Gonzie's bumper match a 2007 Buick Regal. And guess who owns a blue Regal?"

"Our little old pawnbroker Randy Shindler?"

"Yep. We went by his house with a warrant but his wife hasn't seen him in almost a week. Seems he's skipped bail and possibly skipped town."

"Any idea where?"

"Nope," Meierhoff said. "Know where I might hire a good private detective?"

"Good private eyes don't come cheap."

"If I can't afford a good private eye can I hire you instead?" he asked. This rhetoric was routine for us, well practiced and we occasionally went through the mantra.

"Sorry. I'm all booked up, hanging out at the high school, watching the girls play soccer."

Meierhoff laughed, then his voice turned serious. "On another note, you need to keep a lookout. If Shindler tried to run Gonzie off the road, he might be after you, too."

"I'll watch myself."

* * *

Things became fairly hectic after that, but not because of Randy Shindler. I got another contract with the same insurance company from the pawnshop deal, spent a day picking through purchase invoices and verifying serial numbers on estate sale and antique shop records. Stupefying work but it paid okay.

Kate Morley and I met for lunch again and exchanged books as gifts. I gave her ReJoyce by Anthony Burgess, a stirring tribute to James Joyce and his work. I winced inwardly at the name similarity to our local and menacing Burgess boys, but perhaps this book might serve to dispel the surrounding bad karma. Yeah, sure it would.

She gave me a collection of Van Gogh's letters to his brother Theo, interspersed with an historical commentary on the writings. The relationship was evolving nicely, I thought.

I didn't know how well things were going until Kate phoned the next day, asking me on a date.

It had been ages since a woman had asked me out and I stammered like a nerdy middle-school kid but still managed to say yes.

Chapter 49

Kate Morley drove south on I-45 to Galveston Bay. I would normally be reluctant to spend more time with the loony Albertson family but Kate had asked me, so I was happy to be going anywhere with her. Valerie had invited Kate for a party on their boat and Kate decided to drag a date, me. How could I say no?

The situation with Cheryl's recently terminal ex-boyfriend Kenny gave me pause so I asked Kate about it.

"Don't worry," she said. "Cheryl dumped him after he attacked you. Things had been going bad anyway and that was the last straw."

"She's not angry with me?"

"She doesn't even know you were with the cops when Kenny got himself killed," Kate said. "I didn't tell her. And she didn't actually come out and say, but I think she's glad to be rid of him. He was trouble and she isn't. A little rebellious maybe, but a good kid at heart."

"The times I met her, she was pretty glum."

"She's brightened up since Val got back. Makes all the difference."

That made me feel better, too. I wanted to have a good time to match this gorgeous day. It had been a fairly active storm season but the tropics were quiet for now, a modest cool front keeping the highs in the eighties and the air sparkling clean.

I looked over to Kate as she piloted her muffler-roaring Mustang. She's one of those car lovers who works at the wheel, concentrating fiercely on the traffic ahead, seizing each opportunity to slip between slower cars and maintain a quick pace down the highway.

"Where's their house?" I asked.

"Near Seabrook."

"Ritzy?"

"Very." Kate glanced at me and grinned beneath her huge round sunglasses. She looked great. Her reddish gold hair was knitted into a tight French braid and her fine complexion shone with energy. I couldn't see her eyes but I knew their blue matched the clear high sky. Kate wore a white dress shirt midriff style, the tails tied in a knot across her bare tummy. She had hip hugger jeans with slim legs and leather sandals.

I was a sad match for her, wearing faded jeans, an old Astros pullover and my favorite Nikes. We'd been told to come ready for swimming so I wore my trunks beneath and carried a change of clothes in a gym bag. Along with my pistol.

We turned east onto Nasa Road One and drove past the Johnson Spaceflight Center. Construction and road repair were perpetual and we navigated through the detours with depressing slowness until we were clear. I tried not to look toward JSC because of the bad memories, a host of them. So I glanced to my right and that brought me back to my last visit to The Outpost, the famous astronaut bar, recently closed, burned down and now flattened into oblivion by the freight train of progress.

Thankfully, the wealth of astronaut memorabilia had been rescued prior to the fire and now decorated the walls of a nearby family-owned Italian restaurant. But it was the Outpost where I'd come to know Tarah Jacoby and her Air Force boyfriend Major Trent Collins. Now Tarah was dead and Trent was drinking himself into early retirement, so this part of town bore a graveyard of terrible memories for me. But life happens and eventually Kate got us past the trouble zone and my brain ceased buzzing.

"You're awfully quiet," she said.

"Just reliving some old war wounds. Mental wounds."

"At least they don't show." She laughed. "I don't want to explain your bandages to Valerie and company."

"Thanks for the kind concern, Miss."

"The least I can do is bring a guy with me who doesn't have too many scars."

We both laughed at that but I was faking it. Scars I had aplenty. Question was, would they ever heal?

* * *

The Albertson place was in a luxury townhouse complex. Each residence has a private dock in back where the people moor their boats. I could see some of them between the buildings and they were big and lavish, as intended.

Kate buzzed Albertson at the gate and we were punched through. She parked, we grabbed our bags and walked over where Valerie was standing at her front door, waving. "Hi! Come on." She was smiling and her bright attitude was infectious.

The condo was modern and spacious, vaulted ceiling over the main living space and balcony above. The entire back wall was storm-proofed plate glass, spanning both floors and providing an uninterrupted view of the docks. Beyond, the bay water flashed and rippled with gentle waves.

Walter Albertson was in a jovial mood, at least on the surface. No sooner than I got past the front door, he pumped my right hand generously and stuck a cold Heineken in my left. "Glad you could come, Mr. King, ah, Mitch. We're all happy to have Val back."

Valerie embraced both Kate and me. "Kate promised she'd get you here."

Maybe this would be a pleasant day after all, I thought. And then I saw the girls. Valerie's daughter Cheryl was in the living room, sprawled on a sectional sofa. She was turned to face the cushions and didn't acknowledge our arrival, while Walter's daughter Paula was perched on a chair in the dining area, her nose stuck in an iPad. She didn't look up either. We were being treated to the freeze out, and the gloom emanating from the young women lay like a fog around them. Insolence is a primary job description for teenagers and both of them were fulfilling that assignment quite well.

Walter wasn't about to countenance revolt, however. He spotted the insurrection and took steps to quell it. "Paula? Cheryl? Come on, we're going." He kept his voice cheerful and exerted his considerable managerial influence on daughter and stepdaughter alike.

Valerie joined in the campaign. "Cheryl, hon? Kate and Mitch are here," she announced, as though we'd somehow not been noticed thus far. "Paula? Can you give me a hand? There's salad and boiled shrimp in the fridge."

Reluctant stirring. Paula looked up from her display, did something to bookmark the page and shut the thing off. She sighed glacially at the idea of being forced to interact with other humans. Cheryl turned over to assess the assembled guests.

Both girls bore the studied and affected stare of disdain that all kids inflict upon their elders. Still, they did begin to stir and this was a fragile, tangential victory. Eventually sufficient energy was imparted and we all migrated out the back gate to board for our cruise. There was a low current of animosity between the girls and they managed to keep a large personal space separating them. At least the boat seemed big enough.

* * *

I glanced at the stern of Walter Albertson's boat and predictably saw Val. Valerie caught me looking at the name as we stepped on board and she gave me a brief embarrassed smile. Must be nice, having two boats named after you. But risky. Imagine meeting at a regatta.

Unlike the graceful elegance of its competitor, this Val wasn't made for anything but pleasure cruising. It was about forty feet long and had a flying bridge above the cabin. Walter delighted in pointing out the features, from the inboard Chrysler engines to the fish finding sonar and satellite navigation systems. "All the right stuff," he told me, turned to his daughter. "Paula, take the helm?"

Paula was dressed the part. She wore an ersatz sailor suit, stylishly tailored for her slender frame. A brief white bolero jacket with epaulets and a jazzy stripe down the sleeve, blue silk blouse beneath. Striped pants with wide crackerjack cuffs and blue deck shoes completed the outfit. Paula took the dangled keys from Walter's hand, smiled coyly and climbed up the short ladder to the flying bridge.

After a few seconds the engines fired and Walter waved to me for help. He went to the bow, I went aft, and we both cast off. I curled the rope in what I hoped to be the correct spot, looked over to Walter and saw that it was right. Usually when I'm on boats I just stay out of the way and try not to get in trouble but this time I'd done good.

In my limited maritime experience, Paula was as smooth a pilot as I've seen. She reversed the boat expertly from its slip, gently maneuvered it between other vessels and floating buoys until we reached clear water. She gradually applied the throttle and soon the Val was sliding rapidly over the waves. The chop was nonexistent and the ride a blast.

"Bring your swimsuit?" Walter asked.

I nodded and clapped my hips to show him the trunks were beneath my jeans.

He pointed me down the stairs to the cabin. "Put your stuff anywhere."

I clambered down. The interior was spotless, like the rest of the boat. There were four bunks with two more pulldown hammocks aft. Past this was a small galley and the head. The cabin had a built-in stereo, TV with video player, lots of fancy foldout goodies and gimcrackery extras, like the interior of an executive jet. Right now there was a large metal table in the center of the room, hinged so it could be folded up and stowed aside. The table was laden with iced shrimp, salads, a cheese and cold cut plate and condiments that the girls had set out when we first boarded. I sampled a couple shrimp, shucked off my jeans and shirt, rolled them into my duffel bag. I made sure the pistol was stowed deep inside, next to my phone.

I came back up the stairs wearing a pair of raggedy old tennies, a red tank top and my baggy trunks besmirched with gaudy flamingos. As I got to the top, I heard a wolf whistle. I turned to see Kate grinning, flashing me the okay sign. Valerie and Cheryl were looking on, grinning as well. Foolishly, I performed an amateurish disco bump and spread my arms wide. "Ta daa!" I sang off-key. Thankfully, everyone laughed and none suggested tossing me overboard.

Walter Albertson changed into some sort of fluorescent yellow Euro thing. I thought it a bit over the top, but he was trim and fit for a man in his fifties and if he wanted to show off, what could I say? It was his boat and his shiny butt.

Kate, Valerie and Cheryl were next. Kate came out wearing a fairly conservative two-piece with little diamond cutouts over each hip and one between her breasts. She's all woman, with a nice figure and lovely long legs. Of course I was prejudiced where that is concerned. Valerie's suit showed less skin but was somehow more revealing. White and nearly transparent, it left her nipples clearly visible, only a small modesty panel concealing her pubic region. The suit vaguely reminded me of the one that Liz Taylor wore in Suddenly, Last Summer. I tried not to stare.

But try as I might, I could not help ogling Cheryl. She wore a microscopic black string bikini over her gamine frame, the triangles scarcely covering her smallish breasts and pubis. The suit was nonexistent in back, only two slim strings showing. She had a little jeweled navel ring circled by a curling snake tattoo. I smiled nervously and tried to ignore her but it was impossible. I had no interest in Cheryl personally but my body has its own opinion and it was only a matter of time before I made a biological idiot of myself.

"Think I'll see how the captain's doing," I said and climbed up the ladder to the flying bridge to say hello to Paula. She may be cute but at least she wasn't parading around half naked. As I gained the upper deck, Paula glanced over to me, looked down at Cheryl and viciously grinned. "Getting a little warm down there?"

I mumbled something noncommittal and decided to change the subject. I looked out over the water, trying to determine where we were headed. "What's our destination?"

"My favorite quiet place." She notched up the engines and our speed increased. Paula raised her sunglasses and looked at me, smiling. "Don't mind the little stepsister. She's a whore but doesn't know any better. After all, she has a good example."

I was trapped. Odysseus only had Scylla and Charybdis to contend with but I had Cheryl and Paula. I didn't want to listen to Paula's mean-spirited diatribe and I couldn't trust my body around Cheryl right now.

Then came a rescue sweeter than a Titanic lifeboat. Kate climbed up the ladder carrying two cans of beer and a plastic cupful of shrimp. She never looked as good as she did that moment. "Thought you might be hungry," she said.

"You can't imagine."

One look into Kate's eyes and I knew she understood why I'd fled the main deck. She leaned over and whispered. "Cheryl get to you?"

I shrugged. "I'm a guy. What can I say?"

"You've said enough. Stay close to me." She giggled. "I'll protect you from her."

"What I need is protection from myself," I said. We both laughed at this but I was half serious. Men will be men and I'm certainly a member of the club.

Chapter 50

Kate and I nibbled shrimp and sipped beer as my embarrassment faded. Walter soon mounted the bridge, bringing a bottle of Evian for Paula. He stood next to his daughter and they chatted as she steered. I risked a glance down and saw Cheryl lying on an inflatable float near the fantail. She was on her stomach, soaking up the sun. She'd untied the threadlike halter of her bikini as though that would make any difference. To the sun it didn't, but to my genetics it did, making her that much sexier. I thought about it for a second and I looked at Kate. "Youth," I said, "is wasted on the young." So I borrow from Oscar Wilde. So sue me.

"Youth," she came back, "is overrated." She reached out, put her hand on my arm and gave me a kiss. It was the first time we'd done this and although the smooch wasn't passionate on the surface, Kate managed to convey a sense of electricity. I forgot about Cheryl immediately.

Valerie then bounded onto the bridge. She came up the ladder so fast I thought she was on fire. She barely gave us a glance, turning to Walter and Paula. "Can I get you anything?" she asked them loudly. They'd been talking quietly and her sudden intrusion made them both jump.

Albertson turned and smiled at Valerie. "Maybe another beer," he said. "Paula? Want to take a break, let me drive?" Paula shook her head and continued to stare forward. "I guess just a beer for me, a Bass," he said and smiled again but I couldn't tell whether it was benign or patronizing.

There was tension that stood between Walter and Valerie like a plate of solid steel. Kate and I both sensed it and were uncomfortable as witness. Valerie shot back down the ladder without a word and disappeared below deck.

Kate and I both frowned at this brief interchange. Valerie was upset about something but damned if I knew what.

After a minute, Valerie came back, handing Walter a can of Bass. He took it but didn't thank her. Val then paced around the small deck of the flying bridge, nervous as a ferret in a shoebox. She stared at Walter, he back at her. No words were spoken but plenty of static and baleful looks were exchanged.

Kate took the initiative. "Hey, Val, let's go catch some rays."

Valerie let forth a little sigh and linked her arm with Kate, hugging her close as though she were chilly. Kate led Valerie down to the deck to visit with

Cheryl. The three gals took turns rubbing suntan lotion on their shoulders and they stretched out beside one another, laughing. Kate Morley's personality worked wonders with Valerie's jittery condition and I could see why they were friends.

I left Walter and Paula to themselves, climbed down the ladder, waved at the women, slid past the outer cabin wall to the bow. I sat on the foredeck, leaned back against the slanted windows of the lower bridge and sipped my beer. Spray from the prow flicked across my face, dotting my sunglasses with tiny lenses, each magnifying the view. I was actually beginning to enjoy myself out on the water, despite the veiled antagonism between Valerie and Walter.

Chapter 51

We held course a while until we reached a big signal buoy, far out in the bay. It was one of those radio beacon affairs with automated lights and electronic foghorn. As we drew alongside, Paula throttled back, blipped the reverse to halt our forward momentum. I stood up and watched, picked my way aft.

Paula put the drive in neutral, idled the engines, clattered down the ladder to land with a thump. She hurried forward and grabbed the tie line, skipped nimbly to the flat apron of the big buoy and looped the rope around an upright, snubbing it off. There was a sign on the buoy that said No Mooring but nobody else complained so I figured what the hell. Paula jumped back onboard and went below.

"Why are we stopping?" Kate called up to Walter on the bridge.

"Paula," he said, as though the name was in itself sufficient explanation.

A better answer soon. Paula came up carrying an artist's sketchpad and some charcoal pencils. Self-absorbed and generally ignoring everyone else, she sat on the fantail, dangled her feet over the side and gazed out across the water to her subject. It was a big three-legged drilling rig of the type called a jackup, squatting near the horizon.

I walked over quietly and watched Paula work. She used long bold strokes from a flattened stub to extract the essence of the rig design. The sketch wasn't intended to be literal, instead to capture the basic geometry of the structure and depict it in abstract lines. She had an excellent eye for the underlying physics of her subject and it only took a few seconds.

"Nice sketch," I told her.

She looked up at me. "I had to stop here today. They moved the rig last week and I wanted to get this angle before they moved it again."

"So this is the favored spot you told me about."

"Yes. I come out here even when there aren't any rigs around. It's where I do my best work." She flipped a page in her book and quickly lined out another aspect of the rig. I thought it a bit odd, her fixation on drilling rigs, but considered it unwise to comment. Each artist must be faithful to the muse.

I went back to where Kate and the other women milled about, all three puffing cigarettes.

"When the fuck do we get out of here?" Cheryl asked.

"I think pretty soon," I told her.

Cheryl was upset and kept at it. "I didn't want to come anyway." She turned to Valerie. "You insisted! Come on, Cheryl. You'll have fun, Cheryl. God, I hate it! I hate this boat and I hate Walter and I hate Paula. And I hate you!" Her shoulders shook with anger and she seemed more like a spoiled child than a blossoming young woman. She stomped away and dived down the ladder into the cabin, slamming the door behind her. Everybody was looking at the shut door. None of us knew what to say, so we all pretended not to notice Cheryl's outburst and stayed quiet.

Paula soon wrapped up her sketch session and jumped to the buoy, untying the line and we were off again, Walter now piloting.

Valerie ventured down into the cabin to placate Cheryl and after a few minutes, they both came topside. Cheryl was red-eyed but subdued and there were no further outbursts.

The cruise continued in silence, then the warmth of the day and the perfect weather won us over. We ate shrimp, made sandwiches and drank beer, Paula excepted. "I don't touch alcohol," she informed us haughtily. More for the rest, I decided.

Walter dropped anchor just off the shoreline of an isolated beach and flipped a ladder down to the water. Kate, Valerie, Paula and I dived in and splashed about insanely, hot dogging and tossing a beach ball and laughing our silly asses off. Paula stayed dry and onboard, sketching as we swam.

As promised, Kate was close by to protect me from Cheryl, or maybe to protect Cheryl from me. Regardless, it was delightful having Kate nearby, feeling her body press against mine during the horseplay. Valerie whooped it up too, and Kate's humor and high spirits even thawed Cheryl's dark mood.

Walter stood on the fantail and performed a sharp flat dive, cutting into the water and tearing away like an Olympic sprinter. He swam straight out, back, out again, several laps. During this, he didn't so much as cast a glimpse in the direction of his proclaimed beloved wife, daughter, or anyone else.

Fuck him anyway.

Chapter 52

As the day lengthened, Kate and I switched to Diet Pepsi and iced tea respectively. Walter also quit drinking and went to bottled water. Valerie and Cheryl both got a little tipsy but they were in a cheery state of mind and we were all friends.

Then the shit hit the fan.

Valerie and Cheryl lounged on the deck while Kate and I lay on the fantail. Valerie stood up and glanced to the flying bridge. "Where's Walter?" she asked.

"Don't know," Kate spoke for both of us. "Below, I think."

Val dashed for the stairs and collided head-on with Paula coming up. They stood facing each other on the narrow steps. Ordinarily it would have been a comical Ann Landers moment, something to joke about, but Valerie cursed beneath her breath, pushed Paula aside and disappeared into the cabin. Paula raised an eyebrow in disgust.

Suddenly from below, Valerie screeched.

We heard Walter yell and there was a snapping sound. Kate and I jumped up and ran for the stairs. We both stumbled down and burst into the cabin. Valerie was crouched on one of the beds, holding her head in her hands. Walter was standing over her, his palm raised to strike her again.

I stepped between them, blocked his downward blow with an up thrust forearm, pivoted my arm around his, sending him off balance and staggering across the narrow cabin. He crashed into the big table and knocked it off its supports. Potato salad and shrimp went flying everywhere. Walter recovered his balance and stood there, glowering at me and, past me to Valerie.

He moved to challenge me.

"Stay away from her!" I told him. He took another step, thought better of it, raised his hands in surrender and slowly lowered himself onto a bunk opposite.

Kate sat next to Valerie and embraced her. Val was beginning to cry now and soon Cheryl was there with her mother, while Paula stared down the stairs at all of us like we were some sort of diorama of bizarre hominid behavior on display at the natural history museum.

Kate looked over to Walter. "What the hell are you doing? Are you a total bastard?" She turned back to Valerie and brushed the hair from her friend's eyes. A reddish mark covered Valerie's left cheek where it would soon turn to a big bruise. Cheryl was crying, Valerie was sobbing and Kate was seething.

Hell of a way to end a cruise.

* * *

We weighed anchor and Paula quickly steered us back to the condo. She seemed unaffected by the altercation and for once her icy manner served us well, giving her a cool head to dock the boat with scarcely a bump.

Everyone got off as soon as we touched the dock. I hurried down to the cabin to change into my shore side clothes. I clipped the pistol and its holster inside the waistband of my jeans and pulled out my baggy shirt to cover it.

Once ashore, I joined Kate in the condo where Valerie and Cheryl were sitting on the sofa, arms around each other.

"Where's Walter?" I asked Cheryl.

"Back to Houston, Paula caught a ride with him. She has plans in town tonight anyway, a fuckin' art fair." She hugged Valerie tighter. "Mom and I are staying here tonight."

I nodded. Good that Valerie and Walter were apart for the evening. "What do you want to do?" I asked Kate.

"Let's head out. Val and Cheryl want to talk. They'll be okay."

Chapter 53

We drove back along I-45 toward Houston, the mood vastly different from when we were headed down a few hours earlier. Kate was somber and silent a while, then looked over to me. "I need a drink. How about you?"

The Anvil beckoned.

It's a townie bar on Westheimer near Montrose that features crafted mixed drinks and specialty beers. Kate had a dirty martini up and I drank a Stone pale ale. The night was pleasant and we sat on the patio so Kate could smoke.

After a bit, the atmosphere of the friendly bar relaxed us. The drink helped and soon we were able to talk more about what happened.

"Has Walter hit Valerie before?" I asked.

"Until now, I wouldn't have thought so. Now I'm not sure." She took a drag on her Marlboro. "Val's such a private person that she wouldn't tell me. But I never saw bruises, any kind of marks."

"Maybe it's been escalating, he just shoved her around prior to this. That's the usual pattern. And that has to be why Valerie was so reluctant to go back to the house. She knew what was waiting for her. But I can't figure what set Valerie off in the first place. She was livid just before the fight, angry with Paula and Walter both." I took a small sip of beer, noting that Kate had scarcely touched her drink. Neither of us was really much into in alcohol right now. "Any idea what made her so angry?"

Kate shoot her head. "I'm guessing Paula was starting on Val's case again, down in the cabin with Walter, filling his ear with rumors, badmouthing her. Paula's always talking behind Val's back. That's what must have upset her on the bridge earlier, Paula gossiping to Walter. They were doing more of the same in the cabin. Paula can't resist dissing Val."

"Tell me about it," I said. "In Paula's mind, Valerie's the Whore of Babylon."

"Lots of kids are vehemently jealous of a newcomer step-parent. Look how Cheryl views Walter. She despises him almost as much as Paula does Valerie."

"What a family. Open the dictionary to dysfunctional and you'll see their portraits, all in a row."

"Sad for Cheryl, though," Kate said. "She deserves better. So does Val."

"At least Valerie and Cheryl have a good friend. You."

"I do what I can."

I patted her arm. "You did wonders today, Kate."

She took her other hand and placed it atop mine, squeezed. "So did you."

I was a bit embarrassed.

"No, I mean it," she said, tightening her grip. "You could have pasted Walter, maybe you should have, but you held off." She grinned wickedly. "And you behaved yourself, too."

"How? What did I do?"

"It's what you didn't. With Cheryl." She grinned again and poked me playfully in the ribs. Kate knew that Cheryl had stirred my hormones and she was getting the most out of it.

I smiled. "With you around, it was easy to ignore her."

"Even with Cheryl's itsy bitsy teeny bikini?" She laughed aloud and stubbed out her smoke. "She is a pretty girl."

I nodded. "Yep. Exotic, tattoo and all. But she's just a kid, after all. She's cute but not my age group by a couple decades."

Kate sipped her drink and leaned over to me, whispering. "I've got a tattoo."

My heart leaped. "I didn't see it today."

"That's because it's in a secret place."

"Uh—"

"Let's go," Kate said. "I'll show you."

* * *

We were out of The Anvil in twenty seconds and if I were driving we would have been going about ninety-five. But Kate was behind the wheel so our pace was more measured, also mitigated by her behavior as we drove. She reached over and rubbed my shoulders and the back of my neck. Then she let her hand drop and laid it on my thigh, squeezing gently. I was already getting an erection.

Matter of factly, Kate said, "I've thought about this a while and I want to make a little speech. It sounds silly but I decided that tonight was the time."

"Time?"

"When you first met me I was ready to toss you off. A private detective, I thought. Brutal, stupid, all the stereotypes. When you came through my door it all changed. You're a good man, Mitch. Today was an example. Walter was violent and you were a peacemaker."

"I tried."

"You're ready for this now?" she asked.

"You mean?"

"I mean a relationship. A romance." She stroked my thigh, running her hand up to let it brush almost casually over my penis, back down to my knee where it rested again.

I swallowed. "Yes, I think so." I placed my hand atop hers. I'd been thinking about Kate for a while myself and felt that we had a chance. Not just for sex, but a love affair, a real relationship.

We rode in silence, holding hands, Kate pulling away only to shift.

The sun had set and a cool clear twilight covered the city.

"My house?" she said.

"Sure," I replied, thought again. "Ah, maybe we ought to stop by my place. There's something I need to pick up."

Kate chuckled, then flicked her hand over to press it briefly against my groin. She was flirting outrageously and I wasn't about to stop her. "Protection?"

I was in full stammer mode. "Uh, yes. And I've got a bottle of Moet in the fridge, too."

"Okay, you win. Your place it is."

I gave her directions. She took Waugh north, we cruised into the Heights, drove west on 11th, north again onto my street. As we neared the house, my blood was pounding and my heart tripping. I felt like a teenager.

The street was quiet as we drove up to the house. Kate parked in the driveway and we got out. I came over to her side of the Mustang and we embraced, kissed quickly, again, more deeply. Our tongues met. I reached up and pressed my hand against her breast. It was bare beneath the blouse and I felt her nipple stiffen. Kate moaned and kissed me passionately.

Chapter 54

"Come to kick your ass, motherfucker!"

The harsh voice destroyed our mood like a chainsaw slashing through a rose garden. Randy Shindler stood under the carport. He held a crowbar, swung it like a golf club. He howled fiercely and slammed the bar onto the hood of my MG. A deep dent creased it and Kate jumped from the noise. Shindler swung again, smashing out my headlight and part of the grille.

"Know what, asshole?" he yelled, the vehemence in his throat like a growl from a primeval beast. "I said I'd get you dickheads and I keep my promises! I ran that fuckin' wetback cop off the road and tonight I beat the shit out of that little punk Bobby Carter, busted his fuckin' head open. Now it's your turn, cocksucker!"

He let loose another blow, broke out the other headlight, moved toward us. The crowbar dangled in his big fist and glimmered in the light from the carport. There were bloodstains on his clothes.

I felt Kate at my side, quaking from fear and surprise. I stepped in front of her and faced Shindler.

"Mitch…" Kate said quietly.

"If he comes for us, take off," I said. "Run across the street to the yellow house, holler for Ernie."

Shindler heard me. "She ain't going nowhere!" his voice thick with anger. "After I finish ramming this up your hotshot ass, she's next."

"Don't do it, Shindler!"

"Fuck you!" He raised the crowbar above his head and charged toward us, screaming obscenities and threatening doom.

I reached under my shirt, drew the pistol, and shot him twice.

Chapter 55

Kate Morley yelped but her voice was drowned by the echoing boom of the pistol.

Randy Shindler staggered in his forward rush, stopped. The crowbar clattered to the concrete and he stared down at it with surprise, as though the thing had magically appeared at his feet. He looked up at me and his mouth moved but no sound came out. Then he sagged like someone had let the air out of him, his knees buckled and he pitched forward onto his face.

I stood there, pistol still pointed at him. I glanced to Kate. She was stock still, her face frozen in anguish. I walked carefully over to Shindler, .45 at the ready in case he was faking. He wasn't. There was a channel of bright blood oozing from beneath him, running down the pavement. No movement, no breathing, nothing.

I stuck the pistol back into my holster and turned to see Ernie Banks running across the street from his house, a big flashlight in his hand. "You all right, Mitch? I seen it all. That fella was crazy wild. I seen it and I got 911 coming." Right on cue, a siren whooped and two cop cars dashed up the street, screeching inches from Kate's back bumper. Three cops jumped out.

"I'm a licensed investigator. Mitchell King. I live here," I called to them. I held my hands away from my side, pointed at Shindler's body. "He attacked us. I fired in self defense."

Ernie chimed in. "He's right. I seen it from the start! That guy was crazy. He had this big hunk of iron. He was gonna kill somebody!"

The cops came warily toward us. "Where's your gun?" one of them asked.

"In my hip holster. Right side."

"Slowly, please," I was instructed. "Raise your shirt and pull the gun out, two fingers on the butt. Don't drop it, don't point it at us. Put it on the ground and back away."

I did as told and one of the cops asked for identification. I showed him my license. The other cops bent over Shindler, checked him briefly then stood back, shaking their heads.

A minute later and the situation was explained to the cops' satisfaction, at least for now. Ernie had indeed seen it all, drawn to his living room window by Shindler's shouting. A call to Meierhoff cleared up any lingering doubts. He explained that Shindler was a wanted man, had apparently assaulted a decorated HPD officer, threatened me as well.

Everything fell into place quickly after that. The paramedics arrived, pronounced Shindler dead and covered him with a plastic tarp. A shooting team was on its way.

* * *

Kate was ashen and only responded in monosyllables to the questions she was asked. She stood there stunned, leaning against the hood of her Mustang, cigarette grasped in shaky fingers. She raised it to her lips and tried to take a drag, realized it wasn't lit. She fumbled in her pocket for a light. I stepped up to help.

"Get away from me!" she snapped, turning her back to me. "I never want to goddamn see you again!"

"Kate, he was trying to kill us."

She glanced back over her shoulder, refusing to make direct eye contact. "I know that! But you told me this never happened. You said violence wasn't your way. You lied."

"I had no choice."

She found her lighter, lit up, puffed deeply. "Maybe not. That's not the point. I thought things were different, you were different. I was wrong. Stay away from me!"

The shooting had me shaken, of course. You can't kill someone, even if justified, and walk away like nothing happened. I wasn't thinking clearly and decided it was best not to press her on the issue. Later, when she'd had time to calm down and our minds were more at ease, I'd call her.

Homicide rookie Jesus Ortiz drew the primary on the shooting, the more senior homicide cop Tameka Grant watching over and making sure all the right things were done. The EMTs checked that Kate Morley was okay, Ortiz interviewed her briefly, let her go home. She drove away without so much as a word or glance in my direction.

Meierhoff phoned back soon after. They'd found Bobby Carter, beaten to death. His downstairs neighbor heard a commotion and called the cops. Shindler had taken off, apparently headed for my place next, which turned out to be last stop on the Shindler revenge tour.

Ernie Banks was a perfect fount of information, telling and retelling the story to anyone who'd listen, sometimes repeating it to the same investigator more than once until they were all sick of hearing. At least he stood up for me, and having an uninvolved witness on my behalf was pure gold.

I kept to my legal specifics, saying only that I feared for my life and the life of my companion and fired to protect myself. I deferred any more questions until I had a chance to speak with my attorney. The cops took my gun for evidence, telling me that I'd get it back if everything checked out. Same as the last time, but I carefully avoided mentioning that event.

The case would be sent to the grand jury without charges, meaning I'd likely get off free of criminal liability. Again. Civil was another matter. I was certain to be sued by Shindler's widow, who'd probably testify that he was asleep in bed when I broke in and shot him. Due to the new Texas Castle Doctrine self defense law, the case would go nowhere but I'd end up paying dearly in attorney fees anyway.

All the neighbors either stared from their windows or wandered nearby to see what happened. After the commotion last summer, I wasn't the most popular guy around and this was certain to bring the homeowner's association to my door with yet another complaint letter. More grist for the legal wheel, more cash to dump into my attorney's pocket.

You win, you lose, you live, you die, the lawyers take their slice of the pie.

They hauled Shindler away and the cleanup boys sprayed the driveway with a special detergent and disinfectant. It was nearly four am when everything quieted down and I made it to bed. I would phone Donna Boudreaux in the morning so she could check into the legalities.

I slept pretty well, considering.

Chapter 56

I sat in Dr. Chen's office and tried to describe my desolation. I'd failed again and was terribly afraid.

I'd failed Kate Morley, failed myself, and in some way I'd once more failed my father. It was as though his warnings went unheeded and all his predictions came to fruition. I shared this with Dr. Chen.

"Why do you feel that way, Mr. King? Why does your father appear so deeply in it all?"

"I'm not sure, but I keep coming back to him. Maybe it's related to the haphazard way I live my life, the lack of structure, the disorder I subject myself to."

"This shooting, was there any way for you to have avoided it?"

I shook my head. "No. Other than not be armed, other than let that madman kill Kate Morley and me. He had just killed another person and was stalking me next."

"Yet despite this, you feel in some manner responsible."

"Yes, like it's my fault."

Dr. Chen took off her half glasses, gazed at the ceiling where an overhead fan slowly revolved. "As you know, Mr. King, I counsel a number of police officers."

I nodded. This was one reason I'd signed up with her.

Chen looked back at me. "The psychology of a post-shooting trauma can be quite invasive," she continued. "Even when an officer fires in a clear case of self defense, even if the shooting is completely justified, the officer often feels guilt and remorse. We spoke about this after the other shooting."

"I want to be honest with you, Dr. Chen. I don't feel about this in the same way most others do. I've talked to police who have gone through this and for me it's not the same. I don't feel remorse or guilt about having shot the man. There's something different."

"In what way?"

"I don't feel bad about the shooting itself. And I'm not being coy, either. I've given it a great deal of thought and I can handle that part. What's troubling me is deeper than that."

"How do you mean, deeper?"

"It goes to my choice of career. I left law school to find a more interesting profession. I suppose I succeeded."

"And you disappointed your father, leaving the legal career behind, correct?"

"Yes. I loved him, I honestly did. My mother too."

"You lost both of them in a private air crash some years ago. We talked of this, too."

"Traumatic, but I was married at the time, with my own family. I still miss my parents but I'm reconciled to that. What still bothers me is my having quit law school, like I gave up midstream."

"Having second thoughts?"

"Perhaps. It's been on my mind for several months."

"It's healthy to question your motives, Mr. King. Just don't obsess about it. You're more intelligent than you give yourself credit about this issue and you need to let it rest a while. The solution will come to you and I'll help you find it."

Chapter 57

As I drove out of the parking lot, I thought about what Dr. Chen suggested. Don't obsess. But telling me not to obsess was like telling a politician not to give a speech.

I knew Chen meant well, but right now I wasn't tuned into therapy central. I'd pretty well figured out my dilemma anyway. But knowing about something wasn't a guarantee you would act properly upon it. Especially not the way things had been going for me lately.

Soon as I got back to the office I left another message for Kate Morley. I'd phoned her several times without a callback but I thought I'd give it a few more tries and then quit banging my head against the wall. And it wasn't the expectation of sex that had me so boggled. It was the anticipation of an authentic relationship and the pleasure I had seeing Kate that I really missed.

A few minutes later and my cell beeped, announcing a text message. It was from Kate and it read, "u bastrd I googld and u killed 3 people in 1 yr fuck u" which was pretty final, despite the idiotic truncated texting style and clearly meant I'd be unlikely to hear from her again. So much for that.

I was still fuming over that when the desk phone rang. I snatched it up and blurted, "Kate?" mostly because she was still in my mind, regardless of the brushoff.

"Mitch, it's Sandy. Who's Kate?"

All I need, my ex-wife to call. "Just a friend," I said. "What's up? And how's Chrissie?" I hadn't talked to my daughter in a while and felt guilty for that, too. Another cross to bear.

"It's Chrissie I'm calling about," she said.

"Is she okay?" Fear dried up my throat.

"Oh, she's fine. But I need to ask you something."

"What?" I could feel it coming, the setup.

Sandy hesitated and I knew it was going to be unpleasant. "You've been counting on Chrissie for Thanksgiving."

"But?"

"But she's got a chance to go to Europe. Paris."

"Oh?" My stomach twisted in a knot.

"Yes, Paris. Ted's firm is partners with an architect there."

Ted Forester. Mister Genius Engineer strikes again. "And?"

"And Ted's become good friends with the architectural manager and he has a daughter Chrissie's age. They've invited her to visit during the holiday."

Shit. Cut out my heart and take my daughter too. "So when will she come to Houston next?" I asked.

"Spring Break, I suppose."

"Damn it, Sandy!"

"Mitch, don't get angry with me!"

"Why shouldn't I be angry? You take her away and now you keep me from seeing her!"

"I'm doing no such thing, Mitch. She's going to Paris, for chrissake! It's a great opportunity for her."

"And visiting her father isn't?"

"That's unfair, Mitch, and you know it."

Yes, I knew it but I still used it against her, any weapon I could employ. "I don't think it's good, sending a twelve year old halfway around the world by herself."

"Mitch, Chrissie turned thirteen in March. Or have you forgotten how old your own daughter is?"

Jesus. Daggers at long distance. Sandy and I were experts.

"Why'd you even bother calling?" I said, and I could clearly detect the nagging whine in my own voice. "You could just keep quiet and leave me standing at the airport waiting for her to get off the plane. Surprise, surprise."

"Mitch, this conversation is going nowhere. I try to be civil and look where it gets me."

"Well, it got me pissed off, if you want to know!" I was shouting now. "Go ahead and send Chrissie off on her glorious junket! And in the meantime, you and Ted Forester can go to fucking hell!" I slammed the phone down and of course I missed the connector. It broke off and now I was holding a portable desk phone that couldn't be charged.

I love my life.

Chapter 58

I was in the old fourth ward to meet Karl Unger. He ran a small drive-by auto service. Karl would come to your office or home and perform oil changes, tune-ups and minor repairs on your car or truck. Occasionally he'd cover for me while I searched a target's car. Karl charged me usurious amounts but his time was worth it. Mostly.

I swung by Karl's shop so we could take his truck over to the Med Center. Like a lot of entrepreneurs, Karl Unger worked out of his home. I parked in front and went around to the back. Karl was sitting on the ramp of an empty car trailer, smoking a cigarette and waiting for me. He got up and we shook hands.

Karl is a well-built man in his late fifties. He has long streaky hair, a wispy beard and tattoos up and down his arms. He looks like a mix between an unrepentant hippie and outlaw biker. Karl's an excellent mechanic and his business is steady despite recent fluctuations in the economy. People always need their cars worked on and Karl's prices are fair. Except the inflated rates he charges me, of course.

He drives a vintage '53 Ford pickup that he'd painted bright red and customized by removing all the trim, chopping the roofline and lowering the chassis. He added a rustic fence of oaken stakes around the bed, making the truck into a sort of retro hotrod. There were big signs on the doors that read Karl's Kool Kars. It didn't make much sense but at least it was alliterative.

"Put this on," Karl said, handing me a spare jumpsuit. Like the one he wore, it was a garish red to match the truck and had a big silver lightning bolt on the back. Stealth mode was obviously not in the mix today. The coverall was a good fit and Karl appraised my new look. "We bad, Mitch, we bad. Definitely a pair of sharp dressed men. All we need is the dark sunglasses."

* * *

We headed down to the hospital, excused our way into the parking garage and were soon stopped next to Ray's Impala. I got out and pantomimed unlocking the driver's door. At the same time I blocked the view of my using a slimjim to pop the latch. I'd practiced this a lot and it only took a second.

No alarm. Had I tripped an alarm, we were ready to quickly open the hood and jerk the battery cable. People hear car alarms go off all the time and ignore them, but if anyone was looking, my spiffy uniform would give me the cover needed. After disconnecting the battery, we'd turn around and shrug apologetically at anyone watching, a sham that Karl and I had perfected with repetition. But today the Impala was quiescent.

Karl joined me, setting a small tool cart in front of Ray's car. He opened the hood and pretended to work on the engine while I began the search.

I checked the glove box and found the normal things, old receipts and such, but nothing else. The interior of the car was worn but reasonably clean. I checked under the seat and beneath the floor mats but there was only some spare change plus two old McDonald's ketchup packets. I resisted the temptation to take them to Joe Duggan.

The trunk was full of crap and it took me nearly ten minutes to go through it, since I had to put things back in their place after looking. Ray had two extra spare tires and wheels, assorted tools and a big-ass floor jack. I guess he got a lot of flats. There also must have been a dozen plastic Kroger grocery bags stuffed with old newspapers. Why he had them I couldn't say, but I had to unload all of this before I got to the second layer. I snapped some pics to remind myself of the disarray, just in case.

There was a stack of Texas road maps, including city maps for Dallas, Austin and Corpus Christi. These were all places where the Slicer had struck but none of them was marked with Slicer victim addresses denoted by a skull and crossbones. And the existence of maps certainly doesn't prove anything anyway. Everybody has maps.

Besides maps and old newspapers, the trunk was packed with trash. There were empty beer cans, a small foam cooler, discarded food wrappers and other assorted flotsam. But no knives, marker pens, clamps, or any of the normal accessories that the Slicer worked with.

Then I found it. A small torn section of cardboard packaging, mingled with all the other detritus. All that was legible was the partial word "Pflau—" but it was enough. Ray had definitely been stealing those clamps from the hospital for his own murderous use. One more item to add to the list, maybe enough to persuade a judge but probably not.

I carefully tucked the cardboard away in its original place for later discovery and photographed the piece sticking out.

Nothing else worth checking. The only reasonable place for Ray to hide his things would be a concealed area in his house. That would be next.

I restored all the rest of the trash in the trunk, checked that I'd relocked the doors, and Karl and I packed up and left.

Ray didn't get a free tune-up.

Chapter 59

I had given up on Kate Morley, my ex-wife, my daughter Chrissie, and everything else worthwhile, with days now reduced to a morose, sordid, snail-like routine. I'd get around to checking Ray's house more thoroughly as soon as I could, but there were some pending cases I needed to deal with.

One was an insurance scam, the claimant a so-called invalid with a so-called misaligned spine. Stealthmobile and I trailed him until we taped a video of him playing flag football at a pal's house in suburban Katy. Stupid asshole, thinking he could go twenty miles and be safe.

Next I caught up with a professional skip. Those are people who assume different identities, purchase used cars and appliances, then disappear, selling the merchandise on the black market. They carry dozens of false papers, forged documents good enough to fool the average sales staff. I brought Tony Vee in on this job. I jimmied the door to the guy's apartment and Tony barreled in, tackling the skip and flattening him against one of his stolen refrigerators. Case closed, a few more bucks in the bank and another loser in the slammer.

Do I sound vindictive? I hope to God yes.

Gonzie was in rehab, both physical and emotional. The doctors had him hobbling around on his pinned legs and the alcohol counselors had him attending therapy. He still didn't remember the crash, but that was now moot.

His wife Helena had come back to him and she even had him attending her church, one of those Hispanic evangelical places. Gonzie always referred to it derisively as Our Lady of Selena but he'd undergone a one-eighty, at least for now, and was finding new friends there. Sometimes it takes a major trauma to set someone's head straight. I hope for Gonzie's sake it sticks.

The grand jury met and no billed me on the shooting. I didn't even have to testify. The county attorney presented the case without charges and they let me go. They gave me my gun back again. Naturally, Shindler's family slapped a wrongful death lawsuit on my head. Donna filed a brief to get the case dismissed out of hand but she told me it might still get heard in court sometime next spring. More money and time down the toilet.

Funny how this never happens to my imaginary private eye Bugsy Binton. He goes his merry way, screwing the girls and blasting the bad guys with impunity, his only consequence being a hearty laugh at the end of the TV show, freeze frame so they can roll the credits.

I should be so lucky.

* * *

A few days later I got a call from Cheryl Stern. Her mom had apparently run off again. But with Walter beating on her, it was to be expected. Frankly, I didn't much care. "Is she at Kate Morley's?" I asked.

"No. I called Kate and she hasn't seen Mom."

I was pretty sure where Valerie had gone, back to Julio Cardozo, so I made up something reassuring to tell Cheryl and let it slide. I was tired of that family and all the grief they caused me. The case had brought Kate Morley into my life and just as rapidly whisked her away. That simple fact was enough for me to steer clear of the Albertsons forever.

It was Tuesday evening and I was checking out the Weather Channel. A tropical storm named Glenda had skipped Florida and crept into the Gulf where it was upgraded to a Category One hurricane. Now Glenda was buzzing around, gaining strength and trying to decide where to head next. The best bet was Galveston but the forecasters didn't know for sure. Everyone here was praying that Glenda would follow Ellie and head further down the Texas coast and naturally, folks there were praying for Glenda to hit Galveston and Houston.

I thought things had sunk to a low point but it wasn't even a gentle dip. The real blow came from an unexpected direction, David Meierhoff. It was about nine that night when he phoned.

"Mitch, you been keeping an eye on Ray Burgess lately?" His voice was stressed.

"No, not recently. I've pretty much tapped that well dry, but I still want to look through his house again soon as you guys give me the heads up. Why?"

"Bad news."

I laughed. "Bad news and good news again?"

"All bad, my friend. No jokes this time."

"How so?"

"I just got a call from Galveston County Homicide."

"What did they want with you?"

"There's been a murder," he said. "Looks like the Slicer again."

"Jesus, David. I've done what I can with Ray Burgess. I can't follow him around all day."

"No, Mitch, it's not that. We can't fault you there. You weren't expected to set up surveillance on him. And he's only one suspect on our list of possibles anyway."

"Then what? Why call me about a murder in Galveston County?"

That dreadful pause. I knew it was bad, really bad, and I knew what he was going to say before the words were out.

"It's Valerie Albertson."

Chapter 60

Rain was steady and the puddled water multiplied the flashing lights, as if there weren't enough of them already. I sat quietly in the back of a Seabrook cop cruiser. I didn't want to go into the Albertson condo, even though I felt compelled. But my legs were too weak to respond, so I just stared out the car window at all the comings and goings.

Special Agent Ed Scudder stood beneath a nearby carport, smoking a cigarette and talking to Meierhoff and Texas Ranger Danforth. After a minute, they splashed my way. Scudder got in the back with me, Meierhoff and Danforth in front.

"Mr. King," Danforth said. "Do you know anyone who might want to harm Valerie Albertson?"

"I don't understand. It's the Slicer, right?"

"We don't think it's him," Meierhoff said.

"What do you mean?"

"We think it's a copycat but we want you to see for yourself," Danforth said. "Are you up for this?"

With great reluctance, I said yes.

So we went into the condo and up the stairs to the master bedroom, unwanted replay of that dreaded pilgrimage to view Rhonda Willett. I nearly balked and ran back down, but stuck to the job at hand.

What was left of Valerie Albertson was lying on the bed.

She was naked, on her back, arms and legs spread-eagled, tied with thin rope, abrasions on her wrists and ankles where she'd struggled during the attack. Blood was everywhere, soaked into the sheets and mattress, splattered on the walls and floor. Black marker symbols ran all down her body, the ink smeared and mixed with her blood. She'd been stabbed innumerable times, the wounds concentrated on her face, breasts and pubic region. A slender carving knife was stuck to the hilt where her navel had been. I stared fixedly then turned away.

Meierhoff put his arm around my shoulder. "You gonna be all right, pal?"

I managed to mumble something deferential.

Meierhoff went to talk with Scudder and Danforth while the investigating team snapped digital photos and measured things.

"Piquerism," Scudder said. I looked at him quizzically and he gave me a brief lecture. "Piquerism is multiple stab wounds, far more than necessary to cause death. The wounds are usually focused on the genitals, also the breasts for women. It indicates a psychotic fixation, great personal hatred, or both."

Meierhoff walked back to me. He kept his voice low so no one else could hear. "We're certain this is a copycat."

"Not the Slicer?" I asked. "Not our guy Ray?"

"No," David said. "Regardless of who the Slicer is, this isn't his work. He cuts them laterally, she was stabbed downward. And right handed. Plus, he brings his own knives and this one came from the kitchen downstairs."

I nodded vaguely, not wanting to be forced to hear the details, but oddly fascinated nonetheless.

"There are other things," Meierhoff told me. "She was tied differently, arms not behind her and even the knots aren't the same. Rope was used, but not the same type. No strangulation, which the Slicer always does. Instead, she was stabbed to death." He gestured to the body. "And the diagrams. He makes them post mortem but these were done before the stabbing. And there aren't any pentagrams. Those are his favorite. The public knows about the markings but not the specific designs."

I looked again. From what I remembered of Rhonda Willett's corpse and Ray's chamber of self abuse, these patterns did seem different. Instead of stars and mystical symbols, Valerie's body was covered with long wavy lines that were vaguely familiar. Then I thought back to the Georgia O'Keeffe print hanging in Kate Morley's house and realized that was where I'd seen the lines before. But thinking about Kate while immersed in this horror made me even sicker, so I put it out of my mind.

"One final thing," Meierhoff said, pointing to what had once been a beautiful woman. "No signature."

"Signature?" I asked, too stunned to think clearly.

"No surgical clamp in the labia," he said. "We never release that fact to the press and a copycat wouldn't know to do it. But the Slicer always does."

"So who?" I asked.

"It's got to be Walter Albertson. He doesn't have a record of assault but sometimes it happens all at once, comes in a rush."

Meierhoff and I headed downstairs and out. Meierhoff stayed dry under the carport while I stood in the rain because I wanted to feel cleaner.

It didn't help.

I thought about Walter Albertson and raw anger replaced my revulsion. "Any idea where the son of a bitch went?"

"Not yet. Soon as we found the body, we got a car out to Albertson's house in River Oaks but he was gone. Neither of the girls knows where he went. Overnight contact people at his office, also a blank. We've got a red flag alert out for him, though. He won't get far."

"How are the girls holding up?" I asked.

"Not well, as you can imagine," Meierhoff said, his face downcast. He flipped open his palmtop and keyed it for the names. "Her daughter is Cheryl Stern, right?" I nodded. "She's in shock. I called the house a while back. Their doctor came by, gave her a sedative. Albertson's daughter Paula is a little better but she's in denial. Your friend Kate Morley drove over when she heard. She'll stay with them tonight. And of course a couple officers to stand watch."

The idea that Peter Bally might be a suspect was also discussed. I mentioned how Valerie had dumped him. But his status was quickly cleared because he was in San Francisco with his boss attending a legal conference and a call confirmed his being there the whole time. He wasn't the type anyway and in fact he seemed to be an okay guy. Checking on him was perfunctory.

Murders like this aren't done for hire, either. Hit men need to be cool headed and a savage killing isn't their style. Even the Mob won't mutilate a woman. And it couldn't be faked, either. Only a true psychopath can brutalize someone the way Valerie had been. The deed was personal and hateful, like the murder of Nicole Simpson. So the suspect list was again shortened to one name: Walter Albertson.

I looked out across the parking lot, grinding my teeth in frustration. Some of the police had left but there were still about a dozen vehicles clustered around. A team of cops was busy questioning the neighbors.

"When was the last time you saw either of them?" Meierhoff asked me.

"The twenty-second," I said quickly, the date embedded in my memory because of Shindler. "That was the day of the boat trip. And the shooting." I told him about the argument between Walter and Valerie. With the Shindler thing that evening, everything else had paled by comparison, but now I saw the significance of their marital conflict.

Meierhoff nodded, typing a few strokes as I talked. He snapped off his handheld. "This evidence of violence and abuse is indicative of his behavior over an extended period," he concluded. "It started with verbal, upscaled to physical and finally got her killed."

"I hope he hasn't left the country," I said.

"Don't worry. We'll get the fucker no matter where he runs."

Chapter 61

So Ray Burgess hadn't murdered Valerie. So it was Walter Albertson. So I hadn't slipped up and let Ray get to her. Instead, I had merely delivered Valerie straight into the hands of the man she feared most.

Terrific job, Mitch, one you can genuinely be proud of.

Getting drunk can be a chore, especially if you haven't done it in a while. I decided spur of the moment on this endeavor and didn't really have a chance to prep for the occasion. There were only five cans of beer in the fridge, so I skipped them since it would just fill me up. The champagne I'd planned to open with Kate was there too, but popping a cork on a bottle of vintage Moet didn't seem appropriate, my being alone and all. I went instead for hard liquor.

I continued drinking shots of bourbon long after I lost count. It was now five am, ZZ Top was blasting from the stereo and I didn't give a shit. After a pint or more, it's hard to care much about anything. Like the besotted older brother in Long Day's Journey Into Night, I was drunk as a fiddler's bitch.

Regret filled me even as I was filling the shot glass and I was well aware that alcohol only enhances depression, yet it seemed like the thing to do at the time. Now it was too late for anything except to ride it out and wait for the hangover to hit.

And boy, did it.

At dawn I fell asleep or passed out, whichever, and it was afternoon when I woke. The instant my eyes opened I knew I was in for some serious purgatory. The pounding in my head was worse than the noise made by the Tres Hombres.

I tried to throw up but there wasn't enough in my stomach to make a difference. Next I took some aspirin and drank grapefruit juice so the potassium could restore my electrolyte balance and help the headache go away.

Finally I managed to keep down a bagel, went back to bed for a few hours, felt better. Actually, I felt better regarding the hangover, but the more terrible fact of Valerie's murder still prevailed. About this nothing could be done, because my soul was circling the drain and alcohol had no effect upon that, either way.

I felt that a run might clear my head. I dressed in warmup togs and tucked the .45 into my waistband holster. As I began, my head pulsed in rhythm with each stride, but after a few blocks and some pulls on the water bottle, the throbbing lessened. I got my legs beneath me and worked up a decent sweat but didn't push myself because I wanted to think.

It was about seven, the evening air hanging humid from the recent rain. Several other runners were out and we waved to one another with the secret signal reserved for all the casual warriors of the street, civilian athletes who muddle their way through their exercise routine and through their lives.

And I am absolutely among them, belonging in their middling strife, myself mediocre in all achievement, all endeavors. For years I harbored illusions of superiority, bolstered initially by my upbringing, a family solidly within the social ascendancy of Houston professionalism. Father a successful attorney, mother engaged in the arts, myself benefiting from both. Prep school, college, top grades and accolades, law school the same, my future secure. Attractive and intelligent wife, daughter, the proper appurtenances for a stable existence. All of the trappings and decorations needed and all of it simply bullshit.

Now gone as if it never was.

The days of wine and roses had never existed anyway, but even the faint false memory of such a time was thoroughly burned away. Father and mother prematurely dead. My legal career stunted and forgotten. Family law practice that was so carefully built and nurtured now sold, clients absorbed by a larger firm. Marriage failed, wife and daughter lost to me. Lifestyle? A sham. Friends? A scarce few. Relationships? Not fucking likely.

How had all the plans, the carefully plotted career, the home life evaporated into nothingness? Where had it gone? How had I squandered my soul? Had I, like Prufrock, measured out my life with coffee spoons? Was I now destined to squat within a webbing of my own design and weave, desolate and alone, a stunted withered spider scrabbling desperately at his rotted threads, still hoping for a tug of life from beyond?

And was I also at fault in Valerie's death? Partially, I concluded.

My misguided and stubborn sense of purpose had driven me to persuade her to return home, perhaps against better judgment and certainly contrary to her instinct of self preservation. And I knew full well why I had persisted with this, even in the face of evidence that Walter was abusive to Valerie. It had been done to please my father.

All along there was this undercurrent, this impetus that propelled me to act. I was determined to prove my father wrong, to show him that despite his condemnation of my choice of profession, I could succeed, I could implement at least one single plan and follow it to a proper conclusion.

Yet I could not. Failure was to haunt me even more than the ghost of my dead father. Hamlet had it easy. We both had the spirit of a departed father to prod us on, but Hamlet at least had a tangible foe upon whom to vent his revenge. I have only phantoms.

I also knew that I would continue to strive for the goal of satisfying these strict and austere specifications because I was duty bound. How much more pain would I cause, I wondered? How many sacrifices were requisite, how many ashes would I continue to heap upon that cold and silent altar?

* * *

My mind was made up. I was going to take care of Ray Burgess if I had to shoot him myself. The fact that he hadn't actually murdered Valerie made no difference. He created the climate in which she met her death and he had certainly killed many others.

But revenge wasn't my principal motive. I felt that if I brought him to justice I could somehow mitigate the guilt I felt about Valerie, that I might even the score, set straight the cosmic balance sheet.

My initial searches into his den of perversion had revealed little critical evidence, but I was confident that I'd find something if I looked further. Many serial murderers have hidey-holes where they keep their trophies and tools of the trade, as if they are themselves ashamed of the crimes and need to conceal the truth. So I'd get back to Ray's place and dig deeper. There had to be a loose baseboard or false panel somewhere that I could find. And if I did, I'd frame him, plant his trophies and such where they could be discovered as evidence.

Maybe I could do one damn thing right.

Chapter 62

My shiny new Micro Center office phone rang as I stepped inside the house.

"This is Mitch."

"Oh, sorry. I was trying to reach Philip Marlowe."

"I'm authorized to take his messages." It was Irv Bernstein, calling from Dallas.

"I've got the info you asked for," he said.

"Anything off base?"

"You already know some of it, but there's plenty more. The arson folks suspected Raymond of setting the fire that killed his parents. But there was never enough proof so they didn't file on him."

"Why'd he burn them up?"

"Abuse, the worst kind. The father was physically and emotionally abusive to both boys, probably sexually as well. The mother wasn't involved in the abuse but she was certainly complicit in her silence. An enabler."

"Great. Another family in ruin."

"You enjoying a spate of these lately?"

"Yeah. Another case I've been on. Hubby killed his wife, cut her to pieces."

"Sorry about that."

"A rough one, Irv," I said. "But what else can you tell me about the wonderful Burgess folks?"

"Like many of these extreme abuse cases, one child is singled out. That was Raymond."

"So brother George escaped the brunt of it?"

"No way to tell for sure. Being older, he may have just gotten out of the house in time, or he was abused too, just didn't do anything about it. That happens. More likely, he got too big, the father was afraid of him, so the abuse turned instead to the younger brother."

"Any more details?"

"I don't know them personally, but I do have a name for you. Eddie Dupree. He was the principal arson investigator on the case. Now retired. He's expecting your call."

I copied the name and phone number. "Thanks. Anything else?"

"Nope. The newspaper clippings don't give much. But I'll get somebody to scan them, e-mail them to you anyway. That okay?"

"I think I've seen most of them, but anything that helps is welcome. What do I owe you?"

"Nothing. Someday I'll have something I need from your end of the line, you can recip me."

"Thanks again."

"Glad to help. Come up to the big city and say hello sometime."

* * *

Irv had indeed helped, if only to confirm what I suspected. Raymond Burgess had been bred to the cause and was to the manner born by his own parents, manufactured and customized in a facility of depraved evil.

Love is grand.

I grabbed a bottle of Ensure from the fridge, sat at my desk and phoned the retired arson guy, Eddie Dupree.

"It was pretty bad, Mr. King."

"How do you mean? The way the couple was killed?"

"No. I've seen lots of fire deaths, this was typical. The fire spread fast and they died of smoke inhalation. It wasn't that."

"Then what?"

"The other things we found in the house. In the basement."

Dupree was willing to talk but he liked to be drawn out, which was okay by me. "Go ahead."

"The old man had a damn torture chamber set up."

"For his boys?"

"Yeah. At least the younger one. Had these big leather straps where he'd tie him to this frame, like a rack in the Inquisition. There was a lot more, whips and chains and everything. Weird clamps and hooks."

I saw little point in telling him I'd seen the same thing less than a week ago.

"And worse, he kept fuckin' notebooks. Most of them was burned up, but we had a few pages left. He'd write down how he'd beat the boy. Cleansing the devil, counting the demons, he called it, how many lashes, how tight he'd pull the straps, all of it."

"His own child. Makes my head want to split open."

"Yeah," Dupree said. "Gave me fuckin' nightmares. Those damn demon signs, too. His notebook was full of 'em."

"Demon signs? What did they look like?"

"Well, like I said, most of the notebooks was burned up, but a few of the pages had these goofy occult markings, triangles and all. What do you call those upside down stars?"

"Pentagrams." I knew precisely, because I'd seen them, drawn on Rhonda Willett's body and emblazoned on Ray's wall. "Any photocopies of the notebooks?"

"Sure. Criminal records has them stored away somewhere. You need a court order or police request to get them, though."

"That can be arranged," I told him. "You may get a call from the Houston police to verify the dates and all."

"Sure."

"So what did the court do with the boys?" I asked.

"Not a damned thing. They tried to get Raymond into some kind of therapy but didn't have any luck."

"Why not?"

"Combination of things. George, the older brother, was already of age and his brother's legal guardian. He refused anything they offered. Then he moved down your way, right after Raymond got out of the hospital from the burns. Took him along. There wasn't any other family, least none we could find. So they couldn't really keep the boy in custody. They tried."

"I understand. And I appreciate your help."

"Glad to be of assistance." He hesitated. "And can I suggest something?"

"Sure."

"The way I imagine it, that poor boy Raymond has got a lot of stuff bottled up inside him. Bad stuff. He'd bear watching. Not that it's really his fault, you know. But if it ever bubbles out, comes to the surface, there'll be hell to pay."

Hell to pay? Of that, at least, I was certain, because it had already surfaced into my life. Surfaced in great layers of sin and pain.

Chapter 63

Five minutes later I was in the kitchen and thinking about fixing a sandwich when my cell rang, Kate Morley calling.

"Terrible about Val," she said, apparently skirting our own problems, for which I was grateful, at least for now.

"Yes. I was there, Kate."

"My God. Was it as bad as I heard?"

"Worse. I never want to see anything like that again as long as I live."

"Any word on Walter?"

"Nope, nothing yet. I checked with Homicide a while ago. But they'll find him."

"Soon, I hope," she said.

"How are the girls? I understand you've been to see them."

"Cheryl's a wreck. Her girlfriends from school came over, she's visiting with one of them now. And the neighbors are helping. Paula's not much better off. She keeps insisting that Walter didn't do it. You know, protection mechanism. She's always been that way about Walter."

"And you? How about you?"

"I'll be okay. I'm still numb about the whole thing, though. I can't believe Val's gone."

"Anything I can do?"

"Not that I can think of," she said. Then she added, "Mitch?"

"Yes?"

"This isn't the time to talk about it, but I'm sorry about what happened between us. Your friend Detective Meierhoff phoned, we talked a long time. He explained things, how you weren't responsible. I gave it some thought and maybe I overreacted."

"Me too. I behaved poorly with you."

"Give things a while, Mitch. It's too soon."

"Take as long as you need, Kate. I care about you and I want things to be right. In the meantime, keep in touch."

"Sure," she said. "You do the same."

"Will do."

Finally, some good news. I decided to hit the shower, so I slipped the pistol out of my waistband and laid it on the kitchen counter.

"Glad you did that," a voice behind me said.

I looked around to see Ricky Perdon standing in the doorway, cousin Angel behind him. "Saves me the trouble of searching you." He smiled. "And you oughta keep your back door locked."

Chapter 64

We were in the Lincoln again, headed to see Julio Cardozo. Ricky drove slowly and was quiet the whole time. His round face was puffy and drawn and it looked as though he'd been crying. Perhaps he had.

Angel didn't speak either, just sat beside me and stared ahead. But just as we were pulling into the fenced lot of Pease Trucking, a thought hit me: Was I going to my execution? Did Julie Cards blame me for Valerie's death?

If so, it was too late for me to do anything about it. Ricky had already stopped the Caddy and the two sullen guards were stationed at the car. We got out and the Perdon boys escorted me into the warehouse, past the boat and into the back. The personal bodyguard Carlo stood there, drinking a can of Jumex, that sweet Mexican fruit punch. He nodded to us and opened the door to the private office where sat Julio Cardozo.

Cardozo got up, came around the desk and faced me, saying nothing. His expression was unreadable. Suddenly he threw both arms around me and hugged me with intense passion. After a bit, he stepped back and looked at me squarely. Tears welled in the corners of his eyes. Cardozo nodded to the other men and they turned and left us alone, closing the door.

"My Valerie is gone, Mr. King," he said finally.

"This is terrible for you. I know how much you loved her."

"She was the true love in my life."

"I'm very sorry. How can I help?"

His gaze turned fierce. "Find the man to did this to her, Mr. King. Find him and bring him to me."

"The police may locate him first," I said. "Or he may turn himself in."

Cardozo shrugged. "If that occurs, so be it. But if you can find him, I wish to spend some time with him."

"You're very angry."

"Mr. King, you do not know anger. Do you remember I told you of Valerie's stepfather, how he… how he treated her?"

I nodded.

"One day Carlo and I flew to Oklahoma and paid him a visit. He died, eventually."

Spend time with him. He died eventually.

I knew what that implied. And frankly, I was not all that opposed. After what Albertson had done to Valerie, he deserved it. Still, turning vigilante wasn't my style. I tried that once and the results were disastrous.

"I must be honest with you, Mr. Cardozo. I can't promise I'll be able to deliver on your request. If I find Albertson, I may decide to turn him over to the police."

He nodded. "I only ask that you consider it. But I do want you to work at finding him, nevertheless." He turned and opened a desk drawer, handed me a stack of hundred dollar bills. "This is ten thousand. Will it be enough for you to begin? You can have more if you wish."

I looked at the cash, handed it back. "The money isn't necessary, Mr. Cardozo. This job is personal for me. I considered Valerie my friend and I somehow feel responsible for her death. If I hadn't intervened, she might still be with you, and safe."

He shook his head. "No, Mr. King. It is not your fault. She had already decided to return to that evil man, that animal." A look of disgust crossed his face and I almost pitied Albertson if Cardozo got his hands on him.

Cardozo distractedly tossed the money onto the desk and held out his hands to clasp mine. "You will search for him and if you find him, you will at least consider giving him to me?"

"Agreed," I said.

We shook.

Cardozo went to the door and opened it. He said something in Spanish to Ricky, who went out the back. A moment later, he returned. With him was Cheryl Stern.

* * *

We sat in a circle, Cheryl on the sofa with Ricky, Cardozo and I in nearby chairs.

"She knows everything," Cardozo said.

Ricky put his hand on Cheryl's arm and smiled. "We're your family now."

Cheryl lunged and embraced Ricky, kissing him on the cheek. "Uncle Ricky. You've always been so sweet to me." She began to sob and Ricky patted her shoulders, blushing at all the attention. Cheryl let him go and sat back, dabbing at tears.

Cardozo smiled at this and nodded approvingly, then turned to me. "I know this was a hasty decision on my part, bringing Cheryl here, but I thought it best.

I am after all her true father and I love her. She is welcome to stay here as long as she wishes."

I wondered at the wisdom of dumping all this baggage in Cheryl's lap right now, but again, she had nowhere else to turn. Imagine her stuck in that big house with the austere and spiteful Paula, relatives descending for the funeral, casting Cheryl aside like an unwanted and embarrassing leftover. At least here, the affection was genuine. How she'd eventually feel about having a crime boss for a dad I couldn't say, but it was certainly a way out of the present situation.

"It may not be a good idea for Cheryl to remain here long, at least for now," I offered. "The police consider her in danger until Walter Albertson is caught and they'll be looking for her if she disappears."

"Let them look," Cardozo said. "If they waste time searching for her instead of searching for Albertson, so much the better. Our chances of finding him first are therefore improved."

"Perhaps," I said. "But when she does return, there will be difficult questions which may lead back to you. Remember how important it is that you keep a low profile, especially where Cheryl is concerned."

Cardozo smiled at Cheryl. "She was surprised, finding out her father exists and in the same day, learning that he is, as they say, in the rackets."

"I don't give a damn," Cheryl said. "I can't stay another second in that crappy house." She placed her hand in Cardozo's. "He's my father, and like Uncle Ricky said, this is my family now."

In a strange way I was happy for her. She was obviously running on empty, loss of her mother not yet hitting her completely. But when it did, at least there was someplace to go for solace.

"But Mr. King is correct," Cardozo told her. "You must go back, if only for a while. And there is also your mother's funeral to consider."

That set Cheryl off. She collapsed into Ricky's arms and began to sob continually. He patted her on the head, consoling her as she wept.

Cardozo tilted his head to me, indicating we should leave Ricky and Cheryl alone. We walked into the reception area where Angel and Carlo sat waiting.

"Mr. King," Cardozo said, "I am asking again that you let me have Walter Albertson, if only for one hour."

"I can't promise that, but I'll give it serious thought."

He nodded, reached in his pocket and handed me a business card. There was a phone number printed on it and nothing else. "Call any time, day or night," he said. "Someone will pick up the phone but will say nothing. You speak the word

Madrid and they will connect to me immediately. Ask for anything and it will be done."

Better than a Get Out of Jail Free card.

I thanked Cardozo, said goodbye to Cheryl, who had cried herself out for now and was sitting on the sofa, leaning against Ricky Perdon, a giant convenient teddy bear. Ricky was telling her how much her father loved her and that she would be all right.

The former was certainly true but I doubted the latter.

Angel drove me home and on the way, we stopped by Jack in the Box to grab a couple of burgers. Could this be the beginning of a beautiful friendship? With Major Strasser dead, who could say?

Chapter 65

Finding someone wealthy is easier than finding a lowlife. Rich folks are used to a certain level of luxury and they don't readily give it up. They're also accustomed to credit cards instead of cash and that leaves an audit trail. And of course they're less self-sufficient, accustomed to having things done for them instead of going it alone, so they aren't able to hide as well as the average thug.

This time however, Walter Albertson did a pretty good job of digging a hole and pulling the dirt in after himself. From a review of his belongings, he apparently grabbed a few clothes, his toothbrush and razor, and a Colt Python .357, the empty box left on his desk. Then he'd driven by his bank, cashed a check for five thousand and that was the last time anyone had seen him. They found his Mercedes on a side street near Fannin not far from the bank, but it offered no clue to his whereabouts.

Naturally, the cops had his photo stuck up everywhere. The airports were checked but since you can't get on a plane without six IDs and a full set of chest X-rays these days, it was unlikely he'd take that route. Family, friends and business associates were questioned but it was a dead end.

And everyone was cooperating, too. It might be one thing to pretend ignorance if a guy was running from the IRS, but if he's wanted for a vicious murder, it's something else entirely.

I did my best to follow up leads but they were cold. None of my usual contacts had anything. Ricky Perdon phoned me but nothing had come out yet. Tony Vee heard on the street that some rich but shady guy had put up a reward of fifty thousand dead, a hundred grand alive to anyone who'd deliver Walter Albertson. Apparently, Julie Cards was working his own end of the game. I sympathized with anyone who bore a resemblance to Albertson. It was open season on tall athletic white guys in their fifties.

Kate and I kept in touch as promised. We didn't see each other but we did talk. Paula had apparently bucked up pretty well and was managing her father's home responsibilities in his absence. Albertson's corporation stepped in, too. Kate told me that Cheryl had been spending a lot of time elsewhere, probably with a new boyfriend. I said it was a good thing and wished her well, knowing in fact that the boyfriend was actually her father.

Then came Valerie's funeral, a quick and fairly painless ceremony at the Episcopal church where George and Barbara Bush were members. Kate and I went together. Walter Albertson's sister and brother in law were there, having flown in from Atlanta, staying to help wrap things up.

Cheryl stood tall during the whole thing and I was proud of her. Paula was her usual unctuous self but she thankfully stayed out of Cheryl's path. I glanced around the church for Ricky Perdon or even Julio Cardozo but neither showed. Sensible, their staying away, because the cops were also hanging about, hoping Walter Albertson would sneak a peek. But he didn't attend.

Neither did the Bushes.

Chapter 66

I got the call from Meierhoff the next day. Walter Albertson had turned up, dead.

"We found him."

"How?"

"A magnificent example of tireless police work combined with the pursuit of excellence. Not to mention a little shabby residence hotel on South Main, where the neighbor complained about the smell in number twelve."

"Walter did himself?" I guessed.

"Yep. Swallowed his Colt. Made a real mess. He was pretty ripe when they cracked the door, no air conditioning and an open window, flies having a picnic. Whiskey bottles all around."

"Nobody heard the shot?"

"That part of town, you hear gunfire all the time."

"Case closed," I said.

"Yeah. Like Duggan says, done is done. CSI checked everything, a typical suicide, no doubt. He also left a suicide note. I'll e-mail you a scanned copy if you want."

"May as well," I said. Meierhoff confirmed my e-mail, we talked a bit, promised to meet when I had more on Ray Burgess.

I phoned Kate and gave her the news. She'd gotten to know Walter's sister while she was here and Kate said she'd drive over and help her through the mess. "It's an awful thing," Kate said. "Finding out that your brother's a murderer. Now she has to bury him, too. Terrible."

I agreed. The whole thing was sour and rank. How many lives had this poison affected, how many people had their world turned upside down? Walter Albertson's abuse and eventual murder of Valerie had twisted everyone near him.

Thank God, it was finally over. Cheryl could try to put her life back together. I even felt sorry for Paula.

No sooner than I hung up, the phone rang. It was Julio Cardozo.

"I heard a rumor that Walter Albertson is dead. That he killed himself."

Julie Cards sure had the fast track to inside news. "Yes," I said. "It's true. They found his body this morning."

"Are they certain it is Albertson?"

"Yes. Flies had gotten to him so he was chewed up by maggots, but all the other things fit. Dental records and DNA will verify, but yes, they're certain."

"A fitting end for such a man. Food for flies."

"Yes."

"Then it is finished."

"Yes."

"Thank you anyway, Mr. King. You have been very helpful to Cheryl. This she tells me."

"She's a good girl. Whatever I can do to assist."

"Perhaps we will see one another again," he said, and hung up.

Chapter 67

Today I didn't care about Viola snooping from next door, fake uniforms, or anything else. I wore my leather jacket, shoulder holster beneath, jeans and no hint of a nametag. I was going in for the stuff and didn't give a damn. I had to somehow fix what I'd screwed up. When I found the evidence, I'd figure a way to plant it elsewhere to be discovered by official investigators. So I simply went around to Ray's back door and picked his lock.

I started in the dungeon room because I figured he'd be hiding most of his things there. I tried not to look at the rack or the straps, but instead concentrated on finding his murderous toys, especially the knives.

But the room was empty except for the torture gear and rigging. So I checked the closet, looking beneath all the bondage costumes and spare ropes. Again, no knives.

I found Ray's notebook right away, however, a log of his personal experience in self-destruction. There were dates and lists of what he'd done to himself, all the finer points of how tight he'd pulled the restraints, whether he'd ejaculated and how many milliliters, estimates of when he'd passed out and regained consciousness. And yes, alongside the meticulous record keeping, rows of the satanic symbols, the same as I'd seen on Rhonda Willett's body. Ray's father had trained him well. I had to put the book down for a bit to catch my breath.

I finished the upstairs. No weapons or incriminating materials. Maybe the stuff was stored downstairs after all.

I was halfway down the stairs when the front door opened and Ray Burgess and his elder brother George walked in.

* * *

I stopped midstride and said nothing, but they were surprised as I was. Ray's face blanched and he stood stock still. George frowned and said "Hey!"

"Hi, Ray," I said. I considered drawing my pistol but George was in civilian clothes and didn't seem to be carrying a piece. So I kept my cool and waited to see what would happen.

"You know this guy?" George asked his brother "And why the hell is he here?"

Ray obviously didn't remember meeting me, know the answer to either question, and I was myself at a loss to provide one.

George squinted at me. "I don't know you. But this isn't a robbery, is it?"

"No, it's not. But you'll wish it was."

"Why? And who the fuck are you, anyway?"

"Do you have any idea what you've been doing?" I asked George. "Do you realize that you've been aiding and abetting a killer?"

"Killer? Who?" This was the first we heard from Ray. I could see how he deferred to his brother, cowed in George's presence, standing slightly sideways, a timorous look on his face, almost waiting for permission to speak. "Who's a killer?"

"I know what you are and I've seen your playpen," I said. "It doesn't help to deny it, the people you've murdered."

"I never killed nobody," Ray said.

George tried to seize the initiative in our little three-way debate. "Ray, call 911 and tell them we've got an intruder. I'll hold him."

"Don't do it, Ray," I said. "You don't want the police here. We all know what's upstairs." I turned to George. "And I know you've been helping him, enabling a killer."

"I'm not a killer!" Ray insisted.

"Ray, shut up," George said. "This guy doesn't know shit. Don't say another word."

"I didn't kill Mom and Dad. That was an accident."

"Shut up!"

"May as well let it all out, George," I said. "How long do you think it will take the cops to tear this house apart? They'll find all the secrets that your brother has hidden. He's finished."

"Ray needs help," George admitted.

"Maybe so, but he sure doesn't need the kind of help you've been giving him."

"You got no idea what Ray needs. I'm his brother."

"I'm not going to—" Ray continued.

"Ray, shut the fuck up!" George angrily ordered.

But Ray was on a roll. "No!" he shouted. "It's all my fault! You know how it is, George, I've got it all down in the book. It's my job to heal, my job to take all the demons into my own soul. Into my body."

This wasn't working out like I expected. Ray was babbling denials and protesting about demons. What did that have to do with anything? But he was a nutjob anyway.

George tried again to placate his brother. "Ray, don't get excited. You know what happens when you do. Calm down and let's deal with this logically."

"How?" Ray asked. "I'm doing everything I can! I take in all the evil, mine and yours and everyone else's!"

I needed to regain control. "Okay, everybody take it easy. I know what's happening and I'm going to put a stop to it."

"You can't stop me!" Ray yelled. "I'll show you! I know the truth!" Then he ran toward me, catching me off guard. I pulled my pistol from the shoulder holster but he ignored me and scooted past, further up the stairs and toward his dungeon, the fact that I had a gun in my hand apparently unimportant. So I came right behind Ray, George following us both.

"I'll show you!" Ray kept saying. "I'll show you!" He fumbled with his keys, trying to unlock his secret door.

"Ray!" George yelled. "Stop!"

Ray was sobbing. He turned to us, breath rasping, body shaking. "I need to show him, George, show him the truth. I want to show him the demons, how I cancel them out for you, how I fixed things for you, George. How I protect you!"

"Take it easy, Ray." George talked over my shoulder, trying to calm his brother down. We were all at close quarters, jammed together on the small landing at the top of the stairs.

"You take it easy yourself, George!" Ray insisted. He was near tears. "I can't bind any more demons for you. I can't!"

"Ray, we'll get help for you," I said. "We'll get George involved, too."

"Involved?" Ray's voice was hysterical. "George is already involved. He's the reason I keep binding the demons! I do it every time for you, George!"

"Shut up, Ray!" George said.

Ray's eyes suddenly bugged out and he reached for me. "George! Don't!"

He was unarmed and I didn't want to fire, so I stepped back, hoping to trip him and take him down without anybody getting hurt.

Suddenly I felt a terrific blow to my left side. George had apparently sucker punched me in the kidney, hard. The pain flared throughout my body and I couldn't catch my breath.

George hit me again, even harder, and as I turned to meet him, I felt a strange hot wetness. Everything slowed down and for some reason I was unable to think clearly.

Ray was shouting "George, don't!"

But George went ahead and punched me a third time.

I was light-headed and weak and I got all the way around and saw that George Burgess was holding a bloody knife.

My blood.

Chapter 68

The knife looked too big to be real, but it was. A part of my mind was lucid and in that faraway consciousness I knew I had to shoot George before he stabbed me again. I tried to tell my right hand to follow instructions but it wouldn't behave.

Nothing worked and I was frightened. I began to slide down to the floor.

George loomed above me and came closer, the shiny blade reaching toward my chest. Ray then grabbed his brother and pulled him back, George struggling against him.

I was now somehow flat on my back, the brothers wrestling above me. I knew they were fighting but for some reason I couldn't figure out why. It was as though I was watching a slow motion TV episode on a tiny screen, everything squeezed in. There was a disconnect, a barrier between me and what was going on. Even so, I knew there was something important I needed to do but I kept forgetting.

There was blood on my clothes and I thought that some of it had come from inside me, even though I didn't know how. I didn't feel much pain. Or if there was pain, it came from a distant source, far beyond my realization and scope.

Ray kept yelling and his voice was now annoying me. I wanted him to be quiet so I could concentrate. But the yelling continued, the pushing and shoving. I had to make it quit.

Then I knew the solution to the problem. I had to shoot George to make the fighting stop. But where was my gun? Had I lost it?

I looked at my right hand and felt relieved to see the pistol there. It was now simple and I was angry at myself for not having figured it out earlier.

I raised my pistol, sighted on George and pulled the trigger.

I think the gun went off.

Chapter 69

It seemed I lay in Ray's hallway for hours but it must have only been a few minutes.

The initial shock had passed and pain woke me fully, raging through my side and back, forcing me to suck in my breath sharply. Dizziness surged through my head.

At first I panicked, searching for George and his knife, aiming my pistol up and down and around, but George wasn't there. As I moved, bolts of pain rippled from my left side and cascaded through my body. Breathing was difficult.

I rolled to my knees and grabbed the balcony railing for support, pulled myself to my feet. It was hard to stand and the pain made me dizzy again, but I had to look for George and make certain he was no longer a threat.

There was a trail of blood down the stairs. I halfway believed the blood trail was mine, but it wasn't. I hadn't gone downstairs yet. Or had I, and just forgotten?

Although the pain was blinding, the bleeding seemed to have somewhat subsided. I hoped it didn't mean that I was dying. I kept wavering in and out of reality, not understanding what needed to be done.

"Ray?" I called out.

Nothing. So I held onto the wall and slid along, keeping mostly upright. "Ray?"

Silence.

I saw that the door to Ray's special room was ajar, so I headed in that direction.

I turned the corner and there was Ray.

He was hanging from his frame and he had strangled himself. But it was no erotic fixation this time. It was his final exit. He'd quickly set up a noose and rope over the pulley and down to his ankles. When he passed out, the legs would sag, the loop would tighten, finishing the job.

Ray Burgess had finally exorcised all his demons. And those of his brother as well.

"Hello? Hello? This is the police! Is anyone here?" A female voice from downstairs. "We got a call about gunshots. Is everyone okay?"

"Up here!" I hollered. "I've been stabbed. Call an ambulance!"

I began to drift to the floor again.

I had the presence of mind to lay my pistol down before I passed out.

246

Chapter 70

I was spending an inordinate amount of time in hospitals, back in Memorial Hermann and in recovery.

I was a day out of surgery and I'd been relentlessly hovered over and harassed by nurses and lab technicians, all of whom wanted to wake me up to take vital signs, give me pills or draw blood. They also seemed to be waking me up to check if I were asleep and ask earnestly if I was getting enough rest. If they left me alone I'd probably heal faster, but there is the continued employment of hospital staff to be considered.

And rules are rules.

Surgery for me had been quick and successful. George's knife was evidently deflected by the straps of my shoulder holster, just where it crossed my back for support. The blade slid across my ribs, carving out sizeable, very painful, but non-lethal fillets of muscle and connective tissue. If George had been right handed or if I'd worn my hip holster, I'd be dead.

When I was in the recovery room and first came out of anesthesia, I had an allergic reaction to the drugs and hallucinated. I thought George was still attacking me, teaming up with a bunch of pool sharks who wanted to steal my money and my custom cue. I tried to fight them off but I didn't have my cue or pistol so I had to use bare hands. I succeeded in giving one of the postsurgical aides a split lip before they got me restrained.

When the drugs wore off, I was immensely embarrassed and apologized to anyone who would listen. They told me it was a common reaction to anesthesia but I still felt awful about it.

Connected to my saline and antibiotic drip was a tube that ran up to a little black plastic box on my IV stand that simply said, in big block letters, MORPHINE, with a cord running from it and a button on the end to push.

This is possibly the most elegant and useful device in medical history. You press the button, you get your fix. However, I quickly discovered that the damn thing was on a timer so I couldn't simply lie there and keep pushing the button like a rat in a Skinner box. Instead, I had to wait for the timer to click out between reloads, like using the super shotgun in Doom.

So nothing is perfect in this world, not even the morphine drip. Such as it is with other things, appearances and promises that never carry over into reality.

Our letdown comes in drips and is apportioned like my rationed painkiller, or in one large gusher, when, at the end, we finally descend into that wormhole of our own darkness.

I kept drifting in and out, letting the healing begin and what morphine was allotted me help with pain. Kate Morley had come by while I was sleeping and left some flowers and a card. And a few other folks also visited, Tony Vee, Donna Boudreaux and my neighbor Ernie Banks, who assured me that Krazy Kat was getting fed just fine.

Meanwhile, Captain George Burgess was nowhere. Duggan, Meierhoff and Agent Scudder had all been to see me, asking questions and filling me in on the latest. "You must have only grazed him in the arm," Joe reported. "We found a hole in his jacket sleeve but not a lot of blood."

"Where'd you find his coat?"

"A rest stop on I-45 near Huntsville. In the john. His car was parked there."

"Where is George, then?"

Duggan was uncomfortable with this. "It went bad."

"How?"

"Ranger Danforth worked the case, found a guy, throat cut, stuffed in the trunk of George's car. The guy's own car and wallet, missing. George knew we'd be looking for his car so he made the switch."

"Who was the guy?"

"Random victim. Sales rep for an offshore supply company. Poor bastard picked the wrong place and time to take a piss."

"God, Joe. I feel responsible."

"Don't. If it wasn't for you, he'd still be killing people. This way, he's on the run and we know who he is. And we'll get him."

"But—"

"Look. If you wanna wallow in pity and bitch and moan, be my guest. Just don't do it on my time. I don't want to hear it."

So I kept quiet and fumed inwardly. My specialty, after all.

* * *

A few days later the stolen car was towed from a lot near Greenville Avenue in Dallas, but George was still on the run. Meierhoff filled me in on the other details. "We got the proof we needed in George's house, extra knives, those surgical clamps, rope, all the goodies. Found the Smith-Corona typewriter and it's sure to match the letters. He kept trophies, too, pieces of his victims in little jars, labeled and dated. Had a complete notebook of everything, going back years. Scudder says that Burgess is a lot like Ted Bundy in that respect."

"He and Ray made quite a team, I guess."

"Yeah. You should read George's diary. He trained poor Ray from the beginning, helping his father with the basement torture. The kid never had a chance. Maybe the typed letters George sent to the FBI were his way of trying to stop it all, confession by proxy. We'll never know the logic of it because there is none."

And thanks to me, I thought, I made sure Ray killed himself in some sad, pathetic penance. Not to mention my screwing up and letting his brother get away. Nobody said anything to me about it, of course. Some of them may have even thought I'd done a good job, exposing the killer.

To explain why I was in Ray's house, I flat lied about breaking in and made up a cock and bull story about a client who was planning on suing Ray. Duggan and Scudder whispered into the ear of the county attorney and I was off the hook. It helped that nobody was left to complain.

But I knew better. I knew the truth.

I had failed, failed in a terrible, deliberate way. Again it had cost me, my perverse drive to prove that I could succeed, that I was worthy, that I was a man who had found himself a stable place in life.

I once more jumped to a conclusion and once more that rash act cost someone a life. First it had been Valerie, herself blameless except for having too much passion. Now it was Ray, guilty perhaps of his parents' death but surely innocent due to his warped mind, harming no one but himself.

So I lay in the hospital and wished myself dead. Nonetheless, they soon had me walking around and kicked me out not long after.

Chapter 71

It was late morning and hurricane Glenda was bearing down on Galveston like a rhino in full charge. Near landfall, it was downgraded from a Cat One to a major tropical storm but it was still dangerous. Intense rainfall, high winds and heavy tides were on their way to Galveston and the surrounding coastal area, and everyone was getting out of town, headed up I-45 to Houston and beyond.

We were guaranteed a ton of rain ourselves, but the fifty miles of dry land between Houston and Galveston Bay meant that most of the bad stuff would fall short of the city proper. Nevertheless, everyone stocked up supplies against possible power outages and storm damage. This consisted of running to Kroger and buying batteries, duct tape and most important, beer.

My wounds were healing. I stopped by the clinic and they checked the surgical staples. Those would come out next week and I'd be fine.

What was not healing was my soul. If I still had one, that was. Maybe I'd bartered it all away, leading both Valerie and Ray to their terrible and lonely deaths. But I was nevertheless trying to get back into some modest semblance of normality.

I was sipping coffee and reading the Van Gogh book that Kate Morley gave me. If I couldn't see her, at least I could maintain the psychic connection.

Outside the wind was picking up and it had been raining hard for an hour or more. I'd already covered my MG and made sure the 4Runner and Stealthmobile's windows were cranked up tight. Krazy Kat was fed and snoozing, all tucked in for the duration. I would sit here in my study, listen to Bach and enjoy the fury of the storm. If the power went off, what the hell. My beer would stay cold for hours.

I tried to relax, recuperate and enjoy a day off, but Walter Albertson's suicide note began to intrude into my thoughts. I'd read it once and there was something in the text, something that bothered me which I couldn't put my finger on.

The note nagged me until I gave up, hobbled downstairs and fired up my computer, printed the scanned image that Meierhoff e-mailed me I went back upstairs and sat reading. The handwriting was neat and precise.

It has been my fault from the beginning. I bear responsibility for all the grief and pain that has fallen upon my family. Do not blame Paula. After all, I am an adult and she is still a child.

That's strange, I thought. What did Paula have to do with Walter murdering Valerie? I read further.

I should have known it would come to this. When Paula's mother took her life, I knew that I had driven her to it. Even then it was my fault. But still I continued. I am helpless and I cannot stop, even though I know it is wrong. Now Valerie is gone and I am solely to blame.

Another odd turn of phrase. He spoke of her murder in a detached way.

I cannot live with the guilt of what I have caused. I ask Paula to forgive me. Tell her that I love her. I know that I have also wronged Cheryl, and for that I am sorry. There is no hope for me and I must now do what I should have done long ago. If I had the courage then, fewer people would have been harmed and Valerie would still be alive.

I set the printout aside and reflected on Albertson's bizarre choice of words. He asks for forgiveness, not for killing Valerie but for unknown deeds in the past? I concluded that he was crazy anyway. No wonder the note made little sense.

The power flickered, my music stuttering. The house was taking a pounding, the storm whipping through the trees and slamming the rain against the windows. I turned up the TV volume and checked the news.

Galveston and the Bay were really getting it now, the only people left in town being cops, emergency workers and hordes of remote broadcast news teams. I could only hope for a huge wave to come in during a live remote from the beach and wash all the reporters out to sea, side by side, still talking into their microphones, stylish windswept hair still in place as they slipped beneath the waves.

They cut away to a background report about how the storm had affected shipping and other maritime business. All the drilling platforms had been shut down and evacuated a few days earlier, so the crews were at least safe. But the loss in oil and gas production meant millions down the drain without even counting storm damage. Onscreen were obligatory stock file videos of offshore rigs during the narrative.

That set me to thinking idly about how Paula was so fixated on the drilling platforms, how her abstract sketches depicted their linear structures, her broad dark charcoal lines so severe, so stark.

And it hit me! I knew!

Chapter 72

My God! The revelation was like a Torino Ten meteor strike.

Now I realized where I'd seen the markings on Valerie's body. It wasn't Georgia O'Keeffe's painting. It was Paula! The marks were a perfect match for her charcoal sketches in the library, the symbolism identical.

And now I understood Walter Albertson's suicide note. He wasn't apologizing for killing Valerie, because he hadn't. It had been Paula and he knew why.

His apology was about what had happened between Paula and himself. Father and daughter. Incest. It made me shudder with disgust. And it made me dive for the phone and call the Albertson house. Cheryl was in serious danger.

"Yes?" A woman answered. "This is Marie Phillips." Walter's sister from Atlanta.

"This is Mitchell King, the investigator."

"Yes, I remember."

"Is Cheryl home?"

"No. She and Paula are staying with friends."

"Do you know specifically where? It's important."

"Sorry, I don't. Paula was out early this morning, then she came by and picked up Cheryl. They left together, oh, a couple hours ago."

"They didn't say where they were going?"

"No. Paula seemed quite upset at first. I could hear her arguing with Cheryl. Things calmed down. I didn't want Paula driving in this weather but they left anyway."

"If you see or hear from Cheryl, have her phone me immediately. It's urgent. A matter of life and death, literally. And make certain she stays home."

Next, I scrambled for the card Julio Cardozo had given me. I punched the number, it clicked and I spoke the code word Madrid. There were a couple more clicks and Cardozo spoke. "Yes? This is Julio."

"This is Mitch King."

"What can I do for you, Mr. King?"

"Is Cheryl with you today?"

"No. She is at her house."

"She is not. I just called."

"Is there a problem?"

"I don't know. Maybe. She's apparently missing." I thought about what to do. "Can you ask Ricky and Angel to drive over to my place? Now."

"Yes, certainly. Angel is visiting his family in Juarez but Ricky is here. Is Cheryl in trouble?"

I hesitated. All I had was a hunch and a possibly misguided sense of comparative abstract art styles. "She may be. I'm concerned with her whereabouts, the storm and all."

What I didn't mention was the far greater deluge that might be ready to engulf Cheryl, a terrible force from within the mind.

"I will send Ricky immediately and he will come prepared for any problem."

A quick call to Kate Morley proved fruitless. She hadn't spoken to Cheryl lately and had no idea where she or Paula might be.

"Is something wrong?" she asked.

"I hope not. I'll let you know as soon as I have something."

Next was Meierhoff. I caught him at home. "This better be good," he said. "I'm conducting an intense opera appreciation session with Monique."

"This is serious, David. I think Paula Albertson was intimate with her father Walter, and that she killed Valerie." I quickly outlined my thoughts about the markings and Paula's artwork. "I need your help right away."

"Jesus, Mitch."

"Yeah. The more I think about it, the more I think I'm right."

"Gimme a half hour."

* * *

Ricky Perdon and David Meierhoff stood in my kitchen, drinking hot coffee. At first they eyed one another like adversaries in a wrestling ring, but when I reiterated my concern, they forgot their professional antagonism and joined with me.

"What should we do?" Ricky asked. "How can we find Cheryl?"

"The condo in Seabrook," I said. "I'm sure that's where they are."

"Let me try the cops there first," Meierhoff said. He called HPD on his cellphone and had them patch him into the Galveston County sheriff's office. He spoke with them for a few minutes sand although we could only hear one end of the conversation, we pretty much knew what was happening, Meierhoff being insistent yet getting nowhere. He clicked off, shook his head. "They can't get anyone over there for an hour, maybe more. Everyone's tied up with the storm, pulling people out of flooded houses and cars."

"We have to go down there," I concluded.

"With the roads the way they are?" Meierhoff asked.

"We've got to try."

Ricky agreed. He and Meierhoff grabbed some rain gear from their cars and we all got into my 4Runner. It would be the best vehicle for what lay ahead. I had my pistol, extra magazines and two big MagLite flashlights. Meierhoff brought his Colt 9mm and Ricky pulled a long padded case from his trunk that I assumed held a shotgun.

Ricky got in back and Meierhoff sat up front with me. He stuck a Houston Police placard on the dash. It would get us past the roadblocks but what it wouldn't do was help navigate the washed away streets.

The storm had lessened and it was pretty easy going for the first few miles, with only heavy rain and wind gusts to slow us. The Texas Highway Patrol had I-45 southbound blocked at three points but Meierhoff flashed his badge and we were let through. We did get some curious glances and more than a few warnings to be careful.

"Watch for them copperheads and water moccasins," one officer told us. "You get a big rain, it flushes them outta their dens and they're everywhere. Crawl up your leg and latch right onto your balls." Scant humor to lighten the occasion, and none of us laughed.

I drove as fast as I could and still maintain safe conditions. Meierhoff kept trying to rouse the Seabrook cops, gave up. "A damn semi ran into a Greyhound bus in west Galveston County. Bad. Five known dead and more injured. Everybody's headed there. They'll try to send someone over to the condo but can't promise when. Or if."

I thought we were making good time considering the cascading rain, but I had a backseat driver with an agenda. "Go faster," Ricky urged. "Faster."

So I boosted it. Things were okay for a while, then a gust of wind took us and we went sliding sideways at seventy.

"Dios!" Ricky let out.

"Oh shit!" Meierhoff echoed.

Oh shit, I also thought, eased off the gas gradually and tried to correct the steering. We straightened, fishtailed wildly back and forth until things settled.

After that, nobody asked me to speed up.

* * *

It seemed days until we reached the NASA highway turnoff but it had only been an hour.

Along the Interstate, the lanes had been relatively clear but now we were in a commercial and residential area with debris everywhere. Pieces of siding, shingles, tree branches and various kinds of junk were strewn across the roadway.

Hoping there weren't nails or other sharp edges to slash my tires, we crunched through all of it. The power lines were down at one point and I steered around their broken ends, black sizzling electric snakes lurking in pools of rainwater. There were some big tree branches across the road at one narrow spot so I put the Toyota into 4-wheel drive and bumped right over them.

We could have filmed a commercial.

The rain intensified when another cell swept through. Sheets of water gusted across our path and at times it was hard to see, even with the wipers going full blast. Cop cars were parked at several intersections, their lights flashing to turn back anyone foolish enough to be out. Each time we passed, Meierhoff waved the HPD placard and we were given the high sign, allowed to proceed.

No one got out to challenge us. Cops they might be but they wanted to stay dry as much as the next guy. I think we would have been just as successful waving a sign that said Eat at Joe's.

As we neared the condo, the streets were under water and I maneuvered through some deep spots where the waterline was over the hubs. I took it slow to keep the engine from flooding but fast enough to preserve momentum. One time we broke free and began to float at a precarious angle, then the tires bottomed out again and we continued.

While I drove, Meierhoff and Ricky Perdon were giving me constant instructions and suggesting alternate routes but I steadfastly ignored them and stuck to my original path. Finally, I turned into the complex. The power was out and the electric gate stood propped open, held there by a dented trashcan. We pulled up to the Albertson place and I saw Paula's Honda Civic in front.

As soon as we got out, we were drenched through, our shoes also soaked by the standing water everywhere.

I pounded on the door. No answer. It was locked but one big foot from Ricky Perdon took care of that.

We ran inside, each of us with gun in hand, but the place was deserted. The gushing rain echoed on the skylight in the vaulted ceiling and made the place seem even emptier. We dashed upstairs. The murder bedroom was still roped off by crime scene tape but it was as deserted as the rest of the house. We quickly checked the other rooms but nobody was home.

As we walked back downstairs, I noticed a chair tipped over in the breakfast room off the kitchen. Meierhoff stooped over it and said, "Blood."

There was a trickle on the floor and across one arm of the chair. The drops formed a small trail and we followed it to the rear of the house. It led outside. I looked up and saw the problem.

The boat was gone.

Chapter 73

We all stood there like dunces, staring out the back window at the empty slip.

Neighboring boats were moored and battened down for the storm, but the spot where the Val would be was abandoned.

During the trip I'd emphasized to Ricky and Meierhoff what I suspected and why I feared for Cheryl. I hoped to catch Paula at the condo but she'd apparently taken the boat. How she'd gotten Cheryl to go on board with her I didn't know, but I was certain that's what happened.

"What the hell are we going to do now?" I asked. "If she's where I think, we've got no way out there."

Meierhoff took out his cellphone. "I'll call the Coast Guard."

"No, ese," Ricky intervened. "I have better idea. I have people with boat. A fast boat." Ricky got his own phone, punched the number, spoke in rapid Spanish. After a minute he clicked off and smiled. "We go."

* * *

The rain had finally begun to let up. We drove further east until we came to a large marina, one of many in the area. We turned in and Ricky pointed us to a boat shed toward the end of the complex. Two young, casually dressed Hispanic men were waiting for us. As we came to a stop, Ricky looked to Meierhoff. "Don't tell you're a cop, okay? Makes them nervous."

We got out and Ricky greeted the men. "This is Hector and Alonzo," he said. "They work for Julio." They led us into the shed.

It was one of those covered affairs you could moor your boat in and sitting there was quite a boat indeed. The thing was sleek and pencil thin, with huge engines at the stern and a hull that seemed to be zipping forward even as it rode at anchor.

This was a cigarette racing boat, but I'd bet the type of racing it did, they didn't hand out trophies. I wondered how many kilos it had delivered to the Texas coast.

We jumped in, Hector at the controls, Alonzo staying ashore to help release the mooring lines and swing open the big rear door to the bay. Hector fired the twin engines and a throaty rumble vibrated inside the metal shed, roaring like a lion trapped in an oil drum.

We cast off and Hector eased the slender shape forward. He didn't speak much English, but with Ricky interpreting I got the destination across and we were soon headed out to the buoy where Paula did her best work.

I only hoped she wasn't doing it yet.

* * *

Seas were rough and we hopped across the waves in a clip-clop motion that could make anyone seasick. Most of us managed to keep it down, but eventually Meierhoff bent over the fantail and let go. Nobody cared.

Rain pelted into the open hull and we got even wetter, if that was even possible. It had cooled off and with the wind on our sopping clothes, we were soon chilled. But we kept on. Hector was an expert pilot and was stroking the throttle faster and faster until we skipped across the crests, barely touching the water at all. The motor's noise was enormous, the sound bouncing across the curling sea and filling our ears with its power. Any other time and this would be a major treat, but now it was a solemn rescue mission and there was no fun in it.

We seemed to be making good speed and then another squall hit.

Hector backed off the throttle. He frowned and mumbled something to Ricky, who turned to Meierhoff and me, wiggling his hand sideways. "Got to slow down. Capsize."

With our reduced speed, the long boat settled into the wave troughs again, dipping and tossing us around, making us queasy once more. We held on and hunkered down as low as we could. At every bounce of the boat my stitches ached, making me long for that little black box named Morphine.

The rain increased again and this time we were in danger of swamping. Hector set the engine to neutral, came back to the stern, cursing in Spanish and English mixed.

He opened a compartment, brought out a plastic hose and tossed the end of it overboard. He pressed a button and a small electric bilge pump began to stutter, sending a stream of water out the hose. He cautioned Ricky to keep the hose pointed outboard, returned to the controls and set off once more.

It was getting hard to see because the rain brought its share of mist and fog and, with the boat riding low in the water, there was no vantage point to get our bearings. But Hector seemed to know where we were going and he gradually pushed the speed up a notch, fighting the controls but keeping us steady.

We'd just settled down for the duration when a spot on the horizon rapidly grew to become a boat. It resolved itself into the Val, moored to the automated buoy, just where I expected. There was no sign of anyone on board, no running lights, nothing. A ghost ship.

As the cigarette boat drew alongside, we realized that getting onto the other boat would be difficult. The railings of the Val were higher than where we sat, and with both boats jouncing and heaving in the water, there was no way to grab onto the other rail. We each made a try but risked getting caught between the hulls. Neither boat was huge but they were slamming together hard. It could sure as hell break your leg.

"Let's try the buoy," I said, gesturing a circular route.

Ricky spoke to Hector, who nudged the racing boat forward, steering it in a sharp arc to clunk against the buoy's metal casing. As soon as we touched, I leaped across. My momentum carried me along, then my sneakers skidded on the slippery surface and I slammed sideways against an upright. The pain in my ribs rippled through me but I was too pumped to let it slow me down. I quickly covered the remaining few feet to where the Val was tied. I jumped onto its deck and this time I didn't slip.

There was still no sign of anyone aboard. I pulled out my pistol, glanced over my shoulder to ensure that Meierhoff and Ricky were following me across, and headed down into the cabin.

Chapter 74

It was a surreal nightmare world, bizarre as Ray's fetish bedroom.

Cheryl lay stretched on the big foldup table, naked and on her back, just as her mother had been. Her wrists and ankles were tied to the table legs and she was writhing to pull free. Tape was wrapped around her mouth and her body was covered with the abstract linear markings now so familiar.

Ranged about the small cabin were Paula's charcoal sketches, propped up all around. Some were Paula's oil rigs, but most were figure studies. There was Walter Albertson, nude and erect. Other sketches depicted Walter and Paula copulating. A larger drawing with Paula and Walter, both nude, standing together, embracing. It was viewed as in a mirror, self portrait and homage to her father and lover.

I'd suspected the truth when I snapped to the origin of the markings on Valerie's body, but having it displayed so graphically was still a shock. Seeing this in these charcoals stopped me and it was a hesitation that nearly cost me my life.

A noise from behind made me swing around. Paula was pointing a small automatic at my head. There was a crooked smile across her face. I had a pistol in my hand but could not bring it up in time.

"Mitch!" came a shout and I was shoved aside just as Paula let out a strange giggle and fired.

Meierhoff knocked me over and we both went sprawling on the deck. I banged my head and I saw stars for a second. Meierhoff simply lay there and then I saw the blood on his jacket.

Paula kept giggling. I was dizzy and my gun hand was being tardy. Meierhoff tried to sit up and kept slipping back.

Paula raised her gun again, aiming straight at me.

"Puta!" Ricky Perdon had come into the cabin and Paula turned to him.

A flurry of motion from Ricky, almost too quick to follow. There was blast and in an instant, Paula dropped to the deck, unmoving.

Ricky held a big revolver and he'd just shot Paula Albertson between the eyes.

Chapter 75

Chaos at first. Ricky and I waited until we realized that Paula wasn't going anywhere. Then he dived for Cheryl and I went for Meierhoff. David was fully conscious, sitting up now, bleeding from his upper right arm. He'd already pulled off his jacket and together we got his shirt down. Blood was oozing from small spots at the front and back of his bicep. Apparently the bullet had gone straight through.

He looked at the blood. "She shot me! The bitch shot me!"

"You okay?" I asked foolishly.

"No, I'm not okay!" Meierhoff protested. "I've never been shot before. Hurts like hell."

I glanced over to Ricky. He'd pulled his coat off to cover Cheryl's body and was now picking away at the tape over her mouth. There was dried blood on her temple but as far as I could tell, she'd not been otherwise harmed.

A sudden clumping on the stairs and Hector burst in, holding a tricked out AR-15. He glanced around the room. "Madre," he said quietly, crossing himself. Ricky spoke to Hector and he laid the gun down, rushed over to help untie Cheryl.

Meierhoff wasn't bleeding much, just a little puncture. Of course, I wasn't the one who had a hole in his arm.

I went into the head and grabbed a towel, came back and fashioned a compression bandage of sorts, wrapping my belt around it and slipping it through the buckle to pull it tight.

Meierhoff grunted, grabbed the end of the belt away from me. "Damn. She didn't kill me so you want to finish the job?" He began to pull on the belt himself.

I wouldn't leave David until I was sure he was going to be okay. He'd taken a bullet for me, after all. But he was fine, the bleeding slow, no large blood vessels hit. So I finally got around to checking out Paula. Ricky's shot was perfectly centered on her forehead, the hole a gory splatter like some silly Halloween gimmick. Threads of blood ran from her nose and ears and I looked at the back of her head. Most was missing.

Paula's pistol lay where she'd fallen. It was a little .25 auto, which accounted for the modest degree of injury to Meierhoff. A .25 can kill you, sure, but it has to hit squarely in a vital organ or tear up an artery.

Cheryl was untied now, and Hector wrapped a blanket around her. She was grey with shock but seemed okay.

I got her to lie back again and we stuck a pillow under her feet to keep them elevated. Ricky patted her arm and cooed soothing words to her, promising her it was over and telling her everything would now be all right.

And maybe that was finally true.

* * *

Meierhoff wanted out of this hellhole so I helped him up to the deck. He favored his arm but walked steadily and insisted he wasn't going to die right away.

Most of the rain had passed us now and the sun was trying to break through the cloud cover. The waves subsided too, both boats rocking and thunking against the big buoy in a gentle rhythm. We sat on the bench and leaned against the railing. "You feel faint or anything?" I asked.

"No." He shook his head. "You'd think getting shot would be more traumatic."

"You got lucky, pal. Out here, no quick way back. If she'd hit an artery you'd have bled out."

Meierhoff suddenly leaned forward and put his head down, pivoting at the waist like a dunking bird.

"You okay?" I asked. "Dizzy?"

"Not what's bothering me. I wonder how I'm going to tell the review board." Meierhoff turned to me, his face serious. "I'm out of my territory here. The brass get their teeth into this, only Moses and Aaron know what will come of it."

"You're on the Slicer serial killer team. This could have been a tip. A follow-up maybe."

"Okay. But why didn't I call the local police?"

"You tried, remember? The storm had them busy."

Meierhoff nodded. The lie seemed silly but reasonable. He let out a big sigh then straightened himself. "Maybe we'll be okay," he said. "Maybe things will work out."

Chapter 76

Strangely, things did work out, after a fashion.

Meierhoff's exemplary record carried him past the initial investigation and raw luck took us through the rest. That, along with the shadowy presence of Julio Cardozo. The minute we were in the Galveston County attorney's office we were joined by a team of lawyers from a high-priced Houston firm. They slathered every inch of the court with writs and filings and every other conceivable form of legalese designed to quash any more exploration into the affair. Lawyer versus lawyer, but ours were better.

Meierhoff even earned a commendation for bravery and his gunshot wound healed quickly. My own stitches had opened and had to be restapled but that would be mostly painless, I was assured but lied to. It hurt. The docs didn't let me have the morphine box again, insisting that good old Tylenol would be fine. They lied about that, too.

Paula's shooting was ruled justifiable, Ricky Perdon suddenly acquiring status as a licensed investigator and proud possessor of a pistol permit. It seemed that the law firm had engaged Ricky to protect their client, Cheryl Stern. Who would have thought it?

Most interesting, Cheryl's long lost great uncle materialized overnight from Oklahoma and assumed formal custody. She was now spending most of her time with him, getting stronger and finding herself. I met him afterward, a kindly old guy, sharp minded nonetheless, a man who seemed a bit amused at the goings on. Interesting what money can buy.

The final pieces were filled in when Paula's sketchbooks were discovered, locked in her closet at home. A detailed history of an unbalanced psyche, already fragile, then warped irretrievably by her own father's lust. She had only been a child when it began and unlike most victims of abuse, she had come to relish it, at least on the surface. She sketched with rapture the images of her father's assault, filling the margins around the drawings with vivid and fantastic descriptions of their illicit encounters. What she really felt in the depth of her heart, no one could fathom. It was beyond human reckoning.

No wonder Valerie had been frightened. A victim of abuse herself, she must have picked up vibrations from the beginning, suspecting but not letting herself believe. Her willingness to make things right for Cheryl had led her straight into hell. Paula lured Valerie down to the Seabrook house with promises of reconciliation. It was all in Paula's notes, each detail of the murder carefully illustrated, meticulously documented.

In her insanity, she'd been proud of her initiative, the way she'd cleared the path for Walter and her to finally be together. She'd bragged about it to Walter, showing him the drawings she'd made of Valerie's murder. How could he have endured another moment after seeing that obscenity, knowing his hand was instrumental in creating that monster? It's a wonder he survived long enough to rent that squalid room where he blew his brains out.

Paula's final entries dealt with pure revenge. She refused to comprehend her father's suicide and its implications, instead focusing on how Cheryl had been the cause of his death. She planned to make a sacrifice of Cheryl as she'd done with Valerie.

Truth be told, neither Meierhoff nor I could bear to read these frightening journals. That was left to the psychiatrists, who considered them a treasure trove of aberrant behavior. Even the summaries provided by the forensics team had been chilling enough. I was sick to my stomach for days.

But Paula and Walter's indescribable behavior was not my principal concern. The significant focal point in my life was how to endure the guilt I felt.

Had I let well enough alone, Valerie might have split with Walter Albertson and gone her own way. And she would therefore still be alive. Yet my dogged mindset had driven me to step in where I was not welcome, try to impose a solution that was ill advised. And the consequences were fatal.

The same with Ray Burgess. Yes, I'd unearthed a serial killer and George was now a known and recognizable fugitive. But I had also brought about the circumstances that forced a pathetic broken child named Ray to tie that final knot.

Randy Shindler's shooting? I felt justified, as with Dutch LeBrock. But in each case, I had taken a life and knew it would haunt me, same as had the Victor Allison tragedy.

Yet another link forged in my chains of despair.

I kept telling myself that I should schedule a session with Dr. Chen but I was so miserable that I couldn't summon the courage. I didn't get drunk, either. I'd passed the point where alcohol could be considered a palliative. Instead, I sat slumped in my recliner without the energy even to pet Krazy when he nuzzled my ankle. Mozart didn't help, Bach didn't help and after that I didn't know what could.

But as I've said before, I'm good at sitting and brooding so I did just that. Brooded over my consummate failure, my innate propensity to search out and destroy anything near me that had value. I was good at this too and getting better.

After some time I realized the doorbell was ringing. Whether I'd been asleep or had simply zoned out I couldn't say, but I got the impression the bell had been ringing a while.

Wearily, I hauled myself downstairs, saw it was Kate Morley. I'd phoned earlier and left a message, asking to see her, asking if she'd drive over so we could talk. Seeing her gave my spirits a boost. I unlatched the door and let her inside.

"Mitch," she said. Her eyes were soft and her brow wrinkled with concern. She came in and I shut the door behind her. We were there in the foyer, a parody of the moment we'd halted uncomfortably in her office hallway an eternity ago, when I'd enjoyed some modicum of respect, some modest degree of happiness.

"You look awful," she said.

"I feel awful."

"You need some fresh air, Mitch." So she led me outside to the breezeway near my carport. Kate brushed at my hair with a detached tenderness, as if I were some ailing but cherished pet. "Is this about Val?"

"About Valerie and Cheryl. About Ray Burgess. Remember what I said, that abuse wears many masks? Why didn't I see the situation more clearly?"

"You couldn't be expected to know. How could you? How could anyone?"

"Still, I blame myself. I pushed Valerie back into that house, pressed her to return, even after Walter Albertson fired me, even though I could see Valerie's reluctance. And I created the circumstances that led Ray Burgess to kill himself. I keep screwing up and I can't seem to break the cycle."

"Why? What is it?"

"A long story."

Kate put her hand on my shoulder. "Tell me. Take all the time you need."

"My father," I began.

Then the floodgates opened and it all came out, a torrent of despair and remorse. Words gushed forth in a rant, a litany, a confession. A storm of emotion let go, a storm far more substantial, more pervasive than the hurricane we'd just seen. Any justification regarding my obligations and professional dedication melted into an outpouring of shame.

I embraced Kate Morley, held her close, my knees losing their strength, my body drained. We sagged to the ground and still I held her. My anguish came in great and empty gasps, like I was vomiting up all my misdeeds, my transgressions, and I could not contain them. All was weakness, all failure.

Kate hugged me but there was no physical thrill, only the knowledge that another human being cared.

Eventually the words ran out and tears began. They began and would not stop. They welled from my eyes and rolled down my cheeks, rolled down to drop upon the hard uncaring earth beneath.

About the Author

Recently, Sam's concentrating on his Mitch King private detective novels, based in Houston and the surrounding Gulf Coast region. There are three novels thus far: Blood Spiral, Blood Storm and Blood Vengeance, and he's now writing his fourth Mitch King novel.

Sam worked in science, technology, and research for many years. He was involved in polymer physics, programmed for structural engineering firms, worked with high tech computer ventures, and has also edited petroleum exploration and production specifications as a tech writer. Sam believes that his science and engineering background augments his fiction, in that it provides insight into meticulous details which lend texture and flavor to his mystery novels.

Sam is a longtime fan of classical music and opera, and as a classically trained baritone, sang in opera, chorales, and Episcopal church choirs. He also enjoys classic rock and progressive jazz. A voracious reader, Sam's favorite book is James Joyce's Ulysses, which he's read several times and of which he's made a personal study. He also enjoys books on Imperial Roman history, quantum physics and cosmology, science fiction, biographies and of course, mysteries. Besides Joyce, his favorite modern mainstream authors are Cormac

McCarthy, James Dickey and Joseph Heller. His favored mystery writers are Bill Pronzini, Robert Crais and John Sandford.

Sam enjoys attending opera and classical concerts, pistol shooting, playing chess and pool, and just hanging out at the local pub. He makes his home in Houston. You can reach him at: www.sam-waas.com

Tell-Tale Publishing would like to thank you for your purchase. If you enjoyed this work and would like to read more by this author or our other fine authors, please visit our website:

www.tell-talepublishing.com

Chapter 1

An efficiency apartment neat and spotless, maintained by a young woman who took student life seriously, pride in modest surroundings. Inexpensive bookshelves lining the walls, filled to capacity with paperbacks and collegiate texts. Stacks of notebooks, pristine desk and office-style cubicle, laptop and printer, family photos. Nearby bed made up, sheets tucked. Adjoined kitchenette gleaming, dining counter and two bar stools the same. Bathroom next, also clean, bright.

Except that the apartment was now an abattoir, every surface strewn with her body parts. A vile and perverted display, hacked-off fingers, random pieces of flesh, internal organs and intestines strung across shelves. Other things. Complete reproductive system cut out intact, arranged just so. A kidney. Obscenity of two breasts draped across a chair.

Diorama in blood, meant for us to absorb, for us all to bear witness.

I stood there a moment, stunned, unthinking. Then the stench and blasphemy and evil overtook me and I turned quickly, out the apartment door, choking, spitting up anything in my stomach onto the little lawn. Acidic coffee was all I offered but the spasms persisted.

Hunched over and dizzy, I eventually regained my balance, deep breathing until I was fairly certain I wouldn't simply run down the street screaming, continue running and screaming until I was spent, spent of energy and spent of the sordid life in which I found myself this day.

Instead, I steeled my resolve and walked back inside where Homicide Captain Joe Duggan and Detective David Meierhoff were patiently waiting.

www.ingramcontent.com/pod-product-compliance
Lightning Source LLC
Chambersburg PA
CBHW071138180726
48291CB00007B/2240